"You don't have to be superwoman,"

Finn said. "Why don't you stop being so damned touchy?"

"I am not *touchy*!" Jack said hotly. Just because they'd been stranded together in the jungle didn't mean it was time to get personal.

"You're as prickly as a hedgehog!" Finn snapped. "The way you've been carrying on, you'd think I'd made an assault on your virtue, instead of offering a bit of friendly comfort after a bad dream!"

Jacqueline flinched at the memory of waking up in his arms. "Nobody asked you! I wasn't awake at the time! You took advantage—"

"I *what*?" Finn took one furious step toward her. Suddenly his mouth came down on hers, hard and warm and devastating in its sureness.

Sheer surprise kept her immobile for several seconds. Then a slow, languorous warmth started to course through her. Finally she found the presence of mind to stiffen and push at his shoulders.

Finn lifted his head, and his eyes bored into hers. "That," he said, "was taking advantage. Just so you know the difference."

Dear Reader,

Welcome to the Silhouette **Special Edition** experience! With your search for consistently satisfying reading in mind, every month the authors and editors of Silhouette **Special Edition** aim to offer you a stimulating blend of deep emotions and high romance.

The name Silhouette **Special Edition** and the distinctive arch on the cover represent a commitment—a commitment to bring you six sensitive, substantial novels each month. In the pages of a Silhouette **Special Edition**, compelling true-to-life characters face riveting emotional issues—and come out winners. Both celebrated authors and newcomers to the series strive for depth and dimension, vividness and warmth, in writing these stories of living and loving in today's world.

The result, we hope, is romance you can believe in. Deeply emotional, richly romantic, infinitely rewarding—that's the Silhouette **Special Edition** experience. Come share it with us—six times a month!

From all the authors and editors of Silhouette **Special Edition**,

Best wishes,

Leslie Kazanjian,
Senior Editor

LAUREY BRIGHT
Games of Chance

Silhouette Special Edition

Published by Silhouette Books New York

America's Publisher of Contemporary Romance

SILHOUETTE BOOKS
300 East 42nd St., New York, N.Y. 10017

ISBN: 0-373-09564-3

First Silhouette Books printing November 1989

Printed in the U.S.A.

Books by Laurey Bright

Silhouette Romance

Tears of Morning #107
Sweet Vengeance #125
Long Way From Home #356
The Rainbow Way #525
Jacinth #568

Silhouette Special Edition

Deep Waters #62
When Morning Comes #143
Fetters of the Past #213
A Sudden Sunlight #516
Games of Chance #564

LAUREY BRIGHT

has held a number of different jobs but has never wanted to be anything but a writer. She lives in New Zealand, where she creates the stories of contemporary people in love that have won her a following all over the world.

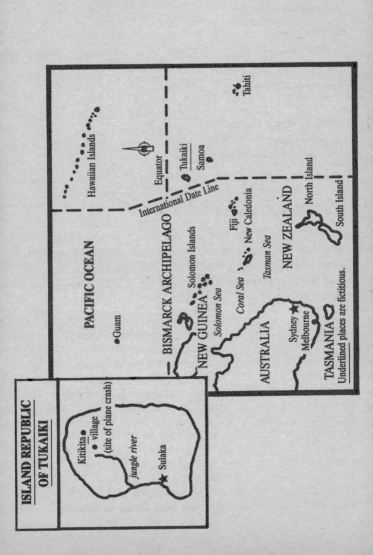

Chapter One

"Jack Renton might do it. Jack's mad enough for anything," said the man leaning on the bar, a huge fist curled about his pint of beer, a sweat-stained shirt almost bursting its buttons over his barrel-shaped chest.

"Is it really that dangerous?" Finn Simonson asked mildly.

The man snorted. "Look, mate. Out there, there's damn all places to land safely, 'specially since the cyclone. Apart from that, the army and the rebels are shooting at anything that moves. You want to fly right into rebel territory. A relief plane went in there coupla days ago to air-drop some food and medicine an' stuff to villages that were cut off by flooding, and it got shot at. The rebels, or revolutionaries or whatever they call themselves, blame the army. The government says they didn't do it. Well, I don't care, but I saw the plane, and I reckon they were lucky to make it back to Panaki airport. I already told you, I'm not risking my neck out there. No matter how much you're offering to pay me." He turned back to his beer with an air of finality.

Finn suppressed a sigh. "Where can I find this Jack Renton?" he asked. It had already taken him hours to track this man to his favourite watering hole, only to find him stubbornly unwilling to undertake the trip.

The man shrugged. "Maybe at the airport. Or come back here tonight. After nine."

Outside, the heat hit Finn like a wall. The bar had been shabby and dimly lit by lamps in atrocious taste made of glued seashells, but it was at least air-conditioned. He paused to get his breath, and then, deliberately curbing his impatience, walked at a leisurely pace along the street. Hurrying in this tropical atmosphere would only get him heatstroke.

The pavement was narrow and crowded. Most of the pedestrians were natives of the island, dark-skinned and black-haired, wearing brightly patterned cotton shirts or dresses. Some of the men favoured a cool pareu tied around the waist instead of trousers, either with a T-shirt or leaving their brown chests bare. There were Indian women in filmy saris, and a few Chinese girls looking cool and dainty in Western dress, with high-heeled sandals on their small, neat feet.

On the roadway, cyclists pedalling along without haste reluctantly made way for sleek, polished cars carrying wealthy businessmen or government officials, and for the occasional tourist bus, although the tourist industry had declined considerably since the government's declaration of martial law, even before the recent cyclone had wreaked its destructive path across the island. Here the storm damage had not been too serious; although a few trees lay across gardens and lawns, the telephone and electrical repair teams were much in evidence still, and workmen perched on several roofs, repairing them.

When a military vehicle roared along the street the cyclists hastily moved aside before its insistent tooting. A couple of soldiers in camouflage fatigues perched on the back of it, holding automatic rifles, their eyes flat and watchful as they surveyed the crowd.

Finn stood still until the truck passed, a coldness shivering down his spine. Last time he had visited the island republic of Tukaiki it had been a tropical paradise, the only signs of a military presence the impressive parade that was staged in front of the governor's mansion each Independence Day, and the guards outside the mansion and Parliament Buildings, sweltering in a colourful and much braided version of military dress uniform.

He bought a bunch of bananas and a fat yellow pawpaw and took them back to his hotel room. The telephone book yielded no entry for Renton, J. He asked the desk to get him a taxi to the airport. The clerk wanted to know if he was leaving. "No," he said patiently. "I will be returning to the hotel later today."

At the airport the military influence was strong. He was not allowed onto the airfield or into any buildings except the arrivals and departures lobby, and when he asked at an enquiries desk about Jack Renton, he got a blank stare and a shake of the head. There were few signs of life, and he realised that he was attracting the attention of the officer in charge of the army guards. After twenty minutes he gave up and left.

When he returned to the bar that evening it was full, and hazy with tobacco smoke. He couldn't see the man he had talked to that afternoon. Most of the patrons were male, but a few island girls in skimpy, tight-fitting dresses or short sarong-like pareus were serving drinks or sitting with men at the round tables. The chatter that hummed all about was mainly in English, although a few island words in common use laced the various scraps of conversation. English had become the official language of the place in colonial times, and most of the native inhabitants except for very old people were bilingual, easily switching from one language to the other.

He waited his turn at the bar and asked the man serving beer from a tap if he knew Jack Renton.

"Over there." The man jerked his head. "Corner table."

The corner table was occupied by a group playing cards, a stack of notes and coins between them. Thin trails of smoke rose from a couple of half-full ashtrays. Finn nodded his thanks and moved towards the table.

The man facing him had a broken nose and a receding hairline, and wore a flowered shirt that had seen better days. He had a cigar clamped in his teeth. On one side of him was an equally rugged character with red hair and deep-set eyes in a craggy face. The third man was round-faced and squat, smoking a limp cigarette that dangled from the corner of his mouth as he surveyed the cards in his hand, his eyes shadowed by the long peak of the army cap he wore. Finn stood behind the fourth player, smaller than the others, dark brown hair with a slight wave just brushing the collar of a khaki shirt.

"Is one of you Jack Renton?" Finn asked.

The man with the broken nose removed the cigar and looked at him warily. "Who wants to know?" he asked, his voice deep and gritty.

The other players had only briefly glanced up from their cards, but Finn had the impression that they were all waiting for his answer.

"My name's Finn Simonson," he said. "Are you—"

"Whaddya want?" the man interrupted.

"I'm looking for a pilot. I believe you have a plane that can carry some cargo and might be able to land where bigger ones can't make it. They tell me you're good—and not afraid to take risks."

The man grinned suddenly. He had a gap in his teeth just to one side. "Is that what they told you?"

Finn grinned back at him. "Mad enough for anything."

The big man laughed out loud, and the redhead and the little fat man joined him. He addressed the fourth member of the party. "Hear that?"

The dark head in front of Finn nodded. The other two had temporarily abandoned their pretended interest in their cards and were openly watching.

The big man tipped back his chair, surveying Finn thoughtfully. "What's this about risks?"

"I want to fly to the interior," Finn told him. "Behind the lines of the fighting."

"You a gunrunner?"

"I'm a doctor. I work for an international relief agency."

"You gonna doctor the rebels?"

"I'm going to help the tribal people in the interior whose crops and homes were ruined by the cyclone. Some are cut off from food and medical supplies, there are bound to have been some injuries, and there's a high risk of an epidemic of some sort. They need help urgently."

"That's a government job, izzen it?"

"It should be," Finn agreed.

"So...? What are they doin' about it?"

"As far as we can tell," Finn answered, trying to keep the bitterness from his voice, "nothing. They're too busy fighting the insurgents."

"You on their side?" the man asked, his eyes narrowing. "The rebels'?"

"I'm not on any side," Finn said. "The people I work for just want to help the innocent victims. We're not interested in politics."

The man grunted. "Ask the government for a plane."

"I have."

"No go, eh?"

"Their planes are all fully... committed."

"To the war," the man said. "Yeah."

The redheaded man removed his gaze from Finn and shifted one of his cards, carefully inserting it in a different place. "Planes flying in there are likely to get shot up."

"So I heard," Finn answered. "I'm prepared to pay danger money."

"Money izzen much use when you're dead," the big man said. "Not worth the risk."

He returned to his cards, but the redhead glanced at his other two companions, then up at Finn and asked, "How much are you offering?"

Finn, calculating the likely effect, decided to offer his limit. Calmly, he named a sum that made the redhead blink, and brought up the big man's head again with a jerk. Finn gazed at him steadily and said, "Well?"

In front of him a hand placing a fan of cards on the table took his attention. He frowned, looking at the hand, lightly tanned and with a gold watch on the wrist. Slender and smooth. Then the dark head turned, and a pair of brown eyes met his. He was still registering the fact that the face was undoubtedly female in spite of the lack of makeup, when she said, her voice firm and slightly husky, "All right. I'll do it."

Before he recovered from his surprise, the big man and the redhead together said, "Don't be crazy, Jack!"

Even the round-faced one who had so far been silent said in tones of friendly tolerance, "You're a loony bitch, Jack. Get yourself killed one o' these days."

She turned back to them. "You heard the man. Mad enough for anything, that's me."

"*You're* Jack Renton?" Finn asked, feeling he had been set up.

"That's right." She scooped some money from the table and stood up, taking a worn denim jacket from the back of her chair. "Sorry, boys, count me out. I've some business to attend to."

She barely reached Finn's shoulder. "No, you haven't," he said, not moving.

Dark brows lifted, and a spark flickered in the depths of her brown eyes. "You want a pilot, don't you?"

Finn looked round the table at the men. "One of you..."

The big man shook his head. "Not me, mate."

"I don't fly," said the redhead. The third man had relapsed into silence.

"Come on," Jack Renton said, turning away. "We'll talk at my place."

She shrugged into her jacket at the door, in spite of the tropical mugginess of the night, and walked with her hands thrust into the pockets as she led the way. Finn followed reluctantly, not quite sure of the reason for the depth of anger that possessed him. He tried to suppress it, but she glanced up at him and said with a hint of laughter, "Are you a male chauvinist, Dr. Simonson? I thought in your profession you'd be used to working with women."

"I'm not a chauvinist," he said shortly, and she laughed aloud then but didn't say any more until they reached a small house set in a square of lawn bordered with coconut palms and flowering bushes.

She opened the door and went ahead of him, entering a room to one side and switching on the light, then motioning him to one of the two cushioned wicker armchairs set on a woven coconut palm mat. For a moment she stayed by the door, apparently studying him as he stood in front of the chair, waiting for her.

"You don't look like a doctor," she commented.

Finn's hair tended to bleach in the tropics, and he tanned easily. He liked swimming and surfing, and that added extra muscle to naturally broad shoulders.

"*You* don't look like a pilot," he retorted.

She didn't smile, but something that might have been humour flickered in her eyes. She said, "Sit down."

"After you," he suggested politely.

She smiled then, but with more than a hint of mockery. "A gentleman, no less!"

She took something from the pocket of her jacket and walked over to place it on a plain occasional table by the other chair before slipping off the jacket and sitting down.

Finn remained staring at the snub-nosed silver pistol on the table. "Do you always carry that?" he asked.

"Insurance," she said. "After all, how do I know you are who you claim to be?"

Slowly, Finn took out his wallet and handed her some papers before taking the other chair.

After riffling through them, she said, "I've never heard of the International Volunteers for Emergency Relief."

"We keep a low profile," Finn told her. "The idea is to conserve what funds we have for the work we do rather than spend it on advertising. We're not so much an organisation as a loose federation of individuals with similar goals. We tend to come in when orthodox methods have failed or are taking too long, and do things that bigger and more established organisations don't feel they can risk, because of political repercussions or misunderstandings about their motives."

"Based in the States?" she asked.

"Yes." Evidently she had recognised the accent. He couldn't quite place hers. Perhaps British, but he thought he detected a hint of Australia in the vowels.

"If you don't advertise," she asked, "where do you get funds? That wasn't peanuts you were talking about tonight."

"You'll get your money," he said. "If you get the job. We have some wealthy patrons, and they have equally wealthy contacts. We manage to maintain our funds quite well."

"Why shouldn't I get the job? I said I'll do it."

He hesitated. "I had the feeling I was being taken for a ride by your friends. No one told me Jack Renton was a girl."

"I'm twenty-five, Dr. Simonson. A woman."

"You don't look it." He was inspecting her face, the broad cheekbones and square chin that were still unmistakably feminine, the smooth golden-tanned skin faintly freckled across the nose, the soft, short hair. Her mouth, he thought, was interesting—firm and yet with a promise of passion in the curve of the upper lip, the slight fullness of the lower one. Surprised at the trend of his thoughts, he brought his mind firmly back to the matter in hand as the mouth he was studying with such attention opened to speak.

"I'm a good pilot," she said, her eyes showing a spark of anger. "Ask anyone."

"We could get shot at."

"I know. I'll take along an automatic rifle in case we get into real trouble."

"No," Finn said. "No guns."

"You just said—"

"I know what I said. I told you we could get shot at. I didn't say we'd shoot back."

She regarded him in thoughtful silence. Then, "You're a pacifist."

"I'm a doctor. It doesn't go with shooting people."

"Even in self-defence?"

"Even in self-defence."

She glanced at the handgun beside her. "I don't go anywhere without my insurance."

Finn hesitated. "If you take this job," he said, "I'd prefer you to leave it behind."

Her eyes were steady and speculative. He had the impression she was wondering if he was snatching at the opportunity to get out of hiring her. Finally she said, "You weren't fooling when you said we'd be taking some risks."

"Nobody's forcing you. I can get another pilot."

Her eyes flashed. "You said you wanted Jack Renton. You've got me. Believe me, you won't find it easy to get anyone else to fly in there."

"Why did you agree?" he asked.

"You pay very well."

Finn's glance roved about the room. The walls were hung with brown-and-black-patterned tapa cloth, the windows dressed with cheap, colourful cotton drapes. He returned his gaze to the young woman across from him, taking in her faded shirt and workmanlike trousers. He said interestedly, "Do you gamble it all away at cards?"

"I usually win," she said. "And what I do with my earnings is my own business."

"Of course." He wondered at the antagonism in her tone. "What makes you so tense?" he asked.

"Tense?"

"You're as tight as a watch spring," he said. "I don't fancy being flown by someone who might break apart at any minute."

"I won't *break apart*, Doctor!" she snapped. "If I'm tense it's because I—" She stopped abruptly.

"Because?" he prompted.

"I don't know. It's . . . something about you."

Finn raised his brows. "Do I remind you of someone else?"

"Maybe." She obviously wasn't going to say any more about it.

"It won't stop you working for me, will it?"

She shook her head. "I told you, I want the money."

He noted that she had said "want," not "need," and regarded her thoughtfully, wondering.... "I'd like to leave as soon as possible," he said. "People may be dying. I've wasted enough time as it is."

"Tomorrow," she said. "If you like."

"Yes. When?"

She thought for a while. "The plane is being checked over. It should be ready to go by noon. How much stuff do you have to load?"

He told her, and she said, "We'll start loading at twelve. Takeoff at two, I'd say. I'll try to arrange it. Just where exactly were you planning to go? I hope you've got an airstrip in mind. I can't land in the jungle."

"A place called Kitikiti." He refused to be nettled. "I've got a map at my hotel."

"It's all right, I know it. The runway's a bit short, but I've landed there before. I'm not sure, though, that it will be usable. If the cyclone didn't wreck it, I should think the rebels might well have sabotaged it. Had you thought of that?"

"It was made unusable by the cyclone, I believe, but a survey plane sent in just after the disaster reported they were trying to clear it. If you've flown into the area before, you'd know if there's anywhere else you could land."

"I wouldn't care to try it. It's rough country. I haven't been into that part of the island for some time, not since the government stepped up the military campaign against the rebels. It's determined to wipe them out. That's probably why officialdom isn't keen to help you get behind the lines." She added cynically, "If the people in the interior are disposed of by disease and starvation, it saves the army the trouble of shooting them."

That thought had occurred to Finn, but he said only, "The military governor has assured me that he has no intention of starving women and children to death."

"You know that was only words. If they hear you've hired me, they'll probably try to stop us from flying."

"Maybe." The possibility had worried him, but he wasn't sure what could be done about it. It was the organisation's policy to try official channels first, and only then go about circumventing them if necessary. He said, "Do you have any suggestions?"

"For a start, we don't tell them where we're heading. But they'll guess, won't they?"

"Probably. I've been trying to get permission and a plane for over a week now."

"Well..." Her eyes ran over him assessingly. "You're a bit big to try and hide. And you'd never pass for a native of the island, with that hair and those Paul Newman eyes. We'll have to brazen it out. Do you have anything with an official signature or seal on it?"

"Yes, I do, but I don't think it would be much good. It starts off, 'The governor regrets...'"

"Never mind. Do you have it with you?"

He dug in his wallet again and handed her a crumpled envelope, leaning across the space between them.

"It might do. Leave it with me."

"Do you number forgery among your talents?"

She laughed. "I have friends. Is it against your principles, being...creative with government documents?"

"Letting people die is against my principles."

"It will cost you," she warned, folding the piece of paper and restoring it to the envelope. "I may need some money to persuade a couple of people to turn a blind eye tomorrow."

Finn took some notes from his wallet. "Take that for expenses," he said. "And here's a deposit for your services. The rest will be paid when you've landed me at Kitikiti."

"You're staying there?"

"That's the plan."

Her eyes seemed to darken further. "For how long?"

He shrugged. "Weeks, months. Whatever's necessary."

"What about getting back?"

"I'll worry about that when the time comes."

"You're taking a chance, but if it doesn't matter how long you stay, I suppose you can afford to."

Finn said, "Why did you let your friend do all the talking when I came to find you? You knew I thought he was Jack Renton."

"Why should I stop him? He was having fun."

"I rather think he was being . . . protective."

She shrugged. "Abe likes to pretend I need his help when I'm negotiating a deal with a stranger."

"And you let him."

"Sometimes I humour him."

Finn stood up. "My supplies are stored near the airport. I'll get them delivered by noon tomorrow to your plane."

She stood up, too, and quickly stepped away from him.

Indicating the pistol just behind her, he said reluctantly, "If you feel you need that for your own personal protection you'd better bring it. Only keep it out of sight, will you? And don't under any circumstances use it unless you yourself are in imminent danger."

"Thanks for the concession. Where are you staying?"

She didn't write down the name of the hotel, merely nodded and said, "Don't send anything out to the airport until you hear from me. It would be too bad to have our cargo confiscated before we started."

He nodded. "I'll wait for a message."

"Fine. That's it, then." She was waiting for him to go.

He held out his hand. Reluctantly, he thought, she put hers into it. Retaining his clasp on her long, strong fingers, he said, "You weren't christened Jack, were you—Jacqueline?"

"Don't call me that" She jerked away from him.

"Why not? It's your name, isn't it?"

She said, "My name's Jack."

Finn made a derisive little sound. "You're not a man."

"I wouldn't want to be!"

Finn's eyes narrowed. "Then why adopt a man's name—Jacqueline?"

"I *said*, don't call me that!"

He could feel that tension again. More than dislike, he thought. Something stronger and more deep-rooted. He wondered again, why?

"I wouldn't feel right calling you Jack," he countered.

"Everyone else does. Why is it such a hardship for you?"

"You look too...female," he asserted.

A hint of colour appeared in her cheeks. "If I'm supposed to be flattered," she said witheringly, "I'm afraid you're going the wrong way about it."

"It wasn't flattery. Just a fact." He thought that if he touched her, she'd quiver and snap. "Why does it upset you to be reminded that you're a woman?"

"I'm not upset. It's irrelevant, that's all."

Finn smiled. "Hardly."

She seemed to stiffen, a sudden scornful enlightenment in her face. "Think you're God's gift, Dr. Do-Gooder?"

He laughed then. "No. And I'm not making a pass at you, Miss Renton. It *is* Miss, isn't it? Or Ms."

"I told you. It's Jack."

Finn shook his head. He wasn't quite sure why, but he wasn't going to give in. "Not to me. I'll see you tomorrow," he told her, and made to walk by her. He was aware that she was holding herself rigid, and he paused, curious, finding her eyes with his. He saw the pupils enlarge; then she stepped back silently. For a moment longer he held her gaze, curiosity sharpening into something else. Then he continued without haste to the door and down the short passageway. At the outer door he turned. She was standing at the entrance of the room, regarding him with faintly hostile eyes. "Good night," he said, and let himself out.

Jack stood looking at the closed door long after his footsteps had faded away. Jacqueline. Nobody called her that now, *nobody*. The men she knew on Tukaiki treated her almost as one of themselves. Sometimes, she could swear, they forgot that she was female.

It had thrown him, finding that his pilot was a woman. She was used to that. But people soon learned to accept it. Anyway, after tomorrow she wouldn't see him again until he sent for transport out of Kitikiti. She almost wished she hadn't offered to fly him. But he paid very well....

That's not why you took the job, a small voice whispered inside her. She pushed it away. She knew she had the reputation that she would do anything—in the way of flying— for money. Even Abe believed it. He would probably tear a strip off her tomorrow, tell her what a fool she was, risking her neck. Again.

She picked up the little snub-nosed gun that Abe had bought for her and taught her to use. Handling it carefully, she made for her bedroom. A few years ago she wouldn't have dreamed of carrying a weapon on Tukaiki. But then the insurgents had started their campaign against the government that they called a collection of imperial puppets, and leaders had arisen who had new and unscrupulous ways of trying to gain their ends. A politician being gunned down in the main street of Sulaka had shocked the community, and a few weeks later a woman journalist had been kidnapped and kept for several weeks until her paper handed over a ransom. She had, of course, written about her experience, and seemed little the worse for it. Violent incidents increased, and gangs of youths had set upon Europeans, apparently regarding them as a symbol of lingering colonialism from the days when the island had been a "dependency" of Britain and administered by the Australian government. Once she and Abe had found themselves in a nasty situation in a dark street, and only his burly bulk and her determined fury had got them out of it.

So Abe had figured that Jack needed protection and made sure she got it, bought her the pistol and showed her how to use it. He had taught her how to use an automatic rifle, too, and told her to keep it in the plane. She could imagine his comments on a man who wouldn't fight. Abe had been a heavyweight champion in his younger days.

She put the gun into the drawer at her bedside and began to undress.

Chapter Two

Finn opened the door to a knock at eleven o'clock the next morning. The redheaded man from the night before, now wearing blue overalls, handed him a note.

"Come in," Finn invited him, and opened the slip of paper. The writing was firm and rounded. *Red will help you load the cargo onto his truck and drive you to the airport. Do as he says and try to look like a delivery man.*

There was no greeting and no signature. Finn read it again, glanced up at the lanky man before him, and said, "When?"

The man shrugged. "Now's okay. Jack said to give you some overalls and a cap. Bit big though, aren't yuh?"

"I'm afraid I can't help that." Finn took the rolled garment the man had been holding under his arm.

Fifteen minutes later, dressed in the overalls and with a peaked cap pulled well down over his hair, he climbed into a rusting truck beside the man known as Red and slammed the door. "Right," he said. "Let's go."

When they had loaded, Red drove to the airport along a narrow road lined with banana plantations and encroaching jungle, and while Finn slumped in the seat with his cap over his eyes and his arms folded, trying to appear bored and sleepy, Red flourished a piece of paper at the armed guard on the gate. To Finn's relief they were allowed to pass through and drive across the short grass to a hangar at the edge of the airfield, where a plane stood outside the doors.

Jack met them, wearing khaki shorts, tattered sneakers and a T-shirt, a cloth hat on her head. "Get the stuff on the plane quickly," she said without preliminary, and started undoing the ties holding the truck's canvas cover almost before the two men had finished getting out of the cab. "I've already refuelled."

They worked fast, the two men unloading, and Jack efficiently stacking the boxes in the plane's cargo space, assessing with an expert eye how to maintain the aircraft's balance. When everything was in place, roped to ensure the load remained stable, they were all sweating. Jack took off her hat and wiped her forehead, and Finn noticed that her hair was curling in fine little feathers about her face.

Looking across to the control tower and the low public buildings, Finn said, "A couple of soldiers are headed this way."

Jack said, "Red, get that truck out of the way. Dr. Simonson, in the plane."

Red ran to the truck's cab, shouting, "Good luck, Jack!"

She gave him a thumbs-up sign and leaped after Finn, who was climbing into the plane. "Strap yourself in!" she instructed him, and threw herself into the pilot's seat beside him as he fumbled with the safety straps. She had lost her hat. The engine coughed and roared, and as Red raced off in the truck, the plane slid out of the hangar and began trundling to the runway.

While Jack checked her instruments and pressed a series of switches, Finn was trying to see what was happening outside. Red had driven towards the two soldiers and jumped out of the truck to speak to them. Delaying tactics, Finn guessed. He hoped Red wasn't asking for trouble.

The plane turned, and the engine noise increased. Jack was talking into the microphone positioned in front of her mouth, but he couldn't hear what she said.

The plane moved forward, gathering speed. An armoured car was leaving one of the airport buildings, coming towards the runway. Finn pointed, and Jack nodded. Her mouth was curved in a smile of reckless pleasure, her eyes alight.

The plane picked up more speed, the buildings and grass slipping by them faster and faster, but the wheels seemed glued to the ground, and the armoured car was making a beeline for them. There was a gun mounted on the back, with a soldier sitting behind it. Finn saw the muzzle swivel and move upwards, and his throat dried.

Then the ground tilted and fell away as the wheels at last left the runway and the plane went into a steep climb. Jack glanced down and banked, flying in a tight circle before straightening out and levelling. She was still smiling like a mischievous child, her cheeks flushed and her eyes brilliant with laughter and triumph.

"Relax, Doctor," she advised Finn. "We're well away."

"You enjoyed that," he said.

"Life's meant to be enjoyed." She was obviously exhilarated. There was no sign of the tension he had observed in her last night.

"What about Red?"

"Red can talk his way out of anything," she said carelessly. "Don't worry, Doc."

"The name's Finn. And you, when you get back? Won't they want to question you?"

Jack shrugged. "Probably. I'll worry about that when it happens." She peered briefly out the side window. Below them the town had slipped behind, and there was a vista of deep green, broken only by a long, winding road and a scattering of houses and small cultivated areas. There were a few places where trees had evidently been flattened by the recent cyclone, but not much major damage. Along the coast on Finn's side of the plane, rippling waves washed endless white coral beaches. This area had been hit only by the fringe of the storm. The northeast end of the island, from the accounts that had filtered through, was much more badly off.

"Is that what you always do?" Finn asked. "Live from day to day?"

"What else is there to do?"

He stared at her thoughtfully, and after a few moments she glanced at him, catching his gaze. "Don't start analysing me, Doc," she said rather sharply.

"Finn," he insisted.

She checked her instruments, and then turned back to him. He still had not taken his attention from her. "Finn," she said, and her eyes slid away again.

He said, "I'm not a psychiatrist."

"Good." She was staring at the instrument panel, then out at the landscape below. Her long, capable hands moved a little, and the plane angled slightly away from the coast, then steadied.

"What are you afraid of?" he asked.

"Afraid?" Her brows drew together momentarily. Then she laughed. "I'm not afraid of anything!"

"Yes, you are. Do you have any women friends?"

Her mouth compressed. "I don't have much in common with women."

"But you do with men?"

"Some men."

"Like Red? And Abe?"

"That's right."

"A taste for cards and living dangerously?" he asked.

She shrugged. "Something like that."

"There's more to life than that."

"Not my life."

He regarded her a moment longer, then turned his attention to the land below. "Where are we?" The road had disappeared, and the country was wild and undulating, with an occasional high rocky outcrop, and no sign of habitation.

"The middle of nowhere," Jack answered. "There's nothing down there but jungle and swamp."

"You're different up here," he said, appraising her again. "Aren't you?"

"Different?"

"More relaxed. Happier."

"I've always been happy flying."

"How long have you been doing it?"

"Years."

"Where did you learn? At home in Australia?"

"That's right," she said again, slightly surprised.

"I'm quite good with accents," he explained. "You lived in the outback?"

"No." Reluctantly, she added, "I was a city kid."

"So what made you want to fly?"

"I liked the idea of it—the freedom."

"Do you have a family?" he asked.

"No. Do you?" She hadn't hesitated, but he had the impression that she had lied.

He said, "Two brothers, a sister, all living in the States and married. My father died a few years back, but my mother is living in New Jersey."

"So what made you want to be a doctor?"

He had the feeling that she was asking only to prevent any more questions about herself, but he answered, "I spent some time in the hospital as a kid. Osteomyelitis. I thought the doctors did a great job."

"So you're repaying your debt to the profession?"

Ignoring the faint sarcasm, he replied, "Not exactly. I get a lot of satisfaction out of healing."

"Well, bully for you."

"Got a chip on your shoulder, haven't you?" he enquired, quite pleasantly.

He saw her blink, and there was a brief silence before she said lightly, "Does it show?"

"What happened?"

She cast him a mocking, scornful look. "Life happened," she said shortly. "And it's none of your business."

After a while he said, "You have very loyal friends. Or did you pay Red for his help?"

"I paid him for the use of his truck. Nothing else."

He watched her for a few minutes, but she kept her gaze steadfastly ahead, ignoring him. He said, "I'll get out of these overalls if you don't mind." It was cooler up here, but he felt rather claustrophobic in the enveloping garment.

"Feel free," she said, and he undid the safety straps and found a clear space behind the seats to wriggle out of the overalls, bundling them neatly before stowing them in a corner.

"Are you okay?" he asked her. "Can I get you anything?"

"A clean shirt," she suggested after a moment. "You'll find a canvas knapsack just behind the seat, here."

"This do?" He thrust a white T-shirt in front of her a few seconds later.

"Fine. Thanks." She unhooked the radio headpiece, and Finn turned his back.

"Okay," she said. "Would you mind putting this in the bag for me?"

He took the stained shirt from her and stowed it away before resuming his seat.

"Do up your seat belt," she said.

They flew in silence for some time, and Finn had almost dozed off when he heard her sudden intake of breath.

He looked at her sharply, but she was eyeing the instrument panel, her teeth digging into her lower lip. He fancied he heard a different note in the engine, and asked quietly, "Something wrong?"

"Nothing I can't handle," she assured him. The engine definitely missed a beat, and her head jerked up; then she scowled again at the instruments, and flicked a couple of switches.

"I certainly hope so," Finn murmured. He added, "Tell me if there's anything I can do." Then he folded his arms and sat tight with his mouth closed, allowing her to concentrate on what she was doing.

The needle on a gauge marked Fuel Pressure was slowly but steadily falling. That couldn't be good. The plane coughed again, and Jack pulled the nose upwards, but then the engine died altogether, and they began losing height. Jack let loose an explosive word under her breath, and Finn quickly shut his eyes, opening them again as the engine spluttered back to life.

Leaning forward to peer through the glass in front of her, Jack said tightly, "Can you see any place that's fairly clear and flat?"

So she didn't trust the engine to keep going. His momentary relief abruptly disappearing, Finn peered out of the window, searching, and the minutes went by. As she had said, there was nothing down there but jungle and swamp.

But there was something else, too. Twisting in his seat, he confirmed it. "There's a river with a stretch of sand. Possible?"

"There's nowhere else," Jack answered grimly. The plane answered to her hands, turning, and then the engine cut out again completely. They were drifting rapidly lower, and she lined up the white strip of sand. It was, Finn thought, terribly narrow.

"Hang on to your hat, Doc," Jack said, busily flipping switches off. "Put your head down as we come in...."

He saw the trees and the murky water rushing up to meet them in eerie silence, took a deep breath and did as he was told. They bounced down quite gently. And he thought the sand must be wider than it appeared. Then there was a frightful bang and a tearing sound, and the plane shuddered violently. He lifted his head to look at his companion. Her face was very white as she fought the controls. He felt a lurch of fear for her, opened his mouth to yell at her to get down, and then there was an almighty crunch and something thumped the back of his head and it was all over.

* * *

Jack was aware that a wingtip had been shorn off just after they touched down. And she saw the driftwood log in their path, but there wasn't a thing she could do to stop them from hitting it. As it went under the wheels, she put her arms over her face, and the plane slewed sideways into the trees. Something smashed through the perspex screen in front of her, and she heard the fuselage crumple and tear. It wasn't until the plane came to a standstill and she lowered her arms that she realised she was bleeding from a long gash in her bare arm, and that her passenger was—at the very least—unconscious.

She fumbled at his wrist and found a pulse. The first thing to do was get him out. If a fuel tank was ruptured the plane could go up in flames within seconds. She started undoing buckles with shaking hands. She hoped he hadn't injured anything that shouldn't be moved, but the risk was a lesser one than being burned alive.

His foot was jammed at an angle under a twisted piece of metal. That ankle might be broken. She pulled at the metal, but it wouldn't budge. Scrambling into the back of the plane, she located a tool kit and hauled out a spanner, wrapped a piece of cloth about the broken metal to prevent any danger of sparks, and managed to lever it away so that she could drag the man out.

He was heavy, and she was afraid she might be making his injuries worse, because it wasn't easy to be gentle. It was all she could do to get him out of the plane without actually dropping him, but fortunately the wheels had been sheared off, and the cockpit door wasn't too far from the ground. She took a good grip under his arms to pull him as far away from the plane as possible, deciding it would be easier to do so along the sand. When, staggering with the weight, she had got him to what she judged would be a safe distance, she manhandled his unconscious body to the shade under the trees, and collapsed beside him, panting.

After her breathing steadied, she lay for a while staring at the trees overhead, the leaves moving very slightly. There didn't seem to be any birds. She supposed the noise of the crash would have frightened them away.

Finn stirred and muttered something. Jack turned to him instantly.

"Dr. Simonson!" she said in his ear. "Finn!"

He groaned and moved his head.

"Finn," she repeated. "Can you hear me?"

He nodded groggily, and said quite clearly, "What happened?"

"We crashed."

"Oh," he said.

"You were knocked out."

His eyelids fluttered, but he winced and mumbled, "We should get out, shouldn't we?"

"We are out."

"Oh," he said again. "Good."

She thought about all the things inside the plane that they might need. If only it wasn't going to burn. It must have taken her a good five minutes to get her passenger out, another five to drag him along the beach. It was maybe twenty minutes since the crash. She looked at her watch. Surely it wouldn't go up now? She made herself wait for another ten minutes. "I'm going back to the plane," she told Finn. "To get some stuff out."

He gave no sign of having heard, but he was breathing evenly, his eyes closed, his face pale.

Jack got to her feet, surprised to find that she was stiff. The first-aid kit and his bag first, she thought. Medical supplies. He needed them himself.

Her arm, too. There was blood all over her clothes, and his. Mostly her blood, although he had a slight cut on his head.

She sniffed cautiously as she approached the wreck, tempted to weep when she saw how bad it was. This plane would never fly again. Her first plane, her very own. Something inside her hurt at the thought, but this was no time for silly sentiment.

There wasn't any sign of fire, but the smell of petrol was strong. She climbed in and began to sift carefully through tumbled boxes, burst sacks and broken crates. The holding ropes had snapped, and the cargo compartment was a mess.

She found her first-aid kit among the chaos, and the two bags that Finn had carried into the plane, and put them outside, then threw out the inflatable yellow dinghy after them. It was meant for ditchings in the sea, but after all, there was a river.... Milk biscuits were spilling out of one of the broken containers. She wondered if the water in the river was safe for drinking, and rummaged for her own bag, knowing there was a bottle of soft drink there.

When she returned to Finn's side, carrying what seemed to be his medical bag, and the plane's first-aid kit, he was sitting up, holding his head in his hands.

He blinked up at her and said, "Who are you?"

"Jack Renton," she said, her heart sinking. "I'm the pilot of the plane."

"Plane?" He looked beyond her, squinting in the sunlight. "We crashed?"

"Yes."

"Where?"

"Somewhere between Sulaka and Kitikiti."

"Sulaka..." He seemed puzzled.

"The capital of Tukaiki."

"I know that! What am I doing here?"

"You don't remember?"

He shook his head, and winced. "Did I hit my head?"

"I think something hit it for you. You've hurt your ankle, too. You're a doctor. Tell me what to do, and I'll try and fix it for you."

"Thanks," he said vaguely. "Who are you, anyway?"

Jack regarded him with exasperation. "We just had this conversation. Tell me what to do with your ankle."

"Yes," he said. "In a minute." Then he lay down and closed his eyes.

"Oh, great!" Jack said to his unconscious face. "You're a wonderful help."

She clumsily bandaged her own arm, and then trudged back to the plane to rescue some more goods. Her survival kit, and food, she thought. They would need a fire. Maybe they should make a signal fire. Only she didn't know who might see it. They must be well behind the rebel lines by now.

The plane had torn off a lot of branches on its progress down the beach. If the wood wasn't too wet it shouldn't be difficult to build a bonfire.

Finn stirred again, and she put the bottle of soft drink to his lips and made him drink some. He opened his eyes and said, "What happened?"

Patiently she explained again. "Do you remember me?" she asked him.

He smiled, and said, "Jacqueline." And then closed his eyes again.

Well, at least this time he had remembered her. She said, "Dr. Simonson? *Finn?*" And his eyes flickered open. "Do you remember hiring my plane?"

"Yes, of course," he said.

"Well, that's a relief. You didn't when you woke before."

"Before?"

"You don't remember talking to me before?"

"Since the crash? No."

"You didn't seem to remember anything."

"I must have been concussed. Have a look at my eyes." They were blue and steady. "They seem normal to me."

"No enlargement of the pupils?"

"No."

"Wait a minute." He put a hand over them. Jack waited until he removed it. He said, "Are the pupils reacting to the light?"

"Yes," she said, watching them shrink.

"Okay. That's a good sign. My ankle hurts."

"I think it might be broken. I offered to try and do something, but you went off again."

"Sorry." He smiled faintly. "Care to try now, if I tell you how?"

His face was rather pale. "Sure you're up to it?" she asked.

He nodded carefully. "I see you got my bag out."

"I thought it might be useful."

"What happened to your arm?" he asked as she reached for the bag.

"It's just a scratch," she answered. "I'm okay."

"Sure?" His eyes searched her face.

"I got you and all this gear out of the plane," she answered. "It's nothing. Now, what do I need?"

It wasn't pleasant for either of them, getting a splint and bandage on the ankle, but in the end she sat back, and Finn opened the eyes that he had closed for a while, his face whiter than ever, and said quietly, "Good girl. I'll be okay in a little while. Then I'll attend to that arm."

She had forgotten about the arm, but blood had soaked through the bandage, and now that she was reminded of it the wound underneath was throbbing rather nastily.

The afternoon was wearing on, and soon it would be dusk. Jack became aware of hunger, and chewed one of the biscuits she had brought from the plane. They were lucky, she supposed, not short of food or medical supplies, and if one had to be stranded in the jungle, a doctor was probably the most useful sort of person to be stranded with. Finn seemed to be sleeping peacefully. She hoped that was what it was—sleep.

There was plenty of wood around. She gathered some and made a fire, and boiled some water from the river. She had put it aside to cool and was sitting by the fire smoking a cigarette when Finn said, "Jacqueline?"

She took the cigarette from her mouth, and contemplated the burning end of it for a moment before turning her head. "I've told you before," she said. "The name's Jack."

"Not to me," he said as he had last night. "I don't remember that."

He remembered perfectly well, she was sure. She said, "What do you want? I've some boiled water here, but it's still warm."

"That'll be fine," he said. "I'm very thirsty."

There had been a couple of cups on the plane, but they were smashed. She poured water into a plastic beaker and handed it to him with a brief apology.

"Don't be sorry," he said. "We're lucky to be alive."

"Well, I've news for you, Pollyanna," she said tartly. "That isn't necessarily a permanent state of affairs."

Finn chuckled weakly. "Two of us could survive for months on what's in that plane. I wouldn't be too pessimistic."

She supposed it was mean, given his condition, to remind him how dire their situation was. She said, "I dug out a carton of milk biscuits. They're dry, but I suppose they're good for us."

"Full of protein," he agreed. "I'll try one, thanks."

"How's your ankle?" she asked when he had finished two biscuits and had some more water.

"Throbbing. Like my head. Otherwise," he said wryly, "I'm fine."

"Can I get you some painkiller from your bag?"

"No. Maybe later. Let me see that arm."

She undid the clumsy bandage, and he held the arm in his hands and said, "Have you disinfected it?"

"No. It looked clean, and I was in too much of a hurry."

"There's a bottle of disinfectant in my bag. Can you wash this yourself, with some of that boiled water? Then I'll stitch it for you."

"Is it that bad?" she asked, taken aback.

"It's quite deep. You've bled a lot. Feeling all right?"

"As well as can be expected. If you're going to start sewing me up," she added, "I hope you've got some local anaesthetic in here. I'm a coward."

He began to laugh but stopped abruptly, a hand to his head. "Damn!" he said feelingly. Then, "I thought you weren't afraid of anything?"

"There's nothing wrong with your memory," she retorted, placing his medical bag beside him. She turned away from him to wash the wound, then sat down at his side. "There. Do your worst."

He had fished out a hypodermic needle and a phial. "Just keep still," he said.

She gazed across the river and tried to think about something else.

As he fastened a clean bandage on the arm, he said, "There you are. Probably not up to my usual standard, I'm afraid, but you'll do."

"Thanks." Jack stood up. "I'll see about some blankets for the night. There's one in the plane's survival kit."

"I've got a sleeping bag somewhere," he said, lying back again.

"Right." She remembered seeing it.

She walked along the sand a little way, then deliberately into the trees where he couldn't see her. She leaned her forehead against a rough trunk, and fought the nausea that threatened to overwhelm her, clenching her teeth. Turning, she slid weakly to the ground, her back against the tree, and rested her head on her arms, propped on her raised knees. After a while the sick feeling passed, and she got up and continued on to the plane.

When she returned with his sleeping bag and a light thermal blanket, Finn opened his eyes and smiled at her. "I'm sorry I can't help much," he said. "We'll have to see if we can manage some kind of crutch for me tomorrow."

She began to unzip the sleeping bag, and he said, "You have that. Give me the blanket."

"This is yours," Jack said. "You're having it."

He said, "Why don't you unzip it all the way? We can both lie on it, then, and use the blanket to cover us. It's not that cold."

She thought about it. "Provided you don't end up with all the blanket," she said finally.

Finn laughed. "Promise." He watched her for a short while, then said, "I'll just crawl off into the bushes for a minute."

"Can you manage on your own?"

"Sure."

She had the sleeping bag spread out when he came back, pulling himself along the ground. He collapsed onto it, gasping, and she said, "You sure you're okay?"

"I will be in a minute."

"Can I get you something?"

"No. Don't worry. It's a bit sore, that's all."

She suspected that was a considerable understatement. She put the blanket over him and slipped under it, beside him. When he was breathing normally she said, "Better?"

"Yes, thanks." He turned to smile at her, and fumbled for her hand, giving it a squeeze.

Jack snatched her hand away.

Finn moved, propping himself on an elbow to stare down at her. "It was just a friendly touch," he said. Then, his eyes crinkling with incredulous humour, "You don't think I've got designs on your virtue, do you?"

"In your condition?" Jack said. "Hardly. It was a reflex, that's all."

He went on staring down at her. "You don't like being touched? Or you don't like being touched by me?"

"Go to sleep," Jack said crossly. The night was descending rapidly now, a couple of stars winking in the purpling sky. "I'm sure you need it."

She rolled onto her side, presenting an implacable back, and making sure there was a foot of space between them. She closed her eyes, but she kept seeing the trees and the beach rushing up to meet the plane, the bleached, lethal innocence of the log lying on the sand in front of them. After a while she could hear by Finn's breathing that he had gone to sleep, and she lay on her back, staring up at the stars.

The water of the river rippled, and the trees rustled. Some insect chirped nearby, and a night bird gave a haunting call in the distance. She wondered if there was any hope that they would be rescued. Abe and Red would start to worry when she didn't return, and Abe might come searching for her. He flew a helicopter, and he had a general idea where to look. But there was a lot of land between Sulaka and Kitikiti to be searched. She doubted that her emergency signal would have been heard before the plane came down, and the radio had been knocked out in the crash. The government probably wouldn't take any action. They hadn't wanted to support Finn's mission, and she was not particularly popular in those circles. Commercial pilots willing to fly anything anywhere so long as the price was right were a natural target of suspicion for officialdom, particularly in a country embroiled in a civil war. Today wasn't the first time that she had skirted close to the edges of the law.

She sat up, and Finn stirred and said, "What's the matter?"

"Nothing. Sorry if I woke you."

"It's okay. Are you worried about our chances?"

Jack shrugged. "I told you, the only way to live is from day to day."

"In the circumstances, that's probably a sensible view to take. Why don't you take your own advice and go to sleep?"

"Soon," she said. She twisted aside from him, rummaging in her knapsack for a cigarette.

"That won't help you to live longer," he observed mildly as she lit a match to the end.

"I'm giving it up," she said flippantly, shaking out the match flame. "Just as soon as this pack is gone. It's all I've got."

"Ever given it up before?"

Jack shook her head. "Why should I?"

"I thought everyone knew that by now."

"Anyway, what do you care?" She took a deep drag, and blew the smoke out satisfyingly, through pursed lips.

"I'm a doctor," he said. "It's my job to care."

"You're not *my* doctor."

"I patched you up this afternoon. You're my patient now."

Jack turned scornful eyes on him. "Look who's talking!"

Finn laughed softly. "Point to you," he acknowledged. And then, as though he had just thought of it, "How did you get me out of the plane?"

"Brute strength."

He studied her assessingly. "I'm no lightweight."

"You don't need to tell *me*!" Jack answered feelingly.

"How long did it take you?"

"About five or ten minutes. Your foot was jammed."

"I don't suppose," he said, "you made sure that the thing wasn't going to blow up before you carried out this rescue act?"

"It didn't."

"No. But I recall being told that when a plane comes down, you've got about thirty seconds before it goes, if the fuel catches."

"About that. But I'd switched everything off."

"It could still have happened, though?"

Jack shrugged.

There was a long silence. Then he said, "Thank you."

"I figured I might need a doctor."

"Sure," he said. "I know."

Jack stubbed out her cigarette and carefully buried the end in the sand. She lay down and pulled the blanket up to her chin. "Good night," she said.

This time she slept like a top.

Chapter Three

When she woke the sun was rising, and the sky had turned a glorious pink. Birdcalls came from the trees roundabout, and the air felt cool and fresh. She turned her head and found that Finn had woken before her, and was lying on his side regarding her with cool curiosity.

Jack sat up, a hand ruffling her hair. "Have you been awake long?" she asked.

"A while. You were dead to the world."

She had slept surprisingly well, but she supposed his ankle was hurting. He looked weary, though the faint stubble on his cheeks quite suited him. "Can I get you anything?" she asked him.

"There's no hurry. Do you always look like a daisy in the morning?"

Startled, she said, "I've no idea. A *daisy*?"

He grinned up at her. "No less. Considering what you went through yesterday, it's nothing short of amazing."

"I thrive on adversity." She tossed aside her half of the blanket and stood up.

"Obviously," Finn said. He moved to lie back with his head propped on his hands. "You like a challenge, don't you?"

"I could have done without this one," she said, gazing along the riverbank at the wreckage of the plane. If anything, it looked even worse now than before. "I'll see if I can find something for breakfast."

"There's a carton of dried fruit in there, somewhere," he said. "It should be labelled."

"Sounds good. I won't be long."

When she came back carrying a small carton, she found that he had relit the fire. She got more water and boiled it, and produced a packet of vitamin-enriched fruit drink from her survival kit.

"How's the head?" she asked him.

"Better. I need something to make some crutches with."

"There's a hatchet," Jack offered. "And I've a Swiss army knife."

"Yes," Finn said, "I was sure you would."

Stirring orange powder into some boiled water, she glanced up.

"Sorry," Finn said. "It slipped out."

"Do you have a girlfriend?" she asked him. "You're not married, are you?" She couldn't imagine a wife putting up with his jaunting about the world on mercy missions of indefinite duration.

"I'm not married. I've had girlfriends."

Past tense, she noted. "Blondes," she guessed. "Feminine and fluttery. And they wear full skirts and high heels, and carry lipsticks, not Swiss army knives."

"I've said I'm sorry," Finn reminded her. "And I've dated mostly nurses. They tend not to be fluttery." He paused. "What about you?"

"Me?"

"Do you date?"

Jack finished her drink. "I haven't dated anyone in years. Do you think it's safe to wash things in that water?" She nodded towards the river.

"I'd boil it first."

"We should fix some kind of signal, in case someone comes searching for us."

"Good idea. If I could just get mobile, I could help you rig something."

She found some fairly straight branches among the wood sheared off by the plane, and took them to Finn, along with a ball of twine and some insulating tape, and the hatchet and tool kit. While he worked on making himself some crutches, she inflated the yellow dinghy and put it on the sand as a sort of signal, firmly tying it to a couple of trees in case the water rose and carried it away. There was a fair amount of driftwood along the bank in addition to the log that had wrecked the plane, and she began dragging broken branches and pieces of old wood, heaping them into the beginnings of a pyre. It wasn't easy, and when she rejoined Finn she felt hot and thirsty and distinctly out of temper.

Tying a crosspiece of wood onto one of the crude crutches, he said, "You'd better put some disinfectant on those."

Her arms and legs had got scratched by twigs and bark. Some of the weals were bleeding, and the bandage over her arm was dirty and had pulled threads hanging from it.

The disinfectant stung, and when she had finished she screwed the cap on the bottle and lay back on the blanket still spread on top of the sleeping bag, closing her eyes.

"You all right?" Finn's quiet voice asked.

"Perfectly. I've only lost my plane and crocked up my passenger and got myself stuck in the middle of nowhere with almost no chance of being found alive ... and wasted the last couple of hours trying to fix a signal that no one will ever see."

"Come on," he said. "Self-pity doesn't suit you, Jacqueline."

Jack lay still for a moment longer. Then she sat up and said, "And if you call me that one more time, I'll ..."

"What?" Finn asked interestedly. As she stood up, he whined, pretending to cower, "You wouldn't strike a crippled man, would you?"

Jack stalked off along the sand, and heard his laughter following her.

She clambered into the plane again. The sun was climbing, making the interior very hot, but she grimly set to work trying to restore some sort of order, noting anything that might conceivably be of use to make their situation more bearable. She found rice and some flour and sugar in the cargo, and dragged them into a corner that still appeared reasonably weatherproof, covering them with a sheet of polythene to make sure.

It was an hour or so before she emerged, and as she stepped out onto the riverside again, she could see Finn standing with his crutches, using them rather clumsily on the soft sand. As she watched, he stumbled and fell, and she heard him cry out.

She ran, and when she reached him he was sitting up, clutching at his ankle and swearing.

Jack crouched beside him. "You haven't damaged it, have you? You should have waited for me."

His face was white, and there was sweat on his forehead. "I didn't know how long you'd be off sulking, did I?"

"I wasn't sulking! I've been sorting out what's left in the plane, if you want to know."

"I don't particularly." He drew in his breath between his teeth, his face tense with pain.

Swallowing a sharp retort, she said calmly, "Tell me how to help."

"You can't," he said. "Just wait . . . until it passes off a bit. I don't think I've done any damage. The bandage is still quite firm."

After a while he said, "Help me up. I'll try again."

This time she stayed close by, and when one crutch sank into the sand, threatening to unbalance him, she was there with a steadying hand.

"Thanks," he said, as he sat down on the blanket. "I'll get better at it. At least the crutches seem reasonably strong."

"Are you hungry?" she asked. "We could have some tinned meat and dehydrated vegetables."

"Sounds good."

"I thought we should put up a tent before tonight," she said, as she set about making the meal. "In case it rains."

"At least I can help you with that," he answered. "What about the plane? It's not weatherproof anymore?"

"Not exactly. I thought we'd rig the tent by the plane. We might as well be near our supplies. If you can get that far on your crutches?"

After they had eaten, Jack helped Finn to hobble to the plane, and while he sat propped against one of the trees, she found the two-man tent and a reasonably clear space to erect it, and spread the sleeping bag and blanket inside.

Finn commented, "Very cosy."

"You didn't tell me," Jack said, "that there's a bale of blankets among the cargo. I found them when I was sorting it."

"I'd forgotten," he said simply.

What with the crash and his concussion, she supposed he might have. Certainly there was no reason he would have preferred sharing a bed with her last night.

"What I'd like," she said, "is a dip in the river." The water was a bit murky, probably because of the recent cyclone and flooding, but it would be cool and wet.

Finn said, "It might not be safe."

"There aren't any crocodiles or piranhas on Tukaiki."

"There could be hidden hazards, though. And you need to keep that arm out of the water for a few days."

"I'll hold it up," she promised. "And stay at the edge. It's really quite shallow there."

She walked over the narrow strip of sand and looked back, finding the plane's bulk between her and the tent where Finn was sitting. Stripping off her shoes and shorts, and the white T-shirt that was now stained and torn, she waded into the river wearing only a pair of bikini briefs. When the water was at knee level, she sank down, carefully holding the bandaged arm up.

It was blessedly cool, and she stayed there with her eyes blissfully shut until her arm began to ache, and she had to reluctantly leave the water. She picked up her shoes and pulled on the shorts and shirt, and padded barefoot back to the plane.

When she came round to the side, she thought a flicker of relief crossed Finn's face. Then it was replaced by something else as he noticed the shirt clinging to her wet body, and she felt her cheeks burn a little as she hurried to the doorway of the plane.

There was a towel in her knapsack, which she used vigorously. She combed her hair, and used her toothbrush and toothpaste, thankful that she always carried them with her on a trip, rinsing with some of the water she had boiled earlier, tipping it out through a handy hole in the fuselage afterwards. She found the shirt she had been wearing yesterday—only yesterday—when they took off from the airport. That needed washing, and the other was still damp. She wrapped the towel about her like a sarong, and carried both shirts outside.

"Would you happen to have any soap?" she asked Finn.

"In my bag." He pulled it over from where she had stowed it in a corner of the tent, and found a bar of soap.

"If you want anything washed," she offered, "I'll do it now."

"Thanks," he said, and stripped off his shirt.

His chest was tanned, with a sprinkling of light, curly hair down the middle. She wrenched her eyes away and took the shirt from his hand. "I'll bring you some water to wash in, if you like."

"When you've finished with the soap."

She spread the clothes out on bushes to dry, gave him a basin of water and the soap, and said, "I'll take a walk along the river.'' So that he knew he could strip in privacy if he liked. "Is there anything else you want?"

"Nothing, thanks. Don't get lost."

She stayed by the river, walking on the sand. On either bank the heavy rain forest was dark and impenetrable. One could easily get lost in there, only a few yards from the river. Birds fluttered from trees in alarm as she approached, flashing coloured feathers under their wings. The water glittered in the afternoon sun, and once she saw a fish leap in a brief silver arc. If tinned and dried foods palled, perhaps they would be able to catch some fish.

When she thought that she had given Finn sufficient time, she retraced her steps, and found him wearing a slightly crumpled but clean shirt and a fresh though faded pair of jeans. He must have had a bit of trouble getting them over the bandage, she thought. He had shaved, too, and combed his hair. She took the basin he had used and poured the soapy water away.

"Are you any good at fishing?" she asked him.

"Haven't tried since I was a kid," he answered. "Do you want me to?"

"If you like. I saw a fish in the river. I expect we could make some sort of fishing line."

"Surgical thread and a safety pin?" he said thoughtfully. "It might work."

"I didn't see any fruit," she told him. "We'll have to rely on the dried variety, I think."

He nodded. "Our worst problem is going to be boredom. I've got a couple of paperbacks in my baggage, if you'd like one."

"Thanks. Later, maybe. I have a pack of cards in my knapsack."

"Don't go anywhere without them?"

"That's right." Suddenly she felt tired. She checked the washing she had done, and found the sun had dried everything. After putting the white shirt back on, she spread the towel out in the shade and lay down, and fell promptly asleep.

* * *

When she woke the sun had lost some of its heat and was below the level of the trees. She sat up, and found Finn gone from where he had been sitting in the tent.

"Finn?" she said. She got up and peered into the interior of the plane. He wasn't there. "Finn!" she called. She hurried round to the river, and looked up and down the sand. She saw him about a hundred yards away, sitting on a driftwood log, the crutches propped beside him. He had a long stick in his hands, and she realised that he had occupied his time making a fishing rod and was trying it out.

She marched along the strip of sand, and when she reached him, said furiously, "What on earth do you think you're doing?"

"Fishing," he replied calmly, his eyes crinkling as he looked at her. "It was your idea."

"It wasn't my idea for you to take off on your own along the river! What if you'd fallen again? Didn't you hurt yourself enough this morning? Why couldn't you fish from nearer the plane?"

"It's more promising here," he said. "See those little eddies in the water?"

She didn't even look. "Next time you want to go walkabout," she said, "tell me!"

"You were fast asleep."

"You could have woken me! Or waited for me to wake up."

"I'm a doctor," he said. "I know what I'm doing."

"You were a doctor this morning, too," she reminded him witheringly. "That didn't stop you being a bloody idiot then, and it didn't stop you this time, either. What are you trying to prove?"

He opened his mouth, his eyes glittery with anger. Then he stopped himself, and his lips took on a rueful curve. "You're probably right. Maybe I was trying to prove that I don't need you to do everything for me, that I'm capable of being the provider, in a modest sort of way."

"With a broken ankle?" Jack said sarcastically.

"Primitive male instinct, I guess," he confessed. "I admit I was a damn fool. Okay?"

Jack bit her lip. He could turn on the charm, she thought. When he looked at her like that, with a half smile on his mouth and a glint of wry humour in his eyes, it was hard not to smile back.

"Just don't do it again," she muttered, scowling, and he laughed outright and said, "I'll try to behave. *Ma'am.*"

She sat down on the sand nearby with her arms round her knees, and asked, "Have you had any bites?"

"Not a thing," he said cheerfully. "But fishing is supposed to be good for the soul, isn't it? Conducive to meditation on the meaning of life, or something."

"So they say. It might be, if your life depended on it."

He grinned. "No doubt." Then he stiffened as the line gave a jerk and tautened. "Hey!" he said. "I think we've got something."

The line jerked again, and Jack stood up. "Can I help?"

He gave her a look that effectively dissuaded her from offering again. Something twisted and leapt at the end of the line, and she said, "It's not very big."

"You do nothing for a man's ego," he complained, and pulled the rod up, then grabbed the line and began hauling it in. "Go and get it," he said, as the fish thrashed about in the shallows.

She took it out of the water, and when it stopped wriggling unhooked it and held it up for him. "Congratulations," she said. "Maybe we should mount this one, instead of eating it." It was all of six inches long.

"It's a start," he said defensively. "We'll use it for bait."

Later he caught one that was twice as big, not huge, but enough to cook for their supper, and along with dried vegetables it made a reasonable meal. Jack had carried it and the fishing rod back to their base, while Finn swung along on his crutches fairly easily. All the same, she held herself ready to drop the fish and rod and catch him if he stumbled.

When they had finished, he said, "That was good."

"And a balm to your male ego, no doubt," she suggested drily.

"That, too. Tomorrow I might get us one each."

"I'll look forward to it."

"How's the arm?" he asked.

"Fine." It hurt a bit, and although she had tried to be careful, she knew she had pulled at the stitching a couple of times when she was sorting the contents of the plane, but the pain was nothing she couldn't cope with.

"I'd better check on it," he said, "before we go to bed."

She held it out, and he undid the bandage. "Good," he commented, and carefully covered it again.

"You think I'll survive?"

"I think we both will," he said, his eyes serious.

Jack hoped so. She had discovered a surprising will to live, in those few seconds when the plane had been careering along the riverbank with the trees tearing at it and leaping frighteningly for the windows.

She said, "I'll make myself a bed in the plane."

Finn looked up at her but said nothing. She walked away from him and climbed into the plane.

When she had made a comfortable bed of folded blankets, arranging a couple more as a pillow, she took some of the extra ones out to him and said, "I thought you could use these as a mattress."

He took them from her. "Thanks. Am I so unpleasant to sleep with?"

"I just thought we could both use some privacy."

"Sure," he said, as though he didn't quite believe her.

"Is there anything you need before I go to bed?"

Finn shook his head. "I'm fine. Sleep well."

Surprisingly, she didn't sleep as well as the night before. The plane creaked, the metal contracting as the air cooled, and when she dozed off she heard screaming in her dreams, snapping awake to realise it was a night bird screeching some way off. The interior seemed hot and stuffy in spite of the numerous tears and holes in the fuselage, and she got up and went to the door. The tent was a pale blur in the moonlight, open in front. She could see the outline of Finn's body with a blanket pulled over it.

Stepping outside, she turned her ankle on an uneven piece of ground. She righted herself, but her startled exclamation had woken Finn. She saw him sit up, and he said sharply, "What's the matter?"

"It's okay," she said, walking carefully towards the tent. "Sorry I woke you. I tripped, that's all."

"Don't *you* go breaking a leg," he muttered. "Couldn't you sleep?"

"It's hot in there. I'll go back in a minute. I just came out for some air."

"Bring your bed out here," he suggested. "There's room for two."

When she hesitated, he said, sounding mildly amused, "I didn't think you'd be one for maidenly scruples. You weren't bothered last night."

She wasn't bothered, of course. In fact, she didn't know why she hesitated. "All right," she said at last. It was a sensible suggestion, after all.

She went back and collected the blankets she had been using, and he shifted over to make room. They were still close, though, when she lay down again and pulled one of the blankets over her. She could hear his quiet breathing, and the last thing she thought before she went to sleep properly was that it was rather a comforting sound.

Next evening Jack made a kind of kedgeree by mixing fish with rice. The fish were biting that day, and Finn was blatantly pleased with himself. Jack had started reading one of the books he had offered her, a thick, juicy tale of intrigue and adventure. But somehow it failed to hold her. All the same, when they had finished their meal she sat by the remains of the fire and carried on reading until the fading light made it impossible for her to make out the words.

She lit a cigarette then from the embers, and sat smoking it slowly. She had only three left, and she was trying to save them.

Finn said, "We should try to keep that fire going and conserve our matches."

He was right. Jack stood up. "I'll find some more wood."

"Don't go too far in the dark," he warned.

She didn't answer, moving along the sandy bank of the river. There were small bits of dead wood here and there, and she collected a modest armful. It had got darker, though, and she had to pick her way carefully on the way back.

"You've been a long time," Finn said, as she fed some of the twigs to the fire. "I was worried."

"You don't need to worry about me. I've been looking after myself for a long time."

"Really?" He was waiting for her to go on, and when she didn't, he said, "Were you an orphan?"

Jack gave a bitter laugh. "No."

He was lounging on his elbow at the other side of the fire. "Was your childhood unhappy?"

"Not any more than most." She shrugged. "I was never sick, like you. A very healthy specimen, me."

"I was only sick for a relatively short time," he said. "Apart from mumps and chicken pox."

"Were you happy?"

"Mostly. Our family was a closeknit one. We still are, in a way, although we don't see a lot of one another."

"Your parents must have been pleased when you wanted to be a doctor."

"I suppose. But they'd have been equally pleased if I'd wanted to be a garage mechanic—as long as I was doing whatever would make me happy."

Jack poked at the fire with a stick. "You were lucky."

"Yes." He paused. "Did you always want to be a pilot?"

"No. I was supposed to go into one of the professions. When I was eighteen I met a man who ran his own airfreight business. He taught me to fly. I knew then I didn't want to do anything else.'' She sat staring into the flames, unaware that her face in the flickering light was starkly revealing.

"Was he your lover?" Finn asked quietly.

It was none of his business, but after a moment she said, "Yes."

For some seconds he said nothing, and then, still quietly, he asked, "What happened?"

Jack stared into the fire, her eyes smarting from the smoke. "He was flying some machinery to a sheep station in the outback. It was almost a year from the day we'd met. We'd been planning a celebration dinner after he got back. He...didn't make it."

"I'm sorry. That was rough."

She said, "It was ages before I was sure he was dead. I knew he must have come down somewhere, but the search parties took days to find the wreckage. I kept on hoping that somehow he would survive. I couldn't believe he would die, just like that. But he had. He was still strapped in the cockpit when they found him."

"It didn't stop you flying," Finn said after a moment.

"No." She looked up at him, over the flames, and the amber light caught her eyes. "Nothing could stop me."

It must have been talking about Brad that brought on the dream. She was fighting her way up a mountain covered in trees and scrub, knowing that if she didn't get there soon Brad would be dead. She had to reach him in time, but the bushes kept tearing at her clothes and clinging, and she had only her bare hands to get through them. She tripped over a vine, and when she made to get up the vine twisted itself round her legs, and she tried to tug it away, desperate to find Brad. She knew if she could only get there quickly enough, she could save him....

She began to sob, and a voice said, "Okay, it's okay. Don't cry." Strong arms came around her and gathered her to a warm chest.

"Brad!" she gasped, and the voice said, "It's all right, everything's all right now. Don't worry." She felt a hand stroking her hair, and she sighed with relief and snuggled into the warm arms and drifted away.

When she woke she found her head was pillowed against Finn's shoulder, his arm loosely about her. She jerked upright, and his eyes opened, so instantly aware that she suspected he had already been awake.

"Good morning," he said. Jack thought she detected a note of amusement in his voice, his eyes.

"Good morning," she said stiffly. "That wasn't necessary, you know."

He didn't pretend not to understand what she meant. "You seemed to appreciate it at the time."

"I was asleep." She had a foggy memory of a distressing dream, and of being comforted. She was appalled to discover that the comfort wasn't part of the dream.

"And having a nightmare," he reminded her. "You were disturbing *my* sleep."

"Well, I'm sorry about that. I'll sleep elsewhere tonight."

"Don't be so silly!" he said, "Anyway, I quite enjoyed having a woman in my arms."

"Is it such a novelty for you?"

"Not entirely. Do you want to know about my love life?"

"No!" Jack got up and, grabbing her towel, moved around the plane to the river, where she had a hasty cold wash.

When she came back he was preparing breakfast, and she kept out of the way, making a production of tidying up her blankets and combing her hair, until he called her.

She felt edgy all day, and when Finn spoke to her she tended to reply in monosyllables. In the afternoon she wandered off along the riverbank, hunting for firewood. She had gone about half a mile when a large black-and-white bird suddenly flew from almost under her feet, startling her, taking off in a flurry of wings.

Jack stopped dead, and there in a hollow of sand and stones lay two speckled eggs, about the size of a bantam hen's.

She gazed down at them, her mouth watering at the thought of fried egg. The bird was circling her, swooping and then lifting, its wings moving silently now. She lifted her head to watch it and said, "All right. You can come back," and walked on.

They were probably too old, anyway, she told herself. The thought of opening one to find a half-formed chick was not appetising.

The trees were thick, with tall palms rising above the shorter, bushier growth. A few of the plants had flowers on them, brilliant reds and pinks, and some small white blossoms. She saw breadfruit trees, but they had no fruit on them. Just as well they had all that food on the plane, she thought again.

She had an armful of wood when she returned to the camp, and as she put it down, Finn said, "We must build up that signal fire. It's not big enough yet, is it?"

"Do you know how long it took me to collect this?" she demanded. "And it's barely enough to last the night."

"I wasn't suggesting you build it all by yourself."

"Well, you're not going to be much help, are you?"

As soon as she had said it, she was ashamed. "Sorry," she apologised. "I didn't mean that."

"I guess it's true," Finn said. "I'm not really much use, am I?"

"Now who's being sorry for himself?"

He smiled faintly. "I hoped you'd feel better after your walk."

"I was perfectly okay before. And I went to collect wood."

Finn sighed. "You know, there's nothing wrong with needing a bit of human sympathy. You don't have to be Superwoman."

"I don't need sympathy! You can save your Dr. Schweitzer act for the poor ignorant savages you've come to minister to, if you ever get to them."

Finn grabbed at his crutches and struggled to his feet. He said angrily, "I don't think of indigenous people as ignorant savages any more than you do! I have *never* patronised them!"

"Then stop patronising *me*!"

"Why don't *you* stop being so damned touchy?"

"I am not *touchy*!" Jack denied hotly.

"As a hedgehog!" Finn snapped. "The way you've been carrying on all day, you'd think I'd made an assault on your virtue, instead of offering a bit of friendly comfort after a bad dream!"

"Nobody asked you!"

"You were glad enough to take it at the time!"

"I wasn't even awake at the time! You took advantage—"

"I *what*?" Finn lifted one of the crutches, and took a clumsy, furious step towards her.

She saw him sway off balance, dangerously close to the fire, and leapt to his side, just as he lurched forward, trying to save himself. She grabbed at him, and they rolled together away from the flames, on the soft, sandy ground. Jack found herself underneath him, his body hard and heavy on hers, his breathing ragged. The crutches had fallen aside.

"You *idiot*!" she spat. "What were you trying to do?"

Finn looked down at her, temper still smouldering in his eyes. "Oh, will you shut up!" he drawled, and his mouth came down on hers, hard and warm and devastating in its sureness.

Sheer surprise kept her immobile for several seconds. Then she stiffened, and squirmed beneath him, pushing at his shoulders.

He grabbed her wrists and wrested them back on the ground, and his mouth began coaxing hers open. A slow, languorous warmth started to course through her, and she clenched her hands and closed her mouth tightly against it, holding her body rigid.

Finn abruptly lifted his head, his eyes boring into hers, which were wide with shock and hostility.

"That," he said, "was taking advantage. Just so you know the difference."

He let her go without haste, and sat up with one arm across his knees as Jack got to her feet.

"Swine!" she said, and wiped the back of her hand across her mouth.

She turned her back on him and strode over to get the blankets she had slept on last night, then carried them round to the other side of the plane and made a bed in the open. She would rather sleep there than spend another night lying side by side with that supercilious male pig.

Chapter Four

A cold splash of rain fell on her face. She opened her eyes, and gasped as the splash was followed immediately by a deluge. Cursing fluently, she struggled up, bundling the blankets into her arms and, already soaked by the tropical downpour, ran for the plane.

The outline of the tent was a blur as she struggled towards the doorway of the plane. Hurling herself inside, she found water dripping and streaming from various places and tried to dodge between them in the dark, making for the rear, where she had stored the perishable foods. Not that there was much point, she told herself ruefully. She was already wet through.

There wasn't room to lie down, but she found a dry blanket and peeled off her wet shirt and shorts, then wrapped herself in the blanket and huddled in the corner. At least it wasn't particularly cold. She leaned her head back and after a while drifted into a doze.

"Jacqueline!"

Her eyes snapped open, and she grabbed at the slipping blanket, staring at the bulky shadow in the doorway.

"Jacqueline! Are you there? Jack?"

"Here!" she said. "Why on earth didn't you stay in the tent?"

Finn clambered clumsily inside. He had a wet blanket wrapped about him, and seemed to be using one crutch. "I was worried about you," he said.

He stumbled and swore, then fell with a bump, and Jack leapt up and hurried towards him. Her own blanket hampered her, and impatiently she cast it aside.

He was still swearing when she reached him. Fumbling for his arm, she said sharply, "Are you hurt?"

"No. Are *you* all right?"

"Of course I'm all right! And if you'd had the sense to stay where you were, instead of wandering around in the dark and getting soaked, you'd be all right, too. A little rain won't hurt me!"

"It won't hurt me, either, particularly," Finn pointed out. "Hell, it's wet in here! I've lost my damned crutch."

His hand touched her bare thigh, and Jack flinched. His eyes becoming accustomed to the gloom, he said, "Aren't you wearing *anything*?"

"I did have a blanket until you came bumbling in! I thought you'd hurt yourself." She backed away from him, groping round for the discarded blanket, and wrapped it about her, sarong fashion.

Finn found his crutch, and sat holding it. "Why didn't you come to the tent?"

"There's a dry part at the rear of the plane," Jack said. "I was quite comfortable."

"Well, lead me to it!" Finn replied. "I don't fancy going out in that again."

Jack sighed. "This way. Can you see?"

"Practically nothing. But I'll get there." He half crawled after her. "Not much space, is there?"

"Not a lot," she replied. "But it's dry."

She passed him a blanket, and he took it and leaned back against the sacks of rice and flour, his shoulder touching hers. He was using his blanket like a cloak, and she felt the texture of the wool against her bare arm. "So it is." The water thundered on the outside of the plane and dripped and trickled from the leaks, but this particular corner was still dry. "Sorry I disturbed you."

"It's all right," Jack said shortly. "But you didn't need to worry about me."

"Can't help it," Finn replied. "I'm built that way."

"Dr. Do-Gooder," she jeered, but without malice. "What on earth did you suppose could have happened to me?"

"A flash flood, perhaps," he answered. "You seem to be a fairly sound sleeper—when you're not having nightmares. The river could rise suddenly and carry you away."

Jack supposed that was a point. Still, "I can take care of myself," she said.

"I don't doubt it. In most situations, anyway. So can I, for that matter. But that didn't stop you from rushing to help just now when I fell."

Jack didn't answer that. It had been purely instinctive, a reflex action.

"There's only the two of us," Finn said softly. "We have to look out for each other, don't we?"

"Don't count on it, Doc," Jack said. "I'll always look after number one first. I always have."

She could hardly hear his laughter, but she felt it, because they were sitting so close.

"Oh, sure!" he said. "That's why you risked your life to get me out of the plane when you knew it might blow up at any minute."

"I told you, it wasn't that much of a risk."

Finn made a scornful sound.

After a while Jack got sleepy again, and let her head fall back against the sacks behind her. When she woke again, light was filtering into the aircraft, and she found that her cheek was pillowed on a warm, blanket-swathed shoulder.

She jerked back her head, and clutched at the sagging blanket in which she was wrapped.

Finn was regarding her with wry amusement. "Don't panic. I've seen the female form before."

"That didn't stop you last night, did it?"

"You were in no danger last night—or any other time. And you won't be. Not from me."

"I know that." She did, too. She'd had a glimpse of his temper, but even then it had been a controlled rage, a deliberate, calculated punishment, not meant to hurt, but only to chasten.

The rain had stopped, leaving a steaming heat. "I'll go out while you get dressed," Finn offered. On the way, he stopped and glanced at her soaking shorts and shirt. "Do you have anything to put on?" he asked.

"Only another shirt."

"You can't wear these," he said, picking up the dripping shorts. "I'll toss my bag in for you. Help yourself to whatever you can use."

His trousers were all much too big for her, and she settled for a buttoned shirt that came to a few inches down her tanned thighs.

"Very fetching," he commented, as she returned the bag to him in the tent. "It looks better on you than it ever did on me."

Jack turned away without answering, and he said, "Don't you like compliments?"

"No," Jack answered, and walked back to the plane.

The rain had added to the humidity, and although she hung her clothes over a dead branch, she didn't think there was much hope of them drying. Water still dripped from the trees, and the ground felt warm and wet.

"Take one of these." Finn held out a bottle of pills to her after their breakfast. "We don't want to add malaria to our troubles."

Obediently she swallowed one of the white pills. Handing back the bottle, she said, "I knew you'd come in handy."

Finn laughed. "We're bound to clash now and then," he said. "The situation makes it almost inevitable. But don't take me the wrong way if I say there's no one I can think of that I'd rather be marooned with."

Jack looked at him and said simply, "Thanks."

"You're welcome. I'm allowed to compliment you on your abilities—but not your looks?"

Studying the ground in front of her, Jack said, "That kind of compliment doesn't mean anything."

"Only if it's insincere, surely?"

"That sort of remark is always insincere. It's a male knee-jerk response to any decent-looking woman."

She got up and began gathering up their meagre breakfast things to rinse them off.

She spent the day collecting lots of wood, which Finn patiently added to their pyre. "It's too damp to burn, now, I suppose," he said regretfully. "But let's hope it'll soon dry out."

As they sat by their fire after supper, Jack said, "I think we should give it ten days. If there's been no sign of searchers by then, we'll have to make our own way out. Or I will."

"Not alone!" Finn interjected.

"I'll send them in for you," she reassured him.

"Of course you would!" he said. "I'm not worried about that. But you can't make the journey alone."

"Well, you wouldn't get far on that ankle."

"We've got plenty of food. Wait until my ankle heals, and I'll come with you—if we haven't been rescued by then."

Jack regarded him tauntingly. "Afraid of being left all alone, are we, Doc?"

His eyes narrowed. "Yes," he said at last. "Sure I am."

She didn't believe him. In his own way he was as tough as they came, an idealist, but no pie-in-the-sky dreamer. Certainly he was not afraid of solitude.

As she started to clean up, he said, "Sleep with me tonight."

She knew he meant only that. She gave an abrupt nod, and later she took her blankets and arranged them beside his in the tent.

On the ninth day, Jack said, "Maybe we could make a raft. To tow behind the dinghy."

Finn was cleaning a fish with her knife. "A raft?" He scrutinised the river. "How far is it navigable, do you know?"

Jack shook her head. "It's a tributary, I think, of a bigger river—if we are where I think we are. I've got charts on the plane. I'll get them out later. Travelling by water has to be faster than going overland in this country. And with a raft we could carry more supplies. If we're lucky, we might go a long way—even all the way to the coast."

Finn deftly scraped the scales from his fish. "It will take a fair amount of wood. And time. Not to mention hard work."

"Well, at least it's something constructive to do."

"Okay," Finn said. "Let's do it."

After the third day of building the raft, Jack was almost ready to give up. Her arm had healed nicely and didn't bother her anymore, but her hands were blistered, her back ached, and she was bone weary. They had prised apart a number of crates, which gave them some quite good boards, carefully saving and straightening nails as they went, and removed the fuel tanks to give the raft buoyancy. They had salvaged a number of good-sized logs for a framework from the havoc left by the plane's progress along the edge of the trees, and painstakingly started to remove the branches. "It'll be weeks before we've finished." She groaned, stretching out by the fire with her last, precious, slightly squashed cigarette. She intended to savour it. Maybe the thought of being able to smoke again when she returned to civilisation would spur her on to finish the raft.

As she blew smoke into the air, Finn began cleaning up. He was managing quite well now with one crutch, and she left him to it.

"I thought you'd finished your cigarettes," he said.

Her eyes closed, Jack said, "This is the last." She inhaled deeply, and blew a plume of smoke into the air.

"I'll leave you to enjoy it."

She smoked it right down to the filter, and when he got back she was sitting cross-legged with the butt in her fingers. Regretfully, she threw it into the fire, and sighed.

"Think of it this way," Finn said. "It's a golden opportunity to give it up for good."

"Perhaps I don't want to."

"Got a death wish, have you?"

Jack gave him a queer little smile, and stood up. "Maybe," she said lightly, and turned her back on him, walking swiftly away along the river.

It was quite dark when she returned, and she crawled under the blankets quietly, hoping that Finn was asleep. But he stirred, propped himself on an elbow, and said, "Why, Jacqueline?"

"Why what?"

"You know."

"I've no idea what you're talking about," she said. "I'm tired. Good night." And she hunched into her blanket and turned away from him.

"One day," he said almost to himself, "I'll get inside that shell of yours."

Silently, Jack stiffened. *Not if I can help it,* she thought. *No way.*

They didn't have enough nails to put all the pieces of the raft together, and Jack went hunting for some palm leaves. She had to climb to get them, putting a loop of rope about her waist and using her feet to push herself up as the islanders did. Although she had tried it before, just for fun, she wasn't as quick and expert as they were, and on the way down, after throwing the leaves to the ground, she skinned her palms badly, the blisters she had on them stinging fiercely as they broke, and for a few minutes she leant against the bole of the tree, holding her hands under her arms and trying not to shriek with pain.

When it was not quite so bad, she picked up the armful of strong, fibrous leaves and made for the camp, where Finn was working on the raft.

"What have you got there?" he asked her.

"Palm leaves. The islanders split them and use them for tying things, and to plait ropes. We can use ties instead of nails." She put the leaves down, and said casually, "I'll just help myself to some disinfectant. I got a bit scratched getting them."

"Show me," Finn said instantly.

"It's nothing. But you're always so insistent on guarding against infection.... I can do it myself."

"Show me," he said again.

"There's no need, really!" She backed away from him as he came closer.

"What's the matter?" he asked, beginning to look amused. "Where are these scratches?"

"It's only my hands!" she said crossly. "It's okay. They'll be all right."

As she turned away, he grabbed at her wrist and held it. "Don't be so childish," he admonished.

Instinctively, she had closed her fingers over the palm. Finn said evenly, "Open it, Jacqueline."

She looked at him mutinously, and he sighed and said, "Jack."

Slowly she opened her fingers. She felt his grip increase momentarily on her wrist. Silently he lifted the other, and stared down as her hands lay in his. "What the hell have you been doing?" he asked roughly.

"I had to climb the tree to get at the leaves. I slipped in the descent and came down a bit fast."

He retained his hold on her wrist and pulled her after him to the plane. He swabbed the raw flesh with disinfectant, glancing at her as she bit her lip against the sting, then smoothed some cream over her palms and covered them with bandages.

"You're not to use them for a few days," he said.

"But—"

"Doctor's orders, Jacqueline. And I'm here to make sure you obey them."

"You are so bossy!" she said feelingly.

Grinning, he said, "It comes with the job." He leaned over and lightly kissed her lips, and before she could react in any way, was turning to rummage in his bag. "I'll give you something for the pain. It'll probably make you a bit sleepy, too. So you shouldn't get too bored."

She did sleep later, lying in the tent, and when she woke, Finn was by her side, with a small fish, nicely grilled, lying on a bed of rice mixed with vegetables.

"Supper," he said. "Seeing you're an invalid, you can have yours here."

"I'm not an invalid," she protested. "But that smells good."

When only the bones of the fish remained, she took the dish out, holding it clumsily in one bandaged hand.

"I'll wash up," Finn said. "I don't want those bandages getting wet. How was your meal?"

"Fine, thank you," she said politely. "Very nice." Actually, the fish had not been as sweet-fleshed as it appeared, but she didn't want to be ungracious.

She sat by the fire until he came back. "I made us a checkerboard," he said. "Do you play?"

Jack shook her head. They had played cards, dredging up all the games they both knew, and using pebbles or leaves as stakes, but she would find it difficult to hold cards with her hands bandaged.

"I'll teach you," Finn said. "It's easy."

The board was made of cardboard coloured with a felt-tip pen, and he had cut circles of card for the pieces. They played for about an hour, and by the third game Jack was getting quite good at it, but he still beat her.

"I'd like to go for a walk," she said. "There's plenty of moonlight." They had a couple of torches, but had decided to conserve the batteries and only use them if needed.

"I'll come with you," Finn said, packing away the checkers in a paper bag and picking up his stick. "I don't want you having any more accidents."

They strolled along the strip of sand, the water rippling quietly beside them. The moonlight made the sand very white, and the river had a silver sheen on it. They walked for some way in silence, then turned to retrace their steps.

"How are the hands?" Finn asked as they approached their camp.

"Not bad. I'd love to go in the water." The murkiness of the first few days had almost disappeared, and she bathed in the river each evening while Finn tactfully kept to the other side of the wrecked plane.

"You can't swim with those hands bandaged," he said. "But you could get into the water for a while, if you like."

"It's a bit difficult undressing," she explained. Her fingers had swollen, and she was wearing the button-down shirt that he had said she could keep, since her own wardrobe was so meagre.

"I'll do it for you," he said. "But I'll wait around, in case you get into any difficulties in the water."

"I won't. And you don't need to—"

"It's okay. Do you want to fetch a towel?"

"No, not really." It was so hot she usually just pulled on her shirt over her damp skin. That way she stayed cool longer.

"Right." His hand on her arm turned her. Deftly he flicked open the buttons on the shirt, then said, "Turn around."

She faced the water, and he slipped the shirt off her shoulders. "Pants off or on?" he asked briskly.

"I'll leave them on," she said hastily.

"Okay. In you go."

She glanced over her shoulder and saw that he had half turned from her, holding the shirt in his hand.

She went cautiously into the water, and when it was deep enough, crouched down in the delicious coolness.

"Are you in?" Finn's voice came.

"Yes."

She turned her head and saw him sit down on the sand, facing her. "Let me know when you want to come out," he said. "And yell if you need me."

"Thanks." She closed her eyes, raising her bandaged hands well clear of the water. "It's lovely," she said.

"I'll go in myself, later," Finn said. He always waited until she had finished, and then fastened a plastic bag tightly over his bandaged foot and went to the river.

"I've had enough," she said at last, and after a moment cautiously stood up. She didn't want to lose her footing on the shifting sand.

When she emerged, Finn was standing with his head turned away, holding out the shirt for her to slip into.

She said, "You don't need to do it up. I'll put on one of my T-shirts instead when I get back. It'll be easier." She wrapped the shirt about her, and held it with her arms. "Thank you, Finn."

"You're welcome," he said easily.

She struggled into a T-shirt on her own while he was having his evening dip, and when he got back she was under her blanket.

"You okay?" he asked. "Do you need some more pain-killers?"

"No," she answered. "No, thanks." She felt a bit queasy, and wondered if the pills he had given her might have caused it. She would rather not take any more.

But in the middle of the night she felt more than queasy, and got up to stumble out of the tent, before she was violently sick several yards away.

When she got to her feet, she felt dizzy. Finn was emerging from the tent, leaning on one of his crutches. "Jacqueline?" he said. "What's the matter?"

"I was sick," she said. "Maybe those pills..?"

"I don't think so." He limped towards her. "Were you feeling ill before?" He kept pace as she returned to the tent.

"Sort of, when I went to bed. I didn't think it was anything...."

"Lie down," he said, as she swayed.

Glad to obey, she practically fell onto the blankets, a hand to her head as the tent seemed to spin. She closed her eyes. "Be all right in a minute," she gasped. She didn't remember ever feeling this bad in her life.

And it got worse. She was sick again, but this time she couldn't even get up to leave the tent. Her head burned, her feet were freezing, and her legs had turned to rubber. Vaguely she was conscious of Finn thrusting a stainless steel basin under her nose, placing a cool cloth on her forehead, and pulling up the blanket to her chin when she had emptied her stomach and was lying very still, hoping that the world would stop whirling and her stomach cease its horrible convolutions.

After a while the world receded altogether, and she was lost in a confused, feverish maze. Sometimes she dreamed, and sometimes she thought she was a child again, back home in Melbourne, or a teenager, falling in love with flying—and with the man who had taught her how to fly—and several times she woke to Finn's soothing voice, his hand on her head, or to a stern command: "Drink this, Jacqueline. Come on, get it down!"

Once she thought he was sponging her body with cooling water, and whispered, "Thank you, thank you, Finn." And at least once she insisted on going outside.

"You don't have to," he said. "I can bring something for you to use." But she said no, she could manage. And she did, somehow. Only she didn't remember getting back to bed.

Then she woke up one day and the birds were singing, the world had come back, and she felt light and empty and tired.

She lay there listening to the birds and admiring the sunshine on the water that she could just glimpse to one side of the tent entrance. And then a shadow fell across the opening, and filled it.

"Finn," she said, surprised at how weak her voice sounded, almost a whisper.

And Finn said, "Jacqueline!" Then he knelt beside her and caught one of her wrists in a hard grip. "You're feeling better?" She realised that her hands were still bandaged, though not as heavily.

She nodded, then said rather doubtfully, "I think so. I feel as though I've...been away somewhere. For quite a while."

"Three days," he said. "You gave me a hell of fright."

"Sorry," she murmured. "You took care of me...didn't you?"

"As well as I could."

She smiled faintly. "I knew..." she said, "...that there was a good reason for me to pull you out of that plane."

Then she drifted back to sleep.

When next she woke, it was to Finn's hand on her shoulder. "I've made you soup," he said. "Try to get some down, will you?"

He held the bowl for her, and she sipped at it. She drank about half, then shook her head. "Sorry, I can't take any more."

"You've done well," he assured her. "It's the only food you've had in three days."

"Is that why I feel like a wet rag?"

"I guess that's got a lot to do with it." He put a hand to her forehead. "You're not feverish anymore."

"What was it?" she asked him. "A bug?"

"I'm afraid it was my fault. That fish I gave you. I think it must have been poisonous."

"You didn't have any?"

"It was my one and only catch that day. I thought I'd give it to you as a special treat." He grimaced. "Some treat."

"Just as well we didn't both have it. I'm glad you were here to take care of me. I knew there were a few poisonous fish around the ocean reefs. I never thought of any of the river fish being poisonous.''

"Neither did I. I guess I should have.''

"You weren't to know.''

He said, "Well, that puts paid to fish on the menu in future. Not worth the risk. I need to dress your hands. I'll be back in a minute.''

They looked better, and he said when he had smoothed salve on them, "I'll just bandage them lightly for the night. Tomorrow we can probably dispense with wrapping them. The swelling's gone down.''

"How's your ankle?'' she asked, and he smiled at her.

"Healing nicely.''

"I suppose you haven't done much to the raft.''

"You're not going to be fit for a raft trip for at least another week. It's a long way to the coast down that river. And according to the maps you showed me, it doesn't seem to come out near a town.''

"There are small coastal settlements not marked on the maps.''

"Mmm,'' he said doubtfully. "I suppose we'd be better off with people, even if they are miles from the main centres, such as *they* are. But they could be hostile, you know. Some of the rebel groups aren't too kindly disposed towards Europeans. They blame us for all their troubles since the colonial era.''

"We have to do something!''

"Yes,'' he agreed, "but not right now. You, lady, are going to be resting for the next few days.''

Gallingly, Jack found that she didn't really have much choice. When she tried to get up she felt as weak as a kitten, and a sickly one at that, and her appetite would hardly have given a bird a run for its money. She also felt peevish, and when she snapped at Finn, who was unfailingly patient and considerate, and then grudgingly apologised, he said, "I'm glad you're feeling better.''

"Do you have to be so nice?" she complained. "It wasn't your fault the damned fish was poisonous."

"I'm not suffering from any guilt complex," he assured her. "It was a mistake, and I'm sorry about it, but there isn't any point in breast-beating. If I find it easy to be patient, it's because I'm relieved that you're still around to be your maddening, prickly self."

Jack bit her lip. "Am I maddening?"

"Frequently," he said cheerfully. "I guess I madden you sometimes, too."

"Like when you call me Jacqueline," she said. "But you do that on purpose."

"Guilty," he admitted. "But also, I...just don't find 'Jack' an appropriate name for a very attractive young woman."

Jack didn't answer, and he said softly, "Please don't do that!"

"Do what?" She looked up at him defensively.

"Slide into your shell like a hermit crab. You do it every time I...every time I say or do something to remind you you're a woman, not...a boy, or some kind of asexual being."

She knew that was true. "In the circumstances," she said stiffly, "I think that's a better way to be."

"Meaning you don't want us involved in a sexual relationship?"

"Bluntly, yes. You can surely see how it would... complicate things."

"Maybe. But a simple admission that I'm male and you're female needn't lead us into an episode of torrid passion."

"But you're a doctor. You must be accustomed to...ignoring a person's sex."

She thought of what he had done for her while she was ill, and flushed a little.

"When the person is my patient, yes," he said. "And I can assure you I wasn't burning with lust while *you* were burning with fever. But I don't ignore the differences in my everyday life. I'm a man as well as a doctor, you know. I don't think that a casual compliment or an acknowledgement of your...femininity...merits the cold shoulder."

"I'm sorry, but I don't know how else to react," Jack said. "I don't play those games—"

"They're not *games*! They're the normal social interchanges between men and women—"

"Anyway," Jack continued, "I don't have any 'femininity,' so you can stop trying to bring it out of me. You're wasting your time."

Finn burst out laughing.

"What's so funny?" Jack demanded suspiciously.

"You!" he answered, still grinning at her. "You really have no idea, do you? You're one of the sexiest females I've ever met. I felt it the first time I saw you, and I assure you, nothing's changed. Jacqueline Renton," he said, savouring the name as though it were a fine wine, "you can deny it all you like, but you are all woman. Jacqueline," he said again, and his eyes smiled at her in challenge, in an awareness that brought a reluctant shiver of answering awareness to her entire body. "Not Jack."

She instinctively shrank back against the piled blankets serving as her pillow. *"Stop it!"* she said fiercely. "Don't!"

Finn frowned. "Tell me why you're so scared."

"You don't scare me!" She injected all the scorn she could into that, but it only made him smile.

"No?" he drawled. "Then why the panic?"

"That's your interpretation."

"It's a fairly obvious one." He paused, his eyes on her face. "What is it?" he asked insistently, and then, "Have you been attacked by someone?"

Vehemently, she shook her head. The action made her feel slightly dizzy, and she swallowed before she said, her voice more husky than usual, "You're way out, Doc. I haven't been raped, and I'm not frightened of men, okay? And I'm grateful for what you've done, but just leave the psychoanalysis out, thanks. I don't need it."

"I thought," Finn said mildly, "that I'd made it clear I wasn't speaking as a doctor."

"You can't help thinking like one. I'm sorry I'm the only subject available for your undoubted skills, but just confine your attention to my physical ailments, will you?"

"Physical ailments often have an emotional connection."

"You said this was caused by the fish," Jack reminded him coldly. "I don't quite see any connection."

He grinned. "There isn't one. That was just a piece of bad luck."

"By the way... Doctor," she said, her hand plucking at the blanket over her knees. "I was about due when we crashed, but nothing's happened. And I'm definitely not pregnant."

Finn shrugged. "Trauma—the shock of the crash. It's not unusual. Don't worry, it'll be all right."

"Okay. Thanks."

He put a hand briefly over hers, and then removed it. "I'll get you some lunch," he promised, and left her.

Chapter Five

He helped her get up later, awkwardly, because he was still using a stick himself. She tried not to lean on him, but she must have been more tired than she knew, and on the way back they collapsed on the sand together.

"You're not hurt?" Jack started to ask anxiously, and was reassured by Finn's burst of laughter.

"A couple of weaklings!" he gasped, and she began laughing, too. They ended up lying full length on the sand, smiling at each other. Then Finn moved closer and leaned over her, and his head came down, and he kissed her gently, questingly, on the mouth.

Her response was instinctive and unstinting, her lips parting, her arms coming up to hold him, her hands spread on the sun-warmed cotton of his shirt. His arm slid under her, gathering her closer, and as her head fell back his mouth left hers and trailed tiny, teasing kisses down the line of her throat.

When his hand touched her breast, she stiffened, and he instantly removed it, slowly drawing back, but without releasing his hold on her. "All right," he whispered, and his mouth brushed her cheek, her still-closed eyes. "It's all right. You're not fit, anyway."

Her eyes fluttered open and she made a small effort at withdrawal, but he kept his arm about her as he rolled onto his back and tucked her head firmly against his shoulder. "Stay there," he murmured. "Please. Just stay there."

After a moment she shuddered and relaxed against him, her eyes closed again. His hand stroked her hair, and his breathing was deep and even against her cheek. She was, she told herself, too tired to fight him.

She must have dozed for a little while. When she woke she felt stronger, and slipped out of Finn's arms to sit up, gazing at the river.

His voice addressed her back. "Don't worry about it," he advised drily. "You haven't given anything away."

"Who's worrying?" she answered, making her voice light, smoothing the frown from between her brows.

He sat up, too, and grasped her arm, with his other hand turning her face to his steady scrutiny.

He ran a thumb over her mouth, and she drew a quick breath, trying not to flinch. She said, her voice full of mockery, "I've been kissed before, you know. It's no big deal."

"Of course," he agreed equably. "No big deal at all."

She stood up and stepped back from him. "I think I can walk on my own now."

"Okay," he said in the same tone of voice. "Try it."

He limped along beside her, but she made it back to the tent, glad to subside again on the blankets. She tried to blot out what had happened on the riverbank, but that night she was wakeful, and her mind kept replaying not only the kisses they had shared that day, but a number of earlier incidents: when they had sheltered together from the rain in the darkness of the plane, and when he had undressed her so that she could bathe in the river. Emotions that she had suppressed at the time, firmly denied, now set her nerve ends quivering, sent waves of heat coursing through her body. She lay with her eyes closed and her hands clenched under the blanket, remembering how Finn looked without his shirt, the way the skin around his eyes crinkled when he smiled, and the feel of the muscles under his light clothing when he had kissed her today, the hard heat of his body pressing hers into the soft sand, the gentleness of his hand caressing her hair. She heard him breathing only a foot away from her, and fought an astonishing, overwhelming desire to close the space between them and wake him, and have him take her in his arms again. And knew that if she did, this time they wouldn't stop at a few kisses.

It was years since she had felt like this. And although there was of course, a fierce, anticipatory pleasure, she didn't welcome it. This was something she had turned her back on long ago. Something she could do without, *must* do without, for her own survival.

I don't love him, she rationalised. *And he doesn't even like me, really—what I stand for, how I live my life. I saw the look on his face when I said I'd fly him to Kitikiti because he paid well. It's simple propinquity that's brought this on. We have nothing in common, a do-gooder and a mercenary. Two young, healthy bodies, no one else around, and nature does the rest. An animal instinct. Survival of the species, and all that. As I said, I've been kissed before. Not lately, of course. But the only reason it's affected me so deeply is the fact that we're alone here.*

Finn stirred in his sleep, and turned, flinging an arm across the space between them. His hand was inches from her, and she thought about twining her fingers into his, then deliberately turned her back, pulling her blanket around her. *No, it's not for me. Never again. I swear it. Never again.*

The next time she got up, she did without his help, and gradually she grew strong enough to sit in the shade splitting palm leaves and plaiting the fibres into rope while Finn carried on building their raft.

He had not attempted again to kiss her. Except for an occasional lingering, speculative glance that she found dif-

ficult to read, but which always sent her finding an excuse
for a hasty retreat from his vicinity, nothing seemed to have
changed.

Progress on the raft was slow. Finn flatly refused to allow her to do anything requiring physical exertion. One day
as he joined her in the shade out of the broiling afternoon
sun, after stripping off his shirt for a dip in the river, she
said, "You haven't been doing a Penelope on me, have
you?"

"Come again?" He mopped his wet face and head with
his shirt, and pushed back his dripping hair.

"Penelope—you know, the wife of Ulysses, who unrav-
elled her weaving every night."

"Oh, yes. Something to do with waiting for Ulysses to
come home. She'd . . . yes, she'd said she would marry
someone else when she'd finished her weaving, right?"

When Jack nodded, he laughed. "Believe me, I find this
far too hard to be undoing what I've done in the heat each
day. Not going fast enough for you?" he asked wryly.

"I didn't mean to be critical. Only I wondered if you were
worried that I'd be wanting to leave before you think I'm fit
for it."

He gave her one of his enigmatic looks, bunched his shirt
in his hand and tossed it down, turning to rest his head on
it as he lay flat on his back, staring at the sky through the
green leaves above them. "If I don't think you're fit, we
don't go," he said. "I may have lost some of my sense of
urgency, because you need a bit longer to recover fully."

"Is that a way of saying I was right?"

A lazy smile touched his mouth, and he closed his eyes.
"It's too hot to argue, Jacqueline. Don't push it."

She gave an impatient exclamation and jumped up,
glowering down at his apparently unconscious face before
stalking away from him along the river.

"Don't go too far," he said without opening his eyes. She
glared back at him, tempted to make some childish retort,
and kept walking.

At this time of the day she wouldn't be going far, anyway. Even the birds tended to remain in the trees when the sun was at its height. Although one was lazily cruising high in the sky some miles off....

She stopped, and her heart seemed to give a great thump, stopping in her throat. She flung a hand up to shade her eyes, absurdly standing on tiptoe as though it would help her to see better. Then she wheeled, running, screaming, *"Finn! Finn! Light the beacon! The fire! A plane, Finn! There's a plane!"*

When she reached him he had already hobbled to the cooking fire and pulled a burning stick from it, but by then the plane had disappeared.

"But they might still see the smoke," Jack urged, as Finn paused doubtfully by the piled wood of the beacon. "It should be visible for miles."

"Yes," he said. "I know."

She guessed what was passing through his mind. "So it's a risk," she said quietly. "I think we have to take it."

He nodded, and thrust the burning end into the stack. There had been no rain for days, and the driftwood and dry timber caught instantly, crackling into a very satisfactory blaze. He had cut some rubber from the plane's tyres, and when the flames reached it the smoke turned thick and black.

"They must see it," Jack muttered, scanning the empty blue sky. "They must!"

They kept feeding the fire, scouring up and down the sand for more wood, and even venturing into the trees, careful to keep the water and the plume of smoke within sight. But after an hour and a half, Finn touched her arm, leaning heavily on his stick, and said, "It's no use. They haven't seen it."

Jack drew in a deep breath, then let it go, her shoulders slumping. "I guess not," she admitted.

Finn's free arm came about her, and she put both of hers around him, and let her head rest on his shoulder. He

rubbed his cheek against her hair, and they stood in silent
disappointment for a long time.

At last he said, "Well, that's that."

Jack nodded. By tacit consent they sat down, side by side
before the still-burning remains of the beacon that they had
so painstakingly built. Moodily, Jack plucked bits of dried
grassy weeds from the sand and threw them onto the dying
flame, watching the brief flare and fizzle of each strand,
before it curled and blackened and then turned to grey ash.

"Never mind," Finn said, and picked up her hand, rubbing it against his cheek. Then he kissed her fingers, his lips
warm against her skin.

Jack bit her lip, and he looked up, a question in his eyes.
For a long moment she looked back at him, feeling her body
yearning towards him, knowing her eyes were answering for
her. But she took a shaky breath, removed her gaze reso-
lutely from his and said with an effort, "We'll have to build
another beacon." It would take even longer, because they
had used all the available wood nearby and would have to
forage farther afield.

"Yes," he said. "I guess we will." His hand tightened for
a moment. Then he got up without releasing her, retrieving
his stick with the other hand, and hauled her to her feet.
"And in case someone *else* saw our fire, perhaps we should
be prepared for visitors."

Jack climbed into the plane, delved into the bottom of her
rucksack and took out the revolver she had packed there,
and the box of ammunition. She efficiently checked over the
mechanism, making sure the safety catch was on, and was
loading the gun when Finn appeared in the doorway.

Looking up, she saw his eyes go cold. "I didn't know
you'd brought that," he said.

"You told me to."

"I told you that you *could* if you felt it was necessary.
And don't forget what else I said."

"That's it's for my own personal protection if I'm in imminent danger," Jack remembered. "Roger." She sketched him a salute.

He didn't smile, merely nodding in a rather tight-lipped fashion before he turned and disappeared.

She finished what she was doing and took the gun with her to the tent, tucking it just under the edge of her makeshift pillow. Finn was making supper, and she looked up to find his eyes on her before he returned them to the packet he was opening.

"Why did you let me bring it, when you feel so strongly about guns?" she asked him.

"I thought I didn't have the right to impose my beliefs on you, if it came to defending your life."

"You're very fair, aren't you?"

"I try to be. I can't say I always live up to my own principles, I'm afraid, but I do make the effort."

"It must be difficult, being so high-minded."

Finn poured the dehydrated vegetables into some water in a bowl and began stirring them. "I don't know that I like that term."

"What else would you call living up to your principles?"

"Everyone has principles of one sort or another that they live by."

Jack shook her head. "Not me."

Finn set the bowl over the fire on the grid they had made from bits of metal, and sat back. "Of course you do. Even if it's only looking after number one, as you tried to tell me. But deep down, your beliefs are a lot more complex than that."

Jack said almost angrily, "Can't you accept that I have a simple philosophy of life—and it's the opposite of yours?"

"No," Finn said, looking directly at her. "Because I know it isn't true."

"It is true," she insisted. "It's all I live by, Finn. And if you believe anything else, you'll be direly disappointed in the end."

Finn rocked back on his haunches. "Okay, so I'll be disappointed."

When he crawled into his blankets later, she was still awake, lying with her hands propping her head.

"I didn't bring the automatic rifle," she said.

"I know." Well, he had asked her not to. And he was paying, after all.

"Abe would flip if he knew," she told him.

"Does that bother you?"

Jack shrugged in the darkness. "Not much."

"Does being without the rifle bother you?"

She thought about that. "Not much," she decided finally.

"How long have you known Abe?" he asked.

"A few years. Why?"

"He seems to care about you."

"I guess he fancies himself as a father figure."

"Does he now?" Finn paused. "What about Red?"

"Why this interest in my friends?" she demanded, turning towards him.

His face was shadowed. "Just making conversation," he said. "Maybe I'm nervous," he added blandly.

Jack gave a disbelieving snort. "Do you think one of us should keep watch?" she asked, wondering if she ought to have thought of it before.

"I'll wake up if there are any unusual noises."

"You must be a light sleeper."

"When I know I might be needed, I am. It's a skill I developed in my hospital training years."

In the early hours of the morning, Jack woke to the pressure of a hand on her shoulder. She opened her eyes, and Finn's hand firmly covered her mouth. She felt his breath on her cheek, and he whispered, "Something's coming down the river."

When he removed his hand she sat up very quietly and eased the gun out from under her pillow. He moved away a little, and his hand came about her wrist, warningly. "We try it my way first!"

Swiftly she pulled on her shorts and tucked the gun into the back pocket, then pushed her arms into the sleeves of the roomy shirt he had given her.

All the time her ears were straining to hear whatever had woken Finn. The rippling of the water against the sandy riverbank seemed louder than usual, and at first she could hear no other sound. Then she thought she did, a gentle, rhythmic splashing. Paddles or oars, and coming closer.

It was no use attempting to hide. If whoever it was saw the wreckage, they would surely search the area, and they probably knew the country well. Implying guilt, fear or hostility by trying to avoid being found would only engender suspicion.

Downriver, she thought. They were coming downriver, so they were unlikely to be government forces. As far as she knew, the army had not penetrated this far. They could be a party of harmless fisherfolk or villagers travelling from one settlement to another. But she couldn't make herself believe that. There was no reason for an innocent party of travellers to be on the river at night. And there was a peculiar stealth about the careful, quiet strokes in the water, the lack of any other sound.

All the same, she didn't fancy being found cowering in a tent, unable to stand upright.

"Let's go outside," she whispered to Finn, and he nodded.

He had a torch in the hand that he didn't need for his stick, but he didn't switch it on. Cautiously they picked their way over the ground between the tent and the crumpled nose of the plane.

They both heard the low-voiced exclamation from the river, and the cessation of paddling. They stopped short, and then, clearly on the night air, came a number of metallic clicks that made goose bumps rise on Jack's arms. Their visitors had guns. And they were getting ready to use them.

They were coming into the bank, with a subdued thumping and a rustle as a keel came to rest on the sand.

Finn edged forward until he could peer through the broken fuselage of the plane, and Jack stayed at his shoulder. The jagged wreckage obscured the view, but she saw shadowy figures against the sheen of the water, and the menacing jut of long gun barrels.

Finn gripped her arm. "I'm going to show a light," he said very quietly. "Keep down."

Jack nodded.

He urged her farther back behind the plane, and switched on the flashlight, throwing the beam beyond the wreckage, out in front of the silent, wary gunmen.

Instantly an order was shouted, and feet pounded on the sand. Then all was silent again, and a voice called, "Who are you? Show yourself."

Jack instinctively clutched warningly at Finn's sleeve. He turned his head and murmured, "It's okay. Just stay here for a minute until I've talked to them." Then he called, "I'm Dr. Finn Simonson. Since my plane crashed, I'm lame. I have to use a cane."

So that they wouldn't mistake it for a gun barrel, Jack realised.

Finn turned the beam of light down to the ground and walked slowly out from behind the plane. Jack eased the revolver out of her back pocket and tucked it into the side one, then strolled out, too, her hands casually in her pockets, the bulge of the gun hidden by her loose shirt.

Finn murmured, "I told you to stay put."

A powerful white light blinded her, and a voice, full of authority, said, "Stop there, please!"

Obediently they halted. "If there are going to be heroics," Jack said without looking at the man by her side, "I want to be in on the action."

"No heroics," Finn told her under his breath. "Not from me."

The voice ordered, "Switch off the light and put it on the ground." Like most of the islanders the man spoke English with an almost indefinable fullness in the vowels, a slight blurring of the consonants.

Finn bent to place the flashlight at his feet. As he straightened, he spread his hands apart as though to show he was unarmed. His faded blue T-shirt and tattered khaki trousers wouldn't have hidden much.

"Keep still, please," the voice said.

Very polite, thought Jack, but there was no doubt that this was an order. The voice said something more quietly, that she didn't catch, and a man came forward out of the darkness, slinging a gun onto his shoulder by its webbing strap. He wore a purple-and-white floral cotton shirt with combat trousers and boots instead of a proper uniform.

The man stopped in front of Finn, and went through the routine that Jack had seen hundreds of times in films, running his big brown hands over Finn's body in a search for weapons. Then he turned to her, and she looked him full in the eyes and said clearly, "No, you don't!"

She heard Finn make a small sound that might have been an exasperated admonition or choked laughter. She didn't look aside to see, instead holding the armed man's rather nonplussed dark eyes with a steely glare.

He turned and said, "A woman!"

Another figure appeared, striding up to them. He was not as tall as the first, and wore khaki shorts with an open-necked shirt, and boots with laces that had been broken and knotted together; but he also had a peaked army-style cap, a handgun in a leather holster at his waist, and an air of confident authority. With the powerful spotlight behind him, his face was shadowed, but his eyes gleamed darkly. He looked closely at Jack, then transferred his gaze to Finn.

"*Dr.* Simonson?" he said, with what might have been a touch of respect. "A medical doctor?" He seemed to lean forward a little, as though the information was important to him.

"That's right," Finn confirmed. "I'm a member of IVER. We were on our way to Kitikiti with emergency supplies when our plane crashed."

"IVER," the man repeated.

"International Volunteers for Emergency Relief."

"Yes. I have heard of them. What kind of supplies, Doctor?"

Finn said, "Blankets, food, medical supplies."

"Why Kitikiti?" the man asked.

"There's a reasonable airstrip there. And there used to be a hospital, of sorts. We hoped we could distribute the supplies from there, and set up a medical emergency base for the area."

The man said, "We will see they are distributed."

Finn said, "They're for the cyclone victims."

"Of course."

"Are you army?" Finn asked.

The man said, "Not exactly, Doctor." Jack supposed that meant that he and his men were rebels. His bearing was unmistakably martial. She wondered if he had once been in the regular army. He glanced at Jack with quick curiosity, and then addressed himself again to Finn. Gesturing toward the wreck, he said, "Who else was in the plane?"

"Just the two of us," Finn answered.

"You and . . . the lady?"

"Yes," Finn said, his hand moving from his side to close tightly about Jack's arm. "Just me . . . and my wife."

Chapter Six

Finn's fingers digging into her arm, Jack closed the jaw that had dropped slightly in astonishment, and brought her teeth tightly together. No doubt Finn had his reasons, and now wasn't the time to enquire into them. She just hoped they were good ones.

Oddly, the man before her made a stiff bow as though he had been introduced at some social occasion. She had the feeling that he had just barely missed clicking his heels, and for a moment she envisaged him in dress uniform with gold epaulettes. "Mrs. Simonson," he said. "I am Captain Tula. I'm sorry about your plane," he said, addressing Finn again. "Is your cargo damaged?"

Jack answered. "Not too badly. Most of it's okay."

The man cast her a slightly surprised look, and Finn looked at her, too, a warning in his eyes. She was annoyed. Obviously they both thought that any conversation should take place between the two of them, presumably because they were male. Tukaikians tended to have rigid ideas about sexual roles, but Finn didn't have to be so ready to relegate her to the position of "little woman." Restlessly, she tried to shift her arm out of his grasp, but his fingers didn't relax by even a fraction.

"I would like to see," the guerilla leader said, as polite as ever, but this was, of course, no request. As if to reinforce that, he added, "Show me," and picked up the flashlight that Finn had left on the ground.

Finn nodded and stepped aside, taking Jack with him as the man walked past them. The other guerilla brought up the rear, and Jack was very conscious of the gun that he now again held in his hands.

The inspection was quick but thorough. When they were all outside the plane again, standing on the sandy ground, Tula said, "You will come with us, please. The cargo will be brought out later."

"Where are we going?" Jack asked him, as he shone the light all about the area, the beam pausing on the tent with her and Finn's tumbled blankets inside it.

He said obliquely, "I'm sure we can find more comfortable accommodation for you, Mrs. Simonson."

Finn looked at her, giving a small shrug of resignation. There wasn't much they could do about it. She was not sure how many men Tula had with him, for in the dark it was difficult to judge, but there were at least four of them, and they were well armed. And they didn't appear to have any intention of harming their captives. For all his air of authority, Tula seemed to have some kind of regard for Finn's profession. She supposed that a doctor would be seen as a useful acquisition by a party of guerilla fighters.

There were, it transpired, six of them. Tula left two men guarding the site and then politely but firmly ushered Finn and Jack into a long native canoe, where they sat together in the middle, with two paddlers in front of them and Tula and another behind. Captain Tula had positively insisted on Finn taking his medical bag, and Jack had her knapsack holding her few clothes and other essentials.

It was eerie on the river at night. The trees on either side cast thick shadows, and the moon kept scudding behind clouds, making the water black and mysterious. The paddles splashed rhythmically, and Jack could hear the men breathing. Travelling against the current would be quite hard work. Beside her Finn's arm brushed hers, and she moved restlessly.

He murmured, "You okay?"

"More or less," she answered. "I can't say I'm completely happy about this, but at least they didn't shoot us."

Finn nodded. She whispered, "Why did you tell him we're married?"

He put a hand on her wrist and gripped briefly. "Later."

They seemed to be going a long way upriver, she thought, almost slipping into a doze. Then Tula gave a low-voiced command, and one of the men in front lifted his paddle, and the narrow craft turned and headed for the bank. Surprised, Jack glanced at Finn. The dark trees rose ahead of them, and the man in the bow brushed aside some low, sweeping branches. The canoe glided under them, into a kind of tunnel of overhanging trees, along a high-banked stream.

Eventually the tunnel opened, and Jack could dimly see rushes growing at the edges, rustling in the night breeze. A bird disturbed by their passage squawked and fluttered across the water in front of them, raising quick splashes of silver. The men had thrown their paddles down before them and unslung the guns on their shoulders before the captain laughed, and they relaxed and laughed, too.

Then they were pushing through the reeds, negotiating some devious channel. The canoe stopped with its nose against a bank, and Tula said, "Please get out."

The two in front jumped onto the bank and helped Finn; then one offered his hand to Jack.

Ignoring it, she leapt onto soft, wet ground beside Finn, her sneakers squelching. Tula came after her and said, "You will follow, please. When we have the boat out of the water."

They carried it, leaving the bags and paddles inside it, while Finn and Jack trailed along behind. The path wound through swamp, and in parts the water ran between lumpy sections of damp ground. Tula stopped once and asked Finn, "Do you need help, Doctor?"

Finn shook his head, and the man nodded and strode on.

Some time later, Finn stumbled, almost lost his stick, and swore under his breath. Jack said swiftly, "Lean on me if you like."

"It's okay," he muttered.

Tula said, "I'm sorry, Doctor. We will go more slowly."

They did, but not much. After twenty minutes or so they came to a shimmer of water again, and the canoe was lowered into another stream, this one wider and deeper than the shallow creek that had ended in the swamp.

Jack found it difficult to calculate the time it took to complete the journey, but the sky was beginning to lighten when the canoe was drawn up again to a bank, and they scrambled out and were taken along a winding uphill path. Jack could hear Finn breathing rather heavily, but when she suggested they ask Tula to let them rest, he said shortly, "I'd rather rest when we get there, wherever 'there' is."

They arrived at last at a cluster of buildings standing on a cleared slope. There was a challenge from a sentry on duty, which Tula answered, and then they were conducted to a native-style house with walls and partitions of woven palm leaves and a thatched roof. The floor was covered in pandanus mats, and several children slept huddled together on a wide mattress in one corner. A woman rose from a single mattress in another part of the big room, and Jack saw that a child lay there, too, his knees drawn up, whimpering rather tiredly and clutching his midriff, as though he had a pain that had been there for a long time.

"This woman's son is ill," Captain Tula said to Finn. "Please, Doctor..."

He gestured, and the woman repeated, "Doctor?" on a note of trembling hope.

Finn knelt by the boy, who would have been about seven or eight, Jack supposed, and gently probed his abdomen.

He put a few quiet questions to the mother, and then said, "It looks like acute appendicitis. He needs an operation."

The woman drew in her breath, and Captain Tula said, "Can you do it, Doctor?"

"You can't send him to—no, I suppose not," Finn answered himself. "Yes, I could do it, while it's a simple job. If it ruptures there will be complications."

"Then it's urgent?"

"Yes. I'll need some help. Is there a nurse here, or anyone with medical knowledge?"

"There is an old woman who treats the sick with native remedies and Western medicine, but she speaks no English. And a teacher who knows some first aid."

Finn thought for a minute, then turned to Jack. He said, "I want you to help."

"Me?"

His eyes cautioned her, *Don't say too much in front of Tula*. "I know I can trust you," he said. "You did well before. You're not squeamish, and you're quick to catch on. All you have to do is what you're told."

Perhaps out of sheer surprise, she thought afterwards, Jack nodded and said, "Yes, all right. If you think so."

"Tell me what you need," Captain Tula said.

Finn told him, and in a remarkably short time the boy had been taken to a makeshift operating room, which appeared to be Tula's headquarters. A large office table covered with a snowy white sheet became the operating table, and a soldier brought in a stainless steel pot of water and placed a spirit burner on a bench for Finn to sterilise his instruments. Hot water had been provided, too, for Finn and Jack to wash in, and clean clothes. Roomy shirts buttoned up the back for them by the boy's mother served for surgical gowns.

Finn administered the anaesthetic himself, telling Jack how to monitor the patient once the boy was asleep. She concentrated on what he told her to do, handed him the instruments he asked for, and kept her eyes averted from what he was actually doing with them. When she hesitated over what he wanted, he quietly prompted her, pointing to or describing the article. It didn't really take very long, and at last he turned away from the table, pulled down the white mask he was wearing and grinned at her. "All over. He'll be fine. I'll keep him on antibiotics for a few days in case of any infection, and in a week or so he'll be up and running."

Jack stepped back from the table, her knees shaky.

"They were lucky to find you," she said, pulling off her own mask. "He would have died, wouldn't he?"

"Probably, if the thing had ruptured, which it seemed about ready to do. Thanks for your help. You did fine."

"I did, didn't I?" she agreed, an enormous relief and unaccustomed pride sweeping over her. "I didn't know I had it in me," she added self-mockingly.

"I did. That's why I asked you to do it."

She glanced at him sharply, wondering if something other than the reasons he had given her had motivated his request. But he was dropping his instruments into a dish with a clatter. "Better get these cleaned up. Then we can move the kid back to his own home before he wakes."

Later, when Finn had roused the child briefly from his anaesthetic sleep, and given the grateful mother careful instructions, he and Jack were led to a small white-painted weatherboard building that appeared to be unused.

"You may wish to sleep," Tula said, as he opened the door. "Please make yourselves comfortable. I can send you some tea, if you would like it."

The thought made Jack's mouth water, and she said, "Yes, please."

"Thanks," Finn added. "We would appreciate that."

Tula came in and lit a lamp that stood on a table at one end of the single room. "I'm sorry, there is a shortage of accommodation since the cyclone," he said.

It seemed to be a disused office, perhaps hastily cleared while they were carrying out the operation. There were two simple wooden chairs flanking the table, and shelves lined one wall, but there was nothing on them except a manila folder and a few papers that had a curled, unwanted air. Along another wall was a broad wooden bench with cupboards under it.

Tula shut the door as he left, and Jack said, "Sleep? Where?"

Finn looked wry. "On the floor, perhaps." There was a thin coconut fibre mat on the floor, rather worn. Jack didn't fancy it.

The tea was brought by one of the soldiers—a silver teapot on a tray, with china cups. The milk tasted a bit odd, and Jack grimaced a little and said, "Goat's milk," but the tea was good, nevertheless. As they sat at the table sipping it, the door opened again and two men entered, almost buried under a large, flopping mattress and a mixed load of bedding.

Jack expected they would drop the things in a corner and leave. Instead, with great care and grave efficiency, they laid the mattress down and made up the bed, smoothing a sheet—Jack blinked, but yes, it was a real sheet—over it, another over that, and then a large hand-sewn quilt like those sold to tourists in Sulaka. Two pillows with starched white pillowcases were carefully placed at the end near the wall, and then the men straightened, nodded in a satisfied way, and left.

Jack transferred her gaze from the bed to Finn's grave face, and saw that he was trying hard not to laugh. Her own lips twitched, and she saw the answering curve of his, and she put her head down on an arm crooked on the table, giggling helplessly while Finn roared.

When their laughter had subsided, she turned to the bed and said, "It does look wonderful, though."

"I agree."

His smile held a wealth of wicked meaning, and she stood up, saying crisply, "A pity we have to spoil it. Do you want the sheet or the quilt? And just why *did* you tell Tula I was your wife, anyway?"

He glanced towards the door and took her arm, not as firmly as before, but obviously as a signal to keep her voice down. "Because lately the rebels have been into kidnapping for ransom," he said very quietly. "And there are other dangers, for women. The medical profession appears to have some clout with Tula. I thought it might be wise to let them think that you and I were...intimately connected."

It made sense, Jack supposed, although her hackles rose slightly at the thought of Finn having to offer his "protection." She said, unaware of the wealth of bitterness in her voice, "They'd be pushed to collect any ransom for me. I can't think of anyone who'd pay to have me back."

He looked at her curiously, but said only, "They won't know, will they? Anyway, we'd better live up to the story I gave them."

"You could have said I was a nurse, couldn't you?" she suggested.

Finn's eyes gleamed in amusement. "You didn't do too badly when you helped me fix my ankle," he admitted, "and you were magnificent tonight, but a nurse you're not. They would have caught on to that in no time, once they started presenting us with patients."

That was a point. Jack nodded, and proceeded to strip the cover and sheet from the makeshift bed. "We could have a sheet each, and share the quilt, I suppose," she suggested.

Finn said politely, "As you like." He watched her arrange the sheets, doubling each one over. "You know," he said, "I'd never have taken you for a woman concerned about the conventions."

Without looking at him she said coldly, "I just think we'll be more comfortable this way."

"Do you?" he asked in a deeply mystified voice.

She threw the quilt back over her handiwork, and straightened, slightly flushed. "I wonder where the nearest bathroom is," she said.

"I'll ask." He limped to the door and spoke to someone outside.

"That way," he said, coming back.

"They've got a guard on us?"

"I guess so. At least, there's a sentry not far away, though he's trying to give the impression that he isn't watching us."

She took the torch, which Tula had returned, and went in the direction Finn had indicated. The bathroom was detached, with a shower cubicle and latrine, and a long concrete tub with a cold tap over it. It was hardly four-star, but it was clean and smelt of disinfectant.

Finn took the torch from her when she returned, then went out himself. Jack slipped under her sheet, and when he came back was pretending to be asleep. She felt him settle down beside her, and before long her pretended sleep had become a real one.

She must have slept late. When she opened her eyes sunshine was streaming in through the windows on each side of the door. There were red cotton curtains, but no one had thought of drawing them last night, and as she gazed out at the blue sky and the green tips of trees, the top of a black head appeared outside, and two round brown eyes peered in at her. A child.

As their eyes met, someone outside shouted, and the child's eyes widened before the head disappeared.

Jack tossed aside the sheet and went to the window. Several yards away, a man with a gun at his back was shooing a small group of children off, waving his arms at them. He didn't appear very menacing, in spite of the weapon he carried, and the children giggled as they ran away up the hill.

Jack pushed back her tousled hair and stepped outside, still in her bare feet. The village was rather bigger than it had appeared last night. The buildings were a mixture—some had weatherboard walls, and roofs of either corrugated iron or traditional palm leaf thatch; others were totally native-style, some with sections of the walls designed to be tied up out of the way like tent flaps in the daytime to take advantage of any cooling breeze. There was a cluster of them in the clearing, but among the trees climbing up the hill were more houses. The thick undergrowth typical of this part of the country, and most of the broad-leaved trees had been cleared away, leaving only palms. Their roots were so far-reaching that they were almost impossible to remove, and they provided some shade for the houses. Spotted black and pink pigs and scraggy hens rooted and scratched about on the bare earth near the houses, and clotheslines strung between the palm trees were hung with washing. Women in native dress sat outside, some with babies in their laps, others dexterously weaving palm leaves into baskets, hats or mats. One group was happily chattering as they pounded bark into tapa cloth. Except for the men with their guns who stood about the perimeter, it was like any Tukaikian village. A couple of recently fallen trees might have been the result of the cyclone, and one house was roofless, perhaps for the same reason. Some other roofs were obviously very new, but if there had been any real devastation the people must have tidied up quite well.

The man who had chased the children away looked over at Jack curiously, and she retreated inside the hut to comb her hair and change the clothes she had slept in.

Not that her others were much better, and she didn't expect her sneakers would last much longer. They were torn and dirty, and she picked them up with the clothes she had discarded, thinking she would try washing them in the bathhouse.

She was about to open the door again when there was tapping on the thin panels, and Finn entered, carrying a woven palm tray, cleverly balanced on one arm.

"Breakfast," he announced, placing it on the table.

Jack put down the bundle of washing she held and approached the table with something like awe. There was fruit—bananas, pawpaws and oranges—and another pot of tea, the cups and saucers nested beside it, some rolls, and two real crystal glasses of fresh orange juice.

"Have you checked on your patient already?" she asked him.

"Mm-hmm. No need for concern. He's a bit sore but I've given him some painkillers as well as an antibiotic."

"Who owns the silver and china?" she asked, fingering the teapot. It was particularly elegant, and the cups and saucers were bone china, covered in roses and edged with gold.

"The wife of the headman of the village."

"Tula?"

"No. Tula's the military commander of the area, I guess. Latu Savusuta is a bit old for that, but he has a great deal of authority. On the surface, at least, even Tula seems to defer to him."

Latu was a courtesy term used for important men who in the old days would have been called chiefs of their villages. "You've met him?" Jack asked.

"Briefly. He received me, I suppose you'd say. All very formal and gracious. His wife would like to meet you later."

Jack nodded, picking up a pawpaw. There was a silver fruit knife on the tray, and she sliced into the juicy, golden flesh with it. She would worry about the meeting later. The sight of food had reminded her how hungry she was after the long journey in the middle of the night.

"How's your ankle?" she asked him. She knew that he had found the walking part of the trip difficult.

"Okay," he said. "I might make a nurse of you yet."

"Not me." Jack shook her head.

"Squeamish, after all?" He peeled a banana and broke off a piece.

"Not squeamish. Except about low pay for unpleasant work."

"It's rewarding work."

"I'm not prepared to accept a warm glow of self-satisfaction instead of the cold hard gleam of real money."

He laughed. "You have a point. They are underpaid for what they do, and they have been more or less told that dedication to their profession doesn't go with expecting more tangible recognition for their work. They should be paid more, I'll admit."

"That's very liberal of you."

A sudden glimmer of temper in his eyes, Finn said, "Why do you *do* that?"

"Do what?" she asked innocently, uncomfortably aware of what he meant.

"Get out the needle every time we come close to having a civilised conversation."

"I don't! And anyway, you started it, by accusing me of squeamishness."

"That wasn't an accusation. It was a question. Lots of people can't stand the sight of blood."

Jack shrugged and said, "Do you want a slice of paw-paw?"

"Thanks," he said, holding out his hand for it. "Is this a peace offering?"

"It's breakfast. The best I've had for weeks."

He smiled faintly, his eyes still on her, but she avoided his gaze, carefully biting into a slice herself. Finn said, "Yes. Me too."

When they had finished, he said, "I'll take you to Savusuta's house. It would be polite to pay your respects before anything else."

He made no comment on her shorts and shapeless white shirt, but he said, "No shoes?"

"They've about had it. And they're filthy."

"Well, most people here never wear them, anyway. And I don't suppose there'll be snakes within the village. Better put something on your feet if you're going farther afield at any time, though."

That was sensible advice, and she nodded.

The headman's house was at the edge of the clearing, shaded by a couple of tall palms and another, bushier tree that Jack couldn't identify. It was bigger than the other houses, and had a verandah running along the front, with two shallow steps leading up to it. Pots of scarlet poinsettia stood on either side of the doorway, and a little cream-coloured dog lying on the mat before the door gave a sleepy "woof" before getting up and moving out of the way, wagging its short tail.

The door was open, but Finn knocked and waited, and a young girl wearing a red-and-white-printed pareu led them into one of the front rooms.

The room was furnished in European style, but with tapa cloth hangings on the walls, and strings of small shells looped above the uncurtained windows as decoration.

A large man rose from a couch covered in a brown cotton print, and held out his hand to Jack. "Mrs. Simonson," he said. "It's a pleasure to meet you."

He made them sit down in the two chairs that matched the couch, and a few minutes later a woman came in, beaming a welcome. She was as tall as her husband but less round, her majestic figure swathed in a tight, long sleeved and much-draped Western-style maroon dress, which Jack guessed she had put on for their benefit. Her black hair was dressed in complicated coils and decorated with tortoise-shell combs, and a yellow flower was tucked behind one ear. Her legs were encased in nylon and her feet in black leather pumps.

She sat on the couch beside her husband and said, "I'm so sorry to hear about your plane. You were lucky to escape."

"Very lucky," Jack agreed.

"But you've lost some of your things?" Mrs. Savusuta took in her visitor's clothes. Without waiting for a reply, she said, "We will find you some dresses. Or get them made for you."

Remembering that she was supposed to be Finn's wife, and that he had been prepared to stay in the interior of the island for some time, Jack didn't attempt to correct the impression that she had somehow managed to lose her luggage in the crash. She said, "Thank you, but I don't wear dresses." She couldn't imagine herself in anything resembling this magnificent lady's outfit.

Mrs. Savusuta was obviously puzzled, her brows contracting over her large brown eyes.

Finn said, "Perhaps a couple of pareus? I'm sure Jacqueline would be quite comfortable in them."

Mrs. Savusuta's face cleared at once. "Of course," she said. "Excuse me for a moment."

It was more than a moment, but she returned with three lengths of material and handed them to Jack with a gracious air. "Please make use of these, and if you want dresses, my sister will make them for you. She has a sewing machine."

"Thank you very much." Jack hoped that her manners equalled those of her hostess. She supposed she would have to wear the pareus, or Mrs. Savusuta would be offended.

She wanted to ask how long they would be expected to stay here, but perhaps it wouldn't be wise. Finn was talking with Latu Savusuta, and she gathered that they were discussing setting up a temporary clinic of some sort. Apparently Captain Tula had sent some men down the river to recover the medical supplies and food from the wreckage of the plane.

When they returned to their own quarters, Finn said, "I'll go out if you want to change."

Jack shook her head. "Later. Do I gather you're going to set up shop here?"

He cast her a gleaming glance at her choice of words, and said, "Might as well. They're keen for medical help, and it certainly doesn't seem as though I'll reach my original destination in a hurry. We must be fifty miles from Kitikiti."

"About that, I guess," Jack agreed. "Have you any idea where we are, really?"

"Probably less than you," Finn admitted cheerfully. "If you're in a hurry to leave, I suggest you contain your impatience."

Jack sighed. "I suppose I'll have to. At least until Captain Tula brings back our supplies. He will bring the dinghy, I suppose."

"I doubt if he'll let you get your hands on it."

"He won't want to, of course. We may have to take it."

"Do you really think we can make our own way out of this? You've just said you have only the haziest idea where we are, and I certainly wouldn't like to try and find my way back to the river through that swamp."

"We can't just stay here indefinitely!"

"I don't think we have much choice."

"Oh, it's all very well for you!" she said bitterly. "You came prepared to spend months in the interior doing your ministering angel thing, but I was supposed to have flown back to Sulaka over three weeks ago! I can't stay here twiddling my thumbs forever!"

Finn sat down, motioning her to the chair at the other side of the table. "So it's different," he said. "But I still don't see what you can do about it."

"I'm going to do something!" Jack assured him sharply.

He looked at her thoughtfully. "Mind if I make a suggestion?"

"Feel free."

"See how the land lies first—in more ways than one. They seem friendly enough, and anxious to make us as comfortable as possible. Just bide your time, and maybe we'll find a way to get you out of here."

"Like what?"

Finn shrugged. "We'll think of something. Perhaps we could say you need hospital treatment. Although I don't know if they'd believe that. You look quite astonishingly healthy."

"Why astonishing?"

"You've been through enough lately to put many a woman in the hospital."

"I'm tough."

He nodded. "So I've noticed." But she didn't miss the speculative, almost sceptical glance he gave her.

"I'll starve myself," she said.

He grinned at her. "Not wise. You might not stand up to the trip out, and you could end up really needing hospital care. Just take it easy for a few days at least," he urged. "We need to know more before we start making any plans."

Jack nodded. Patience had never been the most outstanding of her few virtues, but she could see that he was right.

She put on one of the pareus. She had worn the sarongstyle garments occasionally for relaxing at home or for swimming. Light and cool, the cotton material reached almost to her knees and was firmly fastened above her breasts. She experienced an odd spasm of shyness when she emerged from the hut and found Finn waiting patiently for her outside.

He didn't comment, but said, "Want to go for a stroll around the village?"

She went with him, and they found themselves the object of a great deal of interest. The adults looked up from their work and smiled, and a group of children followed them at a discreet distance, scattering when Finn turned to try and speak to them.

"They're shy," Jack said. "Maybe you frighten them."

"They'll soon get used to us," he said easily. "Just ignore them while they size us up."

By the time they returned to their hut, the children had ventured closer, and one darted forward to touch Jack's hand, then backed away, giggling.

Jack turned and smiled at the bold one, holding out her hand. "It's okay. I won't hurt you."

The child, a girl of about five, stood doubtfully with a finger to her mouth, giggled again and darted away, but an older boy, dressed in a short floral pareu slung about his skinny hips, came forward and touched the gold watch on Jack's wrist.

"What's your name?" she asked, softly.

"Aroko," he answered, staring at her with frank curiosity.

"Hello, Aroko. My name's Jack."

The whole group seemed to find that funny. When he had stopped laughing, Aroko asked, "What's that man's name?"

"Finn," Jack answered.

Again the children dissolved in mirth. Then Aroko said, "Is that man your husband?"

About to say no, Jack hesitated, and Finn said, "Yes, I am."

"He's a doctor," Aroko said solemnly, as though imparting vital new information to her. Then, his white teeth showing in an engaging grin, he lifted one hand and mimed a hypodermic injection into his other arm, gave a dramatic "Ooow!" and fell to the ground holding his arm and writhing in pretended pain, while his playmates, thoroughly enjoying the performance, encouraged him with shouts of happy laughter.

Finn said, "I'm sure you're much braver than that, Aroko, when you get a shot."

The boy got up and boasted, "I'm very brave! I'm the bravest in the whole world!"

Finn cocked an eyebrow at him, and smiled. Some of the other children came closer, and one said, "Your plane crashed!"

"I'm afraid so," Finn told them. Obviously they wanted to know all about it, and Jack slipped inside, leaving him to regale them with the story. It still hurt to think she had lost her plane, the first that she had owned herself, and she didn't want to talk about it, although she could understand the fascination that stories of danger and risk held for the youngsters outside.

When Finn came in some time later, he said, "They're a nice bunch of kids. And pretty healthy. No sign of any epidemic here. I wonder if I can arrange to be taken farther up-country."

"You're crazy!" she told him.

Finn smiled faintly and said, "Maybe."

*   *   *

Late in the day some of the supplies arrived from the plane. Parties of men toiled up the hill with sacks and boxes that were taken to a large storage building that had been a copra-drying shed before the war had disrupted the transport needed to take the crop to town where it could be sold. Finn and Jack helped to identify the supplies and stow them in piles. Captain Tula, who was nothing if not efficient, produced a large clipboard and began listing the items as they were brought in.

"I just hope they get to the people who really need them," Finn said to Jack later, when they had eaten an evening meal provided by Mrs. Savusuta. "I didn't bring this stuff in to feed Tula's fighting men."

Chapter Seven

Men continued to bring stores from the plane over several days, and Tula's list grew longer. Finn set up his clinic in a building near the one he shared with Jack at night, and she spent her time getting to know some of the villagers and trying to discover exactly where the village was and what the chances were of getting out of it. She had taken the bull by the horns on the second day and told Tula that she wanted to go back to Sulaka.

"And leave your husband?" the man asked with surprise.

Damn! Jack thought. She had forgotten that minor detail. "We were supposed to be going to Kitikiti," she reminded him. "I planned to accompany him there, but to return quite soon. Obviously our plans have changed. But I would still like to return to the capital."

"You have relatives, perhaps, who are expecting you?" Tula asked.

Warned by the gleam of interest in his eyes, and remembering Finn's reason for claiming a relationship, she paused.

"No," she said. "No relatives. But I would like to get back to... to my home."

"In America?" Tula asked politely.

Finn, of course, didn't have a home in Sulaka. "Can you tell me when I will be able to leave here?" she asked bluntly, deciding to ignore the question rather than get herself into deeper waters.

"I'm sorry, Mrs. Simonson, I cannot say at this moment. The times are... difficult."

"Yes," Jack said. "I know."

"I'm sorry you're not enjoying your stay."

Oh, no! Jack thought. Now I've offended him. "Everyone is very kind," she assured him. "And it's a very pretty place. But I don't even know the name of the village. Where exactly are we?"

He smiled. "A long way, I'm afraid, from Sulaka. Please tell me, or Latu Savusuta, if there is anything we can do to make your stay more comfortable."

"How long," she asked carefully, "do you think our stay will be?"

He spread his large hands. "I'm sorry, it is impossible to say. So much depends on a number of factors."

Jack gave up.

The village had no electricity, but the running water piped to all the houses came from a stream that fell in a series of small waterfalls down the hillside behind it. The hut she and Finn had been given had a corrugated iron roof, and in the daytime when the sun beat down it was hot and stuffy. She had discovered a tap outside, and a shelter nearby housing a fireplace with a metal grill over the top, which was designed for cooking. Most of the households in the village still cooked outdoors in the traditional style, although a few of them boasted a closed stove that had an oven and also heated water for showers and washing. Meals had appeared for the visitors at regular intervals, brought by different village families, and plates and a variety of utensils had been supplied by Mrs. Savusuta, who visited looking much more comfortable in a loose Mother Hubbard dress and plaited pandanus sandals.

"It's very kind of everyone to supply us with meals," Jack told her. "But if they could just give me the food, I can cook it."

Mrs. Savusuta assured her that there was no need, but Jack said firmly, "I don't have enough to do, anyway."

"I will talk to my husband," the woman promised. Apparently nothing could be changed without the headman's consent.

The next day Jack was presented with a bundle of taro and a string of small fish, and a basketful of sweet potatoes. When she lit the fire with wood thoughtfully stacked behind the outdoor kitchen, a number of women drifted across, apparently to supervise in a friendly fashion. One offered her salt, and another brought a bunch of some green vegetable. When Finn arrived and strolled over to the fire with his stick, they smiled and greeted him and left, and Jack served up the meal.

"Looks delicious," he commented as she set it on the table before him. "Do I take it we're expected to fend for ourselves now?"

"I told Mrs. Savusuta I could do the cooking. I'm sick of having nothing to do but chat with the local ladies."

"You're not the sort to enjoy being idle, are you?"

He was right. The village women had their handcrafts and their families; everyone seemed to have either young children or aged parents to care for. There was a schoolhouse where the children spent half of their days, with two very competent native teachers. And then there were the family gardens, plots burned and hacked out of the forest on land near the village, which provided most of the food, and to which every family member repaired for a part of each day to weed, cultivate and harvest.

"Maybe we should start a garden of our own," Jack said gloomily. "It seems as though we'll be here long enough."

Finn smiled at her with some sympathy. "You could be right."

Frustratedly, she sighed. "No," she said. "I refuse to assume that there's nothing to be done about the situation. I'll go crazy if I have to stay here for months on end. If Tula wants us to stay, he can supply our food. We're virtually imprisoned here."

Finn said, "What about helping me out at the clinic? Word is spreading, and I've had a few patients from other villages trickling in already. Soon I'll be really busy."

"I thought you figured I wasn't much of a nurse."

"As I recall, I said I might make one of you, given time. You could be a natural. You certainly won't fall to pieces in an emergency."

Jack thoughtfully speared a piece of fish. "What would you want me to do?"

"Sterilise instruments, write up notes, watch babies when their mothers are being examined, maybe put on a few bandages, that kind of thing. I could teach you more."

The fish was perfect, white-fleshed and moist, the outside a golden brown with a hint of smoky charcoal taste. Jack swallowed it, and said, "I'm not much good with babies."

"All you have to do is hold them for a few minutes. You're not going to let a little thing like a baby throw you, are you?"

She recognised the teasing challenge in that remark. "Okay," she said. "I'll try, if you like. But if I don't like it, I quit."

"Anytime you want."

Jack was surprised at how much she enjoyed working in the clinic. It was true she had felt an unexpected sense of triumph after the appendicitis operation, but that episode had contained the real and immediate drama of a life-and-death situation, something she had always been well able to cope with. A regular parade of sick people needing medicine and bandages would be quite a different matter.

Looking on it as merely an antidote to boredom, she found the constant procession of disparate personalities a fascinating experience. Most of the islanders were very healthy, but there were sickly babies needing special care, and old people with diseases of the eye, and the occasional accident case.

Finn dealt with them all with cool, friendly expertise. He was good at his job, Jack thought. Unflappable, even tempered, with a way of finding the right questions to ask. She was surprised when one day, as she lifted instruments from the spirit-burning steriliser that was one of the things he had been anxious for Captain Tula to rescue from the plane, he suddenly flung down the pencil with which he had been writing on a card and thumped two clenched fists on the table in front of him.

"What's the matter?" she asked, carefully lowering the instrument she held in a pair of tongs onto a clean cotton towel as he had shown her.

"Oh—" He looked about him with something like despair. "I'm wasting my time here."

"Your patients don't think so."

Finn pushed away the card and pencil, and held his head in his hands. "These people aren't dying," he said. "They weren't too badly hit by the cyclone, and this is a well-organized village. They were able to pick up and go on. Farther up-country, from all accounts, it's a different story. I came to give *emergency* relief. Anyone could do what I've done here. Before this damned civil war started, there was a medical clinic here once a month. A doctor and nurse came in by helicopter and did inoculations and gave basic medical care. If there was anyone needing hospital attention, they took them back to Sulaka."

"They must miss that," Jack commented.

"Yes, but—"

"At least you're doing something. Even if it's not exactly what you came for."

"Yes." Restlessly he got up, pacing the small room, a scowl on his face, his hands thrust into his pockets. "Some of them are only here for the novelty of it, really. Their old woman with her traditional remedies could do just as well, in many cases. She's no fool. But up there—'' he jerked his head as though indicating the other part of the island ''—there could be thousands of people needing help. Immediate help. And—'' a fleeting look of pain crossed his face ''—I've failed them.''

"It's not your fault!"

"What difference does that make?" he demanded angrily. Then, as Jack blinked at him, he added, "Sorry, it's no use snarling at you. It wasn't your fault, either."

"Maybe it was, in a way," she said slowly.

"What do you mean?"

"The plane had just been through a thorough check before we took her up. I've been trying to work out what might have caused the crash. There was something wrong with the fuel, I think. After the cyclone, the fuel tanks at the airport might have been contaminated. Maybe I should have thought of that, before I filled up."

"Is it the sort of routine thing that you might expect a pilot to check?"

"Well—no."

"Then I guess, like me, you did all you could. But sometimes that doesn't help much. Let's go for a walk."

Jack accepted with alacrity. There had not been many patients that day, and if anyone arrived later they would wait for the doctor's return. On Tukaiki there was always time enough for everything. No one hurried, and whatever was not done today could be done equally well tomorrow.

Finn was walking now without a stick, but still limping a little. They strolled out into the sunshine, and across the hard-packed ground between the buildings, making for the shade of the trees around the village. The boy whose appendix Finn had removed that first night ran up, shouting, "Hallo, Doctor!" with the slight proprietary air he always adopted towards Finn. He was terribly proud of his dramatic escape from death, and at first had been in the habit of displaying his new scar to anyone who cared to see it, and plenty who didn't.

"Hi, Kalanui," Finn responded, ruffling the boy's hair. The child hopped alongside them for a few steps, then veered off and ran away to his friends, who were playing a stick game in the shade of one of the trees.

"You did some good there," Jack reminded Finn.

He nodded. "I suppose."

As they passed one of the guards Jack felt a faint prickling between her shoulder blades, half expecting that he would call them back, but when they entered one of the wellworn, narrow paths leading to some of the villagers' garden patches, no peremptory challenge followed them.

Finn, too, seemed to relax slightly when they rounded a bend in the path and were out of sight. He put his hands in his pockets, but casually this time, not as though he were restraining himself from some violent action, and they walked in silence for some time.

A couple of girls with hoes over their shoulders approached them, calling a greeting, and Finn and Jack stood aside to let them pass.

One of the girls whispered to her companion and they both giggled, and Finn looked after them. He glanced at Jack and said, amused, "They think we've come out here because we're in a romantic mood."

They couldn't have been more wrong, Jack thought wryly. The islanders were incurably romantic themselves, and one of their favourite topics of conversation was the latest gossip about who was in love with whom, and if the sentiment was reciprocated, and if so how far the affair had progressed.

She brushed by a flowering hibiscus, with a yellow butterfly busy among its large, open blossoms. Behind her, Finn paused to pluck one of the scarlet flowers; then he caught her shoulder briefly and tucked the flower behind her right ear.

Jack looked up at him, astonished, and he said, "I'd hate to disappoint them. It will look good when we go back."

The two girls were almost sure to be watching for their return, Jack knew. They had probably told all their friends, and the lot of them would be searching for signs that something more than talk had passed between her and Finn on their afternoon stroll. "I don't think it's necessary to encourage them," she said, and Finn shouted with laughter.

"That sounds so prim and proper," he explained. "Quite like a missionary lady."

"I'm hardly that!" Jack said, rather tartly. "One thing I'm glad about is that the missionaries didn't manage to totally eradicate the Tukaikians' sense of the joy of life."

Finn nodded. "So am I." He added, "I sometimes wonder about yours, though."

"Am I such a spoilsport?" Jack asked lightly.

He pursed his lips, looking down at her. "You just have an underlying air of . . . seriousness."

She had the impression that he had been going to use a different word, but she didn't press the matter. She was a little shaken by the probing stare he had given her. She had the fantastic notion that he had just seen into her heart. Or her soul.

"You're the serious one around here," she reminded him. "Not me."

Finn shook his head without answering. He put up his hand, and she felt a gentle tug on her hair. "It's grown," he observed.

Jack jerked her head away from his touch and quickened her pace. They came to a garden patch, and skirted round it. The path ended at a small pool fed by a miniature waterfall, where the islanders sometimes drank when their garden labours made them thirsty. There was a smooth rock making a handy seat by the water, and Jack sat down and trailed her hand in the pool, looking down at the rippling reflection of herself with Finn standing just behind her. The flower in her hair was a bright blur, and she raised her hand and took it out, to toss it in the water.

It floated, swirling gently round the rim of the natural basin, and Finn said, "What did you do that for?"

"I'm not the type for flowers." She stood up and turned, expecting him to move, and found instead that he was blocking her way, standing very close, and that a simmering anger emanated from him.

He leaned over and caught up the flower as it floated by, and shoved it rather roughly back into place behind her ear. "Wear it," he said.

That sparked her own temper. Nobody gave her orders, certainly not in that tone of voice. She raised her hand to remove the flower and found her wrist caught, and when she tried to push him off, the other one was caught, too, in an unbreakable grip.

Her astonished eyes recognised the expression in his, and she felt a kick of adrenaline in her veins, a sizzling antagonism shot with something else, something quite different.

There was a breathless moment when she saw that he had recognised it, too, the flaring of naked sexual awareness, and then his eyes narrowed with decision, and his head came down towards hers.

Instinctively she threw her head back to avoid the kiss, but he followed, his mouth finding hers unerringly, one of his hands releasing a wrist to grasp her hair, his fist nestled hard and warm into her nape while his mouth demanded that she open hers to him.

The shock was intense, sending a shudder of heat through her body, all her senses leaping into a tingling awareness of his hands, his mouth, his body locked against hers. Involuntarily, her lips parted, and he gave a low, satisfied sound in his throat and made the kiss deeper, sweeter, almost explosive in its potency.

One of her hands was clasped in his, the other spread against his chest. She could feel the steady beating of his heart.

When he dragged his mouth away at last, the world was spinning, and she blinked up at the blue blaze of his eyes, trying to get her emotions under control.

Still holding her, he said, his voice vibrant with triumph, "You want me!"

Jack took a deep, gasping breath. "No," she said thinly.

His arms didn't relax their hold. "Yes," he said. "You can't deny it now."

His hand behind her head, he searched for her mouth again, but this time she fought him, thudding her fist against his shoulder, until abruptly he let her go, and she stood staring at him, panting. He was angry again, his eyes glittering, his nostrils pinched.

"Leave me alone!" Jack muttered, and brushed past him, heading back along the path, almost running, so that when she flung open the door of their hut and stumbled inside, she was flushed and sweating.

She sat down on the mattress with her knees drawn up, and dropped her head on folded arms, trying to control her sobbing breath.

She heard Finn come in a few minutes later, and lifted her head to stare at him as he stopped in the doorway.

"Get out!" she said huskily. "Go away."

Instead, he stepped inside and closed the door. "It's my hut, too," he reminded her.

Jack leaped to her feet. "I *want* some *privacy*!" she said between her teeth. "Can't you let me have that, at least!"

"We need to talk."

She whirled, turning her back on him, standing with her shoulders rigid, her arms held across herself. "I don't have anything to say to you," she muttered.

"Well, I have things to say to you, lady!" Finn exploded, and the next moment she felt his hand on her arm, spinning her round to face him. "You can't kiss a man like you kissed me, and then slam the door in his face!"

"I can!" Jack told him, her eyes blazing. "I just did!"

His hands closed over her shoulders, giving her a shake. "Stop it! We need to sort this out."

"There is *nothing* to sort out!" she shouted at him. "And nothing to talk about. I refuse to discuss it—is that clear?"

His hands were still on her shoulders, and she irritably tried to pull away. But Finn tightened his grip and said, "Jacqueline—"

Instantly, they were engaged in a bitter, deadly little struggle, until Jack stepped back and tripped on the edge of the mattress, bringing him down with her on its softness.

Winded by his weight, she gasped and squirmed, trying to wriggle out from under him.

"No, you don't!" he said grimly, and captured one wrist, pinning it against the pillow behind her as he went for the other one, but she evaded him, turning so that he half rolled off her, and as she sought for a purchase to push herself up, the pillow moved aside and her hand found the gun she had hidden there.

Finn moved faster than thought, lifting his hand and bringing the edge of it sharply down on her wrist. With his other hand he pushed the gun off the mattress with a force that slid it across the room to the wall, and it exploded deafeningly in the small space.

He was on his feet and had pulled her up, his fingers like a vise on her arm, when the door burst open and a man with a rifle held at the ready stood there, his eyes sweeping the room.

"It's all right!" Finn said quickly, shoving Jack behind him, and spreading his hands wide. "A slight accident, that's all."

The man stood over them suspiciously, and Jack held her breath, not daring to move.

Then Captain Tula, with a revolver in his hand, came running up, and the soldier stepped aside to let him in, then returned to his watchful stance.

Tula's eyes found the pistol in the corner, and he bent to pick it up, running his fingers over the fresh bullet hole in the wall nearby before turning accusingly to Finn.

"Where did you get this?" he asked.

Jack said, "It's mine. For protection. I—it fired accidentally when I dropped it."

His eyes went from her to the spot in the corner where the pistol had been, and then slowly back to Jack, his gaze sliding over Finn, who had now dropped his hands to his sides.

"You are in no danger here, Mrs. Simonson," Tula said stiffly. "I will keep this, in case of future . . . accidents."

He nodded to the soldier, and they left the hut, closing the door ostentatiously behind them.

Finn turned to Jack, his face white now, but his eyes cold and glittery. "Don't *ever*," he said with deadly quietness, "try to pull a gun on me again. Not *ever*—understand?"

Without waiting for any reply or acknowledgement, he spun on his heel, flung the door open and slammed it hard behind him.

Jack sank down again on the mattress, her knees shaking. She was, she found, shaking all over. Gritting her teeth, she willed herself to stop, and in a few minutes she took a deep, calming breath and lay down with her arm flung across her eyes.

She couldn't believe what had just happened. She felt sick.

When she heard Finn coming back, she scrambled quickly to her feet, pushing back her tumbled hair, and turned to face him as he opened the door.

He cast her a quick glance, then closed the door quietly and stood in front of it. "You all right?" he queried abruptly.

Jack nodded. "Are you?"

"Just fine." His voice was only faintly laced with sarcasm, his face still a bit pale. From the way Jack felt, she guessed hers was, too.

He said, without moving from the door, "Did you think I was going to rape you?"

Jack swallowed. "No. I wouldn't have used it. I just found it there, and I would have let go in the next second if you hadn't . . . hadn't made me."

He halted in front of her. "Did I hurt you?"

Funny, she hadn't been conscious of the vague throbbing in her wrist until now. "I won't hold it against you."

She was rewarded with a faint glimmer of a smile as he picked up her hand to inspect her wrist. "You'll have a bruise. I'm sorry about that."

"You're very quick-thinking," she said.

"When I'm scared. Believe me, I never knew I could move so fast." He searched her face. "I scared *you*, didn't I?"

"Not as much as that gun going off. It shouldn't have...I'm sure the safety catch was on." She almost shuddered, thinking of what might have happened.

He touched the fingers of his other hand to the slight red swelling on her wrist, stroking gently.

"It's all right," she said, and pulled her hand away, pretending not to hear his sharp sigh.

"Maybe we're both a bit more stressed than we realise," he said. "I shouldn't have kept at you when you told me to back off. I guess in some way I was taking out my frustrations on you. I have no right to do that. And if you overreacted, well...the circumstances are a bit unusual."

She said abruptly, "It wasn't only that." Somehow his admitting some of the fault made her want to explain. "Not long ago, I was in a bit of a fight. Luckily, Abe was there, too. Three men jumped us one night in the street. Nothing that...physical...ever happened to me before. I always thought I could handle myself, but at one stage two of them had me pinned down, helpless. I don't know if it was rape they had in mind, maybe not. Certainly not at first, because I don't think they knew in the beginning that I wasn't a man. But I remember feeling suddenly that I wasn't in control, that whatever they wanted, there was nothing I could do about it. It was horrible. I swore I would never let it happen again."

"That's when you bought the gun?"

"Abe insisted. I wasn't about to argue with him."

Finn was frowning. "And do I make you feel the same way?" He looked suddenly appalled. "That first time I kissed you by the river...and today..."

"No," she said. "It wasn't the same, but maybe you triggered a memory, and I was taking something out on you, too. For a second, I wanted to do to you what I'd have liked to do to those thugs."

He nodded. Then he said, holding his voice neutral, "We still need to talk. About what happened before."

"No!" she said. "Please!"

"We can't just ignore what's between us."

"We can! That's exactly what I intend to do."

"Do you really think that will resolve anything?" he demanded.

"Finn—I have enough to cope with here without...without starting a relationship with you, okay? What happened was just a natural result of two people being thrown together day and—and night. *You* ought to know that. That doesn't mean we have to turn it into some big deal. Because it isn't," she finished flatly. "It really isn't important."

"Is that what you truly feel?" he asked quietly.

Jack shrugged. "Yes."

"I think you're lying through your teeth, *Jack*," he said, making the name sound like an insult.

"Oh, for heaven's sake! You know I'm not your type!"

His brows rose. "Would you know what my type is?"

"Well...well, certainly not a hotshot flier with a heart of steel! We have nothing in common—the only thing you like about me is maybe..."

"Is maybe what?" Finn asked politely.

"My...my looks, I suppose. Or the simple fact that I'm female...*I* don't know, do I?" She glared at him.

"I'm beginning to think you don't know a whole lot—about anything at all," Finn replied crushingly. "I think I'd like to teach you a lesson or two."

All her aggression had resurfaced. She faced him like a tigress at bay. "Just you try, mister!"

Finn's eyes measured her for a long moment; then he gave a short laugh and turned, wrenching open the door. He looked back at her, still with that strange, measuring stare. "One thing we do have in common," he said, warning her. "We both enjoy a challenge." Then, leaving the door swinging behind him, he walked away, whistling.

Chapter Eight

For a few days the guards seemed to watch them more closely than before, and when Jack took a stroll outside the village environs, she was followed by one of them at a discreet distance, but nothing more was said about the confiscated gun.

Finn had an argument with Captain Tula. The captain had cut his hand quite badly in the process of helping his men build some kind of fence around the main part of the village. When he came to the clinic with a reddened handkerchief tied roughly about the wound, Finn said, "We'd better see to this right away," and took him ahead of the other patients waiting outside.

"I wanted to talk to you," Finn said, after he had stitched the cut and was carefully winding a bandage about it, rather more slowly than usual, Jack noticed.

"Yes?" the captain said.

"I wondered how you plan to distribute our supplies to the victims of the cyclone."

"It's not possible yet."

"Why not?" Finn persisted, glancing up from his task.

"We have no suitable transport," Tula answered.

"Your men transported all the stuff up here," Finn reminded him.

"I can't spare men to take it to the other districts where the cyclone struck."

"Why not?" Finn asked tightly, completing his bandage. "You need them to build a *fence*?"

Tula spread his hands. "We have a war here, Doctor. The enemy is getting closer. I have to prepare for a battle."

"So you're fortifying the village?"

"Unfortunately that is necessary."

"Are you going to evacuate the noncombatants? Women and children?"

"Where would they go?"

Finn drew a shaky breath. "You're *not*? You're going to make this place into a fortress, which is *guaranteed* to attract the attention of the government troops, and keep families inside your 'fortifications'?"

"Doctor—" Tula stood up "—I am the military commander here. These decisions are not your concern."

"You've made this place my concern!" Finn argued. "You brought us here." He paused, then said, "How long since you were in the capital, Captain?"

Impatiently, Tula said, "That has nothing to do with—"

"How long?" Finn pressed. "Months?" When the other man didn't answer, merely giving him a haughty if somewhat puzzled stare, Finn went on, "Have you any idea of the military capability the government has acquired in the past few months? I don't know where they're getting it from, but their equipment is the latest—and the deadliest—and they've got plenty of it. Guns, men, artillery—they could annihilate this place in minutes!"

"My men are well armed and well trained, Doctor," Tula said. "Don't let the lack of uniforms deceive you."

Finn shook his head. "You know they don't have the kind of weapons you'd need to stand up to a really well-armed force. Don't you understand? The government is determined to crush you!''

"We will not surrender!" Tula said, his eyes flashing. "I thought you were on our side, not that of the oppressors!"

Finn said, "I'm on the side of those caught in the middle of a war not of their making, and not of their desire. I'm on the side of those who may be dying of disease and starvation, while men like you are building barbed-wire fences and preparing to shoot other men in the name of some supposedly noble cause."

"I'm afraid you don't understand," Tula said.

"You bet I don't! I don't understand how you can kid yourself that you're saving your people when you won't lift a finger to help those who could be dying right now!"

"In war, hard decisions must be made. That's my job. Apart from the fact that I don't have the transport or the manpower, as I told you, your stores may be needed here."

Finn went pale. *"For what?"* he asked in a voice like a coiled snake.

"I am expecting reinforcements, and if the enemy closes in on us, it may be necessary for the people to stay in the compound. If it becomes dangerous for them to leave to collect food—"

"Your reinforcements can get their own damn food!" Finn said. "I am not feeding *troops*!"

"No, Doctor, *I* am!" Tula snapped. He swung on his heel and left.

Finn yelled to his retreating back, "Not on my supplies, Tula! No way!"

The people outside stared, and Finn stood for a moment, then turned back inside, slamming the door. He swore, and thumped a fist against the panels, and Jack said quietly, "You can't stop him, Finn. It isn't your fault."

"I'll talk with Latu Savusuta," Finn said, not with much hope. He dragged in a deep breath. "We'd better see to the rest of these patients."

* * *

He went to the headman's house that evening, and when he came back to the hut his face looked grim.

"No luck?" Jack asked.

He shook his head. "Savusuta may be the headman, but obviously Tula has the last word. I couldn't budge him."

"I'm sorry," Jack said.

"Are you?"

She stiffened at the faint disbelief in his tone, and he said, "Sorry, I shouldn't take it out on you."

"My sentiments exactly," Jack murmured, and he gave her the ghost of a wry smile.

"You've done all you can," she told him, "short of sneaking out in the dead of night and destroying the supplies."

"That would serve no useful purpose."

"No, it wouldn't. Neither will anything else, as far as I can see."

"Yes, I suppose you're right," he conceded. "But I'm not giving up."

She studied the set of his jaw, and thought that maybe he was right about the two of them having something in common, after all. Determination not to be beaten, for a start.

In the darkened room after they had crawled into bed, he fumbled for her hand and closed his fingers about hers. "Do you mind?" he asked.

Jack closed her eyes, trying to steady a suddenly racing pulse. "No," she said, her voice decidedly husky. "Not if it helps."

He raised the hand he held and rubbed it against his cheek. "A bit."

She lay awake for a while, and when she went to sleep the back of her hand was still warm against his skin.

She woke to a sound that was familiar, yet unexpected, distant but coming steadily closer, a steady beating. For once Finn was sleeping soundly beside her, until she started up with a shock of recognition, and as his eyes snapped open she turned, her hand gripping his shoulder. "Finn! *Listen*—a helicopter!"

Finn swore, threw aside the bedclothes and went to the door, flinging it open. Jack was right behind him, peering into the dawn light. The sound was loud now; the helicopter, dipping as it flew closer, hovered over the village. It was a big machine, the colouring dull. There was shouting from some of the huts, and people spilled out of them, pointing, exclaiming. Finn's hand closed about Jack's arm, hard. "God, I hope that's not the army!" he muttered.

Captain Tula strode across the compound, gazing upward; then he waved and moved aside, waiting. The helicopter lowered itself gently while Tula's men ringed the compound and motioned off the few people who were bold enough to come closer.

Gradually the blades slowed and stopped whirring, and Jack said, "Tula must have been expecting it."

"Friends, apparently," Finn agreed, as a man came out of the machine and approached the captain to be caught in a hearty embrace. More men were hopping to the ground, grinning, some of them with weapons slung over their shoulders. "Tula's reinforcements have arrived."

That wasn't the end, either. The helicopter made several more trips later on and returned with more men. And guns. The clinic was light on patients that day; the villagers, agog with the excitement of events, seemed content to let their ailments wait, or were too interested to be sick in case they missed something.

The fencing was going up much more quickly now, with most of the new men engaged in it. They had put up formidable wooden posts ten feet tall, and strung barbed wire between then, and a few yards behind the fence, others were building a trench with a wall of earth before it. Finn eyed the preparations bitterly, and about midafternoon he went to where Tula was supervising and accosted the captain.

Jack, standing curiously at the doorway of the clinic, couldn't hear what the two men were saying, but she could see the tenseness of Finn's stance, and the increasing impatience in Tula's gestures.

At last Finn came back, his face set in harsh lines. Jack stepped aside and then followed him into the building. He had flung himself down in a chair, and was scowling at his hands, tightly clasped in front of him on the small table.

"You asked him if you could use the helicopter?" she said quietly.

Finn glanced up. "Yes," he answered shortly.

"And he said no."

"He said no. Or as good as."

"As good as?"

"He 'needs' it for his troops and equipment at present. When he's finished turning this place into a fortress, he'll see about keeping his promise to distribute supplies to people who really need them."

"They may not be in such dire need as you think," Jack suggested. "I expected the devastation would be much worse around here than it seems to be."

"The survey plane that went in there just after the cyclone hit found plantations totally flattened. Most of Kitikiti had been destroyed, and the surrounding country had hardly a tree left standing. Some villages had disappeared. The people at Kitikiti managed to signal that they needed food and medical help urgently—that's why I was sent in."

He sighed, and ran a hand over his hair. Then, in a strange voice, he said, "Can you fly one of those things?"

Jack stared at him. "I could." Dropping her voice, she said, "What are you suggesting?"

Finn said blandly, "I haven't suggested anything."

"No, but..." Jack licked her lips. "Your cargo..."

It was all put away, of course. It would take ages to load.

"Yes," Finn said, scowling again. "Difficult."

"Impossible!" Jack warned him. There was no hope that they could load all that stuff in secret. Or even half of it.

There was a shout from outside, and a babble of voices. The door was flung open, and Captain Tula said, "Doctor!"

Finn jumped to his feet immediately. With Jack just behind him, he followed the captain to where a man lay on the ground, frighteningly still.

"What happened?" Finn asked tersely as he knelt by the unconscious man.

"He was knocked down by one of the posts," Tula explained. "It slipped somehow as they were putting it up."

A girl had come running. Now she knelt by the man's side, her hands clasped, and began wailing softly, rocking to and fro. She was about fifteen and, looking at the still form on the ground, Jack realised that he probably was not much older. She put an arm about the girl's shoulders. "It's all right, the doctor will help him. Are you his sister?"

"I'm his wife," she sobbed, rubbing at the tears on her face with her fingers. Finn, examining his patient, glanced up at her and then returned to his task.

"Where was he hit?" he asked the men standing by who had been working on the fence.

"It hit his head, and when he went down, it...fell on him, and rolled away."

Finn nodded. "Get a stretcher."

When it came, Tula himself helped to lift the man, and two men carried him carefully to the clinic, his wife weeping as she walked alongside.

"Is it bad?" Jack asked when she and Finn were alone with the boy, his wife anxiously waiting outside.

"I don't know yet," he said. "Can't get X-rays here. At the least he's got a concussion and a couple of cracked ribs. I'll have to strap the ribs. Can you help me?"

Jack nodded. "Of course."

While they were doing it, the man came round, and the last part of the process was a bit of a struggle. The patient was groggy and confused, and inclined to hamper their efforts.

Jack said, "The girl—his wife. She might help to keep him quiet."

Finn nodded. "Get her."

With the girl, now tearless and calm, holding his hand, the young man allowed Finn to finish bandaging. Jack breathed a sigh of relief when it was done.

The girl leaned over her husband, smoothing black hair away from his brow, and talked to him tenderly. Jack met Finn's eyes over their oblivious heads, and turned away.

The man stayed in the clinic overnight, with his wife by his side. Finn stayed there, too, keeping an eye on his patient. Jack took him something to eat in the evening and found Mrs. Savusuta there, patting the young wife's shoulder and speaking soothingly to the injured boy.

When Jack left, the headman's wife accompanied her, asking courteously after her comfort, and adding, "I hope you and your husband are finding our village a nice place to stay."

Jack answered carefully, "It's a very nice place. But my...husband is feeling very frustrated. He came to this country to help people who had suffered from the cyclone, and because of our accident he has not been able to take them the supplies and the help that they need."

Mrs. Savusuta nodded gravely. "We too suffered from the cyclone. Some of our crops are spoiled, and three families lost their houses, but of course it's much worse farther north. The villages built on the flat ground near rivers have been the worst hit, I think, because of the flooding."

"Finn said this place seems very well organised, and so you've been able to recover quickly."

"My husband is a good man," Mrs. Savusuta said with proud simplicity. "I was educated in Sydney, but my husband has never been away from this island. But he knows how to look after his people, how to lead them and encourage them to help one another. No one here will be homeless or poor for long. The whole community is one family. That's how it has always been. That's why he supports the movement against the government. Those men in Sulaka have forgotten our old way. They want to copy Westerners—forgive me, Mrs. Simonson—and take up their way.

They talk about profits and free enterprise and the rights of the individual. But the profits are for themselves, not for the people. Free enterprise to them means paying themselves big salaries so they can buy new cars and air-conditioned houses, and giving their own friends contracts on government works. And rights are only for those who don't speak out against the wrongs they see being done.''

Jack said, tactfully refraining from giving an opinion on this assessment of the present administration, ''Would community include the whole island, or only your own village?''

''Ultimately,'' Mrs. Savusuta answered, ''of course it must mean the whole of our people. That's what we are fighting for. The good of all the people—a government that will put the needs of the people first.''

''Does Captain Tula agree with your views on community?'' Jack asked drily. ''Will his movement stick to those principles if they win?''

A flicker of uncertainty crossed the woman's face. She knew, of course, the fate of so many popular uprisings of this sort, which had overthrown one vicious or corrupt regime only to find they had replaced it with something equally bad. ''Sometimes,'' she said sadly, ''power does strange things to men. But my husband and those like him will exert some influence over these young soldiers. In this country, the elders still have power—not the power of the gun, but moral force. Tula is a young cousin of my husband's. He will listen to his words.''

''Will he?'' Jack was sceptical. ''Finn asked your husband to persuade Tula to let him go north with his supplies for the cyclone victims. He had the impression that Tula had the last word.''

''If it is a military decision,'' the woman said with dignity, ''then my husband will defer to Tula. A headman doesn't need to know everything. He needs only to know the best person to ask for an expert opinion.''

"There's nothing military about feeding starving families and bringing them medical help," Jack argued. "Is there?"

The big woman nodded, her expression troubled. "Perhaps the situation may change," she said vaguely. "It has been a pleasure to talk with you, Mrs. Simonson."

The helicopter left again in the morning, and returned just after noon. Jack was cooking a meal of taro, rice and chicken. Finn, strolling across the compound towards her, quickened his pace as the machine manoeuvred into position and touched down on the dusty earth, and he was standing by Jack when the rotors stopped and the pilot and a couple of other men got out. Children scampered up to dance around it. The novelty had still not worn off, Jack thought. Aroko, the little boy who had ventured to ask questions the first morning that she and Finn had been here, was in the forefront. One of the men ruffled his black head and gave him a firm but not rough push out of the way. They were unloading what appeared to be some apparatus that came in pieces. Captain Tula came out of his hut to watch.

Finn drew in his breath as a long, heavy metal cylinder was laid carefully on the ground, and a large tripod of some sort followed.

"Hell!" he said. "I wonder where they got that from."

"A gun," Jack said.

A big one, she thought, and even as she realised just what kind it was, Finn said, "It's a gun, all right. An antiaircraft gun."

The children were jostling one another closer, all curiosity. Tula exchanged a few words with the men who were now picking up the pieces they had unloaded, helped by others, and were carting them away. Finn said, "He's not going to set that thing up in the *village*?" He limped away to intercept the captain.

The smell of burning rice distracted Jack's attention, and she rescued the meal, while trying to keep one eye on the two men arguing—again, she thought—in the middle of the compound.

When Finn finally came back, she handed him without comment a plate of half-cold rice mixture, which he ate in absentminded silence.

"Did you get anywhere?" she asked as she removed his plate.

"What? Oh, he's setting it up in the trees, apparently, farther up the hill. Harder to find, I suppose. He says that's better military strategy, and that he never intended to leave it here."

"He doesn't strike me as a fool," Jack said.

"I never thought he was." He glanced up and said, "I'll wash those."

He usually did the dishes, but tonight Jack shook her head. "I don't mind." He was preoccupied, she thought, as though he had something on his mind.

Finn nodded, and she took the things outside to the tap, rinsing them there before washing them in water heated over the fire.

When she reentered the hut, Finn said, "He's got to let me go."

"He won't." Jack put the plates away on a shelf.

There was a tapping on the door, and Jack opened it to Mrs. Savusuta.

The woman had come with an invitation for Jack and Finn to dine at the headman's house that evening. Finn managed to smile at her as they accepted.

"Apart from anything else," Finn said with unusual bitterness, when their visitor departed, "since we're prisoners here we don't really have much choice."

Neither Finn nor Jack had expected to find that the Savusutas had invited Captain Tula, as well. Finn and the captain greeted each other with determined civility, and after a preliminary exchange of chat about Tukaikian customs and the tourist trade, they sat down to a meal of island

foods served on very English china on a long polished table
flanked by velvet-covered chairs.

The roast pork and sweet potatoes and coconut rice, followed by delicious fruit-based sweets, were accompanied by
rice wine, which Savusuta proudly said he made himself.
Jack, having experienced the effects of it before, was cir-
cumspect with her glass, and she noticed that Finn, too,
sipped it sparingly, but Captain Tula seemed to be imbib-
ing quite a lot. She hoped it would mellow him, and it slowly
dawned on her that perhaps the Savusutas were hoping so,
too.

It was Savusuta himself who introduced the topic of
Finn's interrupted mercy flight, expressing his regret that the
people of the interior who were in such desperate straits were
still unable to be helped.

Jack sensed the quick lifting of Tula's head, and heard the
slight click of his glass going down on the table.

Finn said evenly, "I think it's a great pity, too. I had
hoped by now we would have made some impact on the
plight of the cyclone victims."

Jack caught his eye, feeling that it was perhaps wise to
tread cautiously, and saw by the flicker in his that he
understood.

Savusuta, gently plying a fan made of woven pandanus,
said quietly, "I'm sure Captain Tula will do everything he
can to help."

Behind the benign tone, Jack thought she sensed a steely
note, and she sneaked a quick glance at Tula. He was regarding the glass of rice wine in front of him rather fixedly.
Finn kept his mouth tightly shut.

Tula looked up at his elder cousin and said, "I have told
Dr. Simonson that I will see his goods are distributed as
soon as that is possible."

"It is difficult?" Savusuta queried gently.

"Very difficult," the other man said with a snap. "When
the doctor first asked, I explained that I can't spare the men
to carry them, and it's a long way on foot. The doctor him-

self still limps from the injury he received when his plane crashed. He couldn't make the trip.''

Savusuta smiled. ''But now that we have a helicopter?''

Tula appeared almost sulky, and the older man went on. ''Now it's different, isn't it? You have brought in your reinforcements, your big gun...when will Dr. Simonson be able to leave, with his supplies?''

Tula frowned. He stared suspiciously at Finn, who had schooled his expression to a careful, neutral blankness. ''Perhaps soon,'' he said evasively. ''And...we may not be able to spare all his supplies.''

Savusuta's expression changed to a hard, aloof displeasure. ''What do you mean?''

''We are going to need extra food. It's very difficult to get, since the cyclone. My men are on limited rations now, because I don't want to deprive the people of their food.''

Finn spoke then, his eyes cold. ''I'm not going to give you my supplies.''

''Then maybe I'll take them!'' Tula flashed.

Mrs. Savusuta leaned across the table to her husband and said urgently, ''Savu—''

He silenced her with a quick gesture. ''We will not steal,'' he said with great authority. ''We will not take food meant for our own people whose need is greater than ours.''

Tula said, ''It's not stealing! It's a military necessity—requisitioning. My men can't fight if they don't eat! If Dr. Simonson wants to feed the starving, he can start here!''

''No!'' the older man said unequivocally. ''Here we are not starving yet.''

''Not yet—but later, who knows! The government troops are drawing closer every day, cutting off our supply lines, our lifelines. What the cyclone didn't destroy, they will. Are you going to let your own people die so that this white man can salve his conscience?''

''Those in the north are our own people, too,'' Savusuta reminded him sternly.

''Listen!'' Tula in turn leaned over the table. ''I've said the government forces are closer—soon they'll be attacking us, sending in planes, troops with machine guns. We're going to have to fight—men will be hurt, wounded. We are going to need a doctor!''

''To treat the wounded?'' Finn interrupted.

''Yes.'' Tula looked at him. ''We need you, Doctor. You are needed *here*.'' His clenched fist thumped the table.

Finn met his eyes steadily across the table. ''I won't do it,'' he said flatly. ''I won't treat your wounded, Tula.''

Chapter Nine

Tula gave a disbelieving laugh. "You would refuse medical treatment to a man in pain, perhaps a dying man?"

"Yes."

He looked as though he meant it, Jack thought. He really did. *Could* Finn do that?

He said, "You are denying treatment to a lot of innocent people now, after all. I don't see the difference."

Tula jumped to his feet, his chair scraping back angrily. "Of course there is a difference!"

"Why?" Finn got up in his turn. "Because they're conveniently out of sight?"

Tula glared at him. "You will treat my men, if I have to stand over you with a gun!" he threatened.

Finn said, "You can shoot me first. I'm not patching up men so they can go out and put holes in someone else."

Tula flung out an arm. "You're a *doctor*!"

"And *you* are preventing me from doing my job!" Finn shouted.

Savusuta said, "Sit down!"

Both men looked at him, as he spoke in that voice of quiet but very definite authority. Tula subsided back into his chair, and Finn, his eyes very blue and his jaw determined, did the same.

Savusuta nodded to him. "Doctor," he said courteously, "I'm sure that Captain Tula—" he transferred his gaze to the captain "—will be able to accommodate you shortly."

Tula looked furious, but stayed silent.

"We will have coffee now," Savusuta said, and his wife got up with alacrity to fetch it.

A little later Jack found the woman's gaze on her, with a lurking humour in the dark eyes. She looked, Jack thought, as though she was tempted to wink. Jack smiled, and Mrs. Savusuta smiled back, almost gaily.

As the island woman bent gracefully forward to offer sugar to Finn, Jack met his eyes dwelling on her with suspicion, puzzlement. Then he glanced away, and fixed the same sort of look on their hostess as he declined the sugar.

They walked across the compound together. The moon was almost full, needing only a sliver on the edge, and somewhere one of the women was singing softly in Tukai-kian, perhaps a lullaby for a wakeful child. A night bird shrieked, and a sentry patrolling the new fence turned sharply, then resumed his pacing.

"Do you think we won?" Finn asked, with a measure of disbelief in his tone. "Tula never actually promised anything, did he?"

"Saving face," Jack said. "Savusuta allowed him that."

"Savusuta only made a suggestion, really," Finn worried. "Perhaps it was just a put-up, to make me settle down."

Jack shook her head. "If you want to know who really won," she said, "it was Mrs. Savusuta."

Finn stared at her, bewildered. "What?"

"Mrs. Savusuta," Jack said. "She's the one you should thank, if you want to thank anyone."

They reached the door of their hut, and Finn opened it for her. Inside, the moonlight streaming through the windows made it unnecessary to light the lamp, and neither of them suggested it.

"Why?" Finn asked, not understanding at all.

"She persuaded her husband to assert his authority, by pointing out that this wasn't a military matter."

"How in the world do you know that?" Finn demanded.

Jack shrugged. "We...discussed it. Woman to woman, you might say."

"Discussed it? I didn't know you were matey with Mrs. Savusuta."

"Women don't need to be matey, as you put it, with each other in order to have a sensible discussion and come to some sensible conclusions. We're actually much better at it than men."

"You sound very smug!" Finn accused her.

Jack laughed. "I feel smug. I think we've done it, Finn. I think Tula is going to have to let us go—with your supplies."

Finn said slowly, "I suspect it's you I have to thank."

Shaking her head, Jack said, "Uh-uh! I have no influence with Captain Tula—or Savusuta."

"But you've done it." As though daring to believe it at last, he said again, on a different note, "You've done it, Jacqueline." He suddenly put his arms round her and gave her a hug. "Thank you!"

She hardly noticed his use of the name, grinning as she hugged him back.

"Jacqueline," he said again, his voice soft and almost blurred, and she saw his face, pale in the moonlight, the eyes deep and with a silvery sheen in them.

Overwhelmingly conscious of his closeness, the powerful arms wound around her, his hard chest against the softness of her breasts, she dropped her arms and strained back in his hold. "I can't wait to get out of here, either," she told him, as he reluctantly let her go. "I didn't only do it for you, you know."

"No," he said cordially. "Of course not. You're the woman who's only interested in number one."

It was stupid, Jack told herself fiercely, to be hurt by that. She was the one who carefully protected her image of self-sufficiency and looking out for her own interests.

"Well, I had a contract with you, didn't I?" she said crisply. "I feel an obligation to get you to your destination somehow. That's good business. I'll go and wash." And she collected her towel and the loose shirt she slept in before slipping out of the hut to the bathroom.

After they were both in bed, Finn lying with his head pillowed on linked hands, he said, "I thought you didn't like women."

"I never said that. I said I don't have much in common with most women."

"I wouldn't have thought you'd have much in common with Mrs. Savusuta."

"I suppose not. But she's an intelligent person with a lot of sense."

He turned his head. "You might fit that description."

"Then maybe we do have something in common."

"Was your mother like you?" he asked.

Jack was silent for seconds, in her mind a clear picture of a brown-haired woman with a perpetual, harassed frown between her brows, her mouth thinned by an apparent need to keep emotion in check. "She was very efficient."

"Efficient?"

"A good wife, a good mother. A good teacher, too."

Finn didn't move. After a while, he said, "A disciplinarian?"

And Jack said instantly, with a hardness in her voice, "Oh, that was my father's role. But she always backed him up. They agreed in everything."

"And you were an only child," he said, as if he already knew.

"What makes you think so?" she asked guardedly.

"You told me you have no family. That argues no brothers or sisters."

And he had two brothers and a sister, she remembered, whom he spoke of with a casual warmth in his voice, even without mentioning their names.

"I did have a brother," she said abruptly. "He died young."

Jimmy, the older brother of whom she remembered little but whose brief life had shadowed hers, and shaped it. When he had died of a sudden and virulent illness at the age of twelve, he had already been recognised by his teachers and his parents' friends as unusually intelligent—destined, perhaps, for greatness. Certainly in his parents' doting opinion. And after that, life had changed for Jacqueline, the nine-year-old who had been allowed, until then, to coast through life in his brilliant wake.

"I'm sorry," Finn murmured. "Did you—were you old enough to be fond of him?"

"In my childish way, I suppose I was," Jack answered. "But it was a long time ago. I soon got over it."

She huddled into her sheet and turned away from him, a decisive ending to the conversation. After a while she heard him say, very quietly, "Good night." But she didn't answer.

Once Tula had made up his mind—or had it made up for him—he didn't waste any time. The morning after Mrs. Savusuta's dinner party, he appeared at the doorway of the hut, and when Jack answered his peremptory knock, said, "I would like to speak with the doctor."

She didn't offer to leave, but stood leaning against the bench along the wall, legs crossed and arms folded, while Finn invited the captain to take a chair and sat at the small table opposite him.

"I have a proposition," Tula said harshly, "which I hope you will consider carefully."

Finn nodded, his eyes wary.

Tula said, "I understand your anxiety to complete your mission. I will do all I can to help you."

Finn didn't say, *That's a change of attitude!* He didn't even imply it with the raising of an eyebrow, just gazed steadily at the captain, waiting politely.

Tula cleared his throat. "Your anxiety to fulfill your obligations does you credit."

Finn blinked once, then inclined his head with only a hint of irony. "Thank you," he said gravely.

"I am in a difficult position," Tula explained.

Finn nodded sympathetically. Evidently he was content to let Tula approach this in his own way.

"Your supplies," Tula said, "will be taken to Kitikiti today."

Finn, only a quick flash in his eyes betraying his elation, said, "I'm very relieved to hear it. We are grateful," he added, glancing at Jack, "for your help. We'll pack up our stuff straight away."

Tula cleared his throat again. "It's not necessary for you to leave, Doctor."

Finn showed no surprise. "Yes it is," he said firmly. "I'm needed just as much as my supplies. And I'm not needed here."

"You will be," Tula said. "That is almost certain."

"I told you," Finn said dangerously. "I won't treat your men."

"If I let you go," Tula replied, "until we need you back here . . . will you reconsider?"

Finn looked at him for a long time. Finally he said, "You mean, I'm allowed to go, on condition that I return when you say so?"

Tula nodded. "I'm sorry, Doctor. It's a matter of—"

"Military expediency," Finn finished. "Yes, I see."

"Then you will agree." It wasn't a question.

"Yes," Finn said slowly. "I agree."

"And," Tula finished blandly, leaning back in his chair a little, "I assure you that your wife will be very well looked after in your absence. I personally will see to her comfort and safety."

"I'm going with Finn!" Jack said, even as she knew that *of course* she wasn't going to be allowed to go with him. She was Tula's surety for Finn's return, a hostage against any temptation to go back on his bargain. She wondered if Latu Savusuta knew that Tula had found a way not only of saving face but also of manipulating events to his own advantage.

Tula was looking at her, his brown face expressing nothing but slight, polite surprise. "It is not necessary, Mrs. Simonson. And I'm afraid there will not be room for an extra passenger. As it is, we will be unable to accommodate all the stores Dr. Simonson brought, I'm afraid. And as fuel is short, we can afford only one trip. . . ."

Tula spread his hands regretfully, and Finn said, "If I go, she goes."

"No," Jack said swiftly. She knew that Tula had done all the compromising he was going to. He would only get stubborn if Finn tried to push the issue. The chances of Finn getting any opportunity to leave the area and return to Sulaka were slim, and she was very sure he wouldn't take it, anyway. "I'll be all right," she assured him. "You go, and do what you came for. It's silly for both of us to be stuck here—along with your supplies."

Finn was silent for a long time. Then he said to the captain, "I get to choose which supplies I take."

Tula said, "As far as possible. The load capacity of the helicopter . . ."

Finn cast him a look of resigned grimness, but didn't press it.

"He'd already removed a part of our cargo from the storeshed," Finn told Jack later. "Some bandages and disinfectant and food."

"What he thought his men would need," Jack guessed, remembering the detailed list that Tula had compiled.

Finn nodded. "He claimed he didn't know where they'd gone. Destroyed in the crash, he said, or missed in the move from the wreck. I shouldn't begrudge them, I suppose," he added. "If there *is* a battle before I get back, I'll need them."

"*Would* you have refused to treat his men?" Jack asked. "A lot of them are only part-time fighters, just village people like the rest, really."

"I don't know," Finn admitted. "Probably not, when it came to the crunch. I don't think I could have stood by . . ."

She was sure he wouldn't have. But he had convinced Tula, it seemed.

He was throwing his few clothes into a bag. "Take care," he said, swinging it up in his hand as he made for the door.

She followed him. "You too," she said, acknowledging a deep reluctance to let him go.

They stood outside on the hard-packed earth, and he looked at the helicopter with the pilot climbing inside, the usual cluster of children staring, and Captain Tula waiting alertly with a couple of his men who had helped with the loading.

"They're expecting a fond farewell," Finn said suddenly, his eyes crinkling as they returned to her.

Jack leaned up and planted a cool kiss on his cheek.

He grinned. "You can do better than that." His free arm came about her waist and pulled her closer, and his lips pressed hers under them, trying, she thought, to elicit a response. She rested her hands lightly on his upper arms, and let her body relax against him, but her lips were closed.

Finn drew back, examined her face quizzically, and said, "Goodbye, beloved."

Because there were eavesdroppers, she told herself, as she watched him walk away from her across the compound, and because she was supposed to be his loved and loving wife. Beloved. He'd been joking, of course, using a term that was quaint rather than passionate, with connotations of Victorian married couples. Odd how it had warmed her.

He climbed in beside the pilot, the perspex bubble before them blurring their features. The blades whirred, and the children scattered, Captain Tula and his men moving back unhurriedly while the disturbed air blew their shirts about them and ruffled their hair. Jack saw a hand inside the bubble lift in farewell, and she waved back in return. Then the skids left the ground and the aircraft rocked very slightly, and ascended until the tops of the trees shivered and bent madly in the down-draught before it passed over them and disappeared from view.

Tiare, the girl whose husband had been injured by the falling post, came to visit, bringing a basket of fresh vegetables. "You will miss Dr. Finn," she said, her dark eyes luminous with sympathy. "Please come and visit us when you are lonely."

Finn had asked Jack to keep an eye on the patient, anyway, and told her when and how to remove the strapping about his ribs. She said, "I'd be glad to. Thank you for the vegetables. Is it from your garden?"

Tiare nodded. "It's the first season since we married. My husband and I grew this together."

"How will you get on, while he is recovering from the accident?"

The girl shrugged. "Our two families will help. But since the men have been preparing to fight, there are not so many to work in the gardens. I don't like to see my old grandmother there. She has earned a time of rest, at her age."

"I'll help, if you like."

"But you are a guest...."

A prisoner, Jack thought. But Tiare was too nice for Jack to deliberately embarrass her by spelling out the reality of the situation. "I eat your food. Yours, and other people's. The least I can do is help to grow some of it."

"It's not necessary."

"I might enjoy it," Jack told her. "Really, I'll get very bored with nothing to do. Let me try, at least."

Tiare smiled at last. "If you really want to. I will be going to our garden later, when the sun is not so hot. I'll call for you."

The man Tula had posted on the gate in the fence that now surrounded the main part of the village was doubtful about letting Jack pass. Furious, she nevertheless kept her temper and waited while the captain was sent for, and answered his questions about her intentions with determined civility. "I'm going to help Tiare in her garden, because her husband is ill and she needs extra hands. Also because I'm bored. I need something to occupy my time while . . . while my husband is away."

Tiare was mortified by it all, nervously shuffling her bare feet in the dust while Tula conducted his brief interrogation and then nodded at the guard to let them through.

Tula stood at the gate looking after them for a while, until the trees hid them from view.

"I'm sorry," Tiare said as they strolled along the dirt path. "That must have been awful for you, Mrs. Simonson."

"Not as awful as it was for you, I think," Jack said. The Tukaikians were a very hospitable and courteous people, and Tiare seemed to be deeply humiliated at the treatment of a so-called guest. "And call me Jack, please," she added. "I hope we're friends."

Tiare giggled, as the children had done when Jack told them her name. "Jack," she said. "That's a man's name, isn't it?"

"It's short for Jacqueline," came the reluctant explanation.

"Oh, that's much prettier. Your husband doesn't call you Jack, does he?" Her quick upward glance of mischievous curiosity recalled to Jack's mind the islanders' incurable interest in all matters romantic.

"When he wants to tease," she said, "he calls me Jacqueline."

Tiare giggled again. "My husband teases sometimes," she confided. "He calls me *kakara*."

"Crab?" Jack said. "Why?"

Tiare giggled and shook her head. She was blushing again. "It's just a silly name. I like being married," she added. "Don't you?"

Jack asked, "How long have you been married?"

"Three months. And I think already I'm . . ." She patted her flat stomach under the printed pareu, with a pleased, proud smile.

She was so young, Jack thought. "How old are you, Tiare?"

"Nearly sixteen. Have you been married a long time?"

"Not really." She must seem long in the tooth to this child. Heavens, when she was fifteen, she had been studying for exams, had never even had a boyfriend. But of course, very soon after that was when she had kicked over the traces and made her parents frantic with . . . *shame*, her mind said . . . *anger*. Unfair, she supposed, trying to assess the situation from the objective viewpoint of maturity. They had said—everyone had said—that she had caused them a great deal of worry, that they had only wanted the best for her because they loved her.

"That's our garden, there." Tiare pointed at a neat plot on the hillside. Orange trees grew around the perimeter, and rows of sweet potatoes, corn and taro marched across the slope. From a small shed, shared with other relatives who had gardens nearby, Tiare took two hoes. "We must stop the weeds from growing up between the rows," she said.

Other families were working their gardens, waving before they returned to hoeing, or digging, or pulling up weeds by hand where they grew too close to the roots of the plants. Children walked along the rows picking off insects. The islanders used few artificial sprays to protect their crops, preferring the traditional ways.

A boy with a bunch of green bananas held in his arms called out a greeting as he made his way back to the village. His mother would probably cook the fruit for the family supper. Boiled green bananas were a favourite dish on Tu-kaiki. Tiare returned the greeting, calling the boy by name, and Jack straightened, leaning on her hoe, and waved to him.

They worked for some time, until Tiare called a halt and suggested they cool themselves with a drink of water. Jack remembered the little basin fed by the stream; it was where she had quarrelled with Finn about the flower he had placed in her hair, and he had kissed her. Suddenly she recalled that moment with piercing clarity, the feel of his hands on her waist, the way his lips had tasted hers, savouring the texture, the shape of her mouth as he explored it.

She splashed her hot face with the water, and when they had drunk, Tiare said with sympathy, "You are thinking of your husband."

Startled, Jack stared, and the girl laughed kindly. "You had that special look on your face."

Good heavens! Jack thought, disturbed. Was she really that transparent? Or did Tiare have some particular sensitivity?

"Let's get back to work," she suggested gruffly. There was no way she wanted a discussion of her supposed marital situation.

The work was pleasantly physical, and when they returned to the village at dusk, Jack felt that tonight she would sleep well. They had washed their hands after replacing the tools, and Jack said, "I'll come in and see your husband, if I may. Finn asked me to keep an eye on him."

"Eat with us," Tiare suggested. "The vegetables I brought you will keep until tomorrow."

"Thank you." She had no particular desire to cook for herself. But she must ensure that the hospitality, or at least the food used, was repaid. If Tula was to be believed, the villagers were likely to run short sooner or later.

Tiare's husband was not alone; a couple of young men had been keeping him company, and they rose smilingly when the two women entered, gracefully taking their leave.

Jack checked Finn's bandaging as he had instructed, and assured the young man with more confidence than her extremely limited experience warranted that everything was fine and she was sure he would be as good as new when his ribs healed. There seemed to be no aftereffects from the blow on the head, and she thought Finn would probably be pleased with his progress.

Finn. She wondered what he was doing now. Healing the sick, she supposed. It was his job, his life.

She turned to Tiare, who was chopping into a piece of pork with a meat cleaver. "Can I help? Give me something to do, please!"

It was late when she went to bed. She could smell the rich coconut scent of copra, and hear the palm leaves shivering in the night breeze like brittle paper. Some aromatic flower wafted its perfume across the compound, a blending of sweetness and spice that she couldn't identify.

The moon had acquired a rounded fullness and hung in the sky like a smudged silver balloon. There was an island legend about the shadows that showed clearly tonight on its surface. Not about a man in the moon, but a woman, who had offended the gods and been snatched from her earthly home and condemned to toil forever beating paper-mulberry bark into tapa cloth, under a solitary palm tree. Squinting up, Jack could see the shape of the palm, all right. It was a legend, she knew, that had endured in slightly different versions all over the Pacific, evidence of the relationship between many of the vast basin's different peoples, whose cultures and language had diversified, but had sprung from the same roots.

The hut seemed very empty without Finn, cold in spite of the tropical warmth of the night outside, and echoing with his absence.

Well, she rationalised, she was bound to miss him; after all, they had been constantly together since the crash, and shared some traumatic experiences. It wasn't surprising to find herself waiting for his return from the bathroom, listening for the familiar sound of his breathing before sleep claimed her.

The helicopter returned late the following afternoon. She and Tiare looked up from their hoeing at the sound of its beating progress, and it was sitting in the compound when they returned from the garden. So presumably Finn and his cargo had been delivered, and he was now immersed, no doubt, in assessing and trying to deal with the human damage done by the cyclone. And not, she supposed cynically, giving a thought to her.

Mrs. Savusuta asked Jack to dinner again and offered to lend her some books, apparently feeling that with her husband gone she might need some form of entertainment. The Savusutas had a small but interesting library, and if she was surprised at Jack's first choice of a book on the mythology of the Pacific and a paperback detective story, she didn't say so, merely renewing her offer to let Jack borrow anything she wanted at any time.

Kalanui's mother, who had never ceased to express her gratitude to Finn for saving her little boy's life, also asked Jack to share a meal with her lively family. She understood how Jack was feeling, she said. Her own husband was in jail in Sulaka, for expressing his views against the present government. He had once been the district representative, but his party was out of favour with those in power, and they had rounded up several of its leaders and imprisoned them. According to the government, the woman said scornfully, her eyes flashing, her husband's opposition had taken the form of throwing stones at police, and threatening to topple the government by force. "But my husband is a civilised man!" she declared indignantly. "He's no savage. We've been forced into using arms because the government sent in troops to break up peaceful demonstrations, and has outlawed the only party that threatened their power!"

Jack nodded sympathetically and tried to maintain a cautious silence. She had never wanted to become involved in Tukaikian politics, and had never expressed an opinion one way or the other, but she was aware that the government's dealings with their opposition had become increasingly heavy-handed. It seemed an awful pity for a nation that had fought long and patiently through nonviolent means for its independence from colonial powers to now be divided amongst itself, with escalating violence on both sides.

Chapter Ten

The days settled into a routine. Except when Captain Tula had his men working on some job that he deemed urgently necessary, the pace of village life was slow, as was only sensible in the tropical climate. The helicopter took off again and this time didn't return. Jack gathered that there were other scattered rebel strongholds, and that they, too, had a claim on its services. Tula's men, having hung bits of greenery on parts of the fence, presumably as camouflage, were busy hacking a clearing in the trees some way from the village. No one was saying what it was for, but Jack would have chanced a guess that they were making a helicopter landing area where the machine could be hidden by camouflage nets. She had noticed that it never stayed long in the centre of the village, where it would have been very conspicuous to any government reconnaissance plane passing over.

Jack helped Tiare regularly in the garden, and usually had an evening meal with her and her husband. "I don't feel right if you do the work and don't eat," Tiare said.

"Everyone who helps produce the food has a right to share it."

Her husband concurred, even more strongly, and Jack, realising that matters of pride and principle were involved, gave in.

Sometimes Tiare's younger brothers and sisters would join them at the garden, industriously helping until Tiare gave them permission to play. Then they would scramble up the hillside to climb trees or swing on liana vines, or sometimes slide down a favourite part of the hill, which had become smooth and grassless, sitting on a banana palm leaf and whooping in pretended fright, or laughing all the way until they reached the bottom in a tumble of brown arms and legs.

Aroko was a member of the family, too, not a brother, Jack gathered, but a cousin of some kind. Almost everyone in the village must have been related to everyone else in some way, and although family members could recite exactly how the family tree was organised, she wasn't sure how many degrees of cousinship were involved. She had taken a liking to the little boy, and he showed a marked enthusiasm for her company. His fascination with the subject of aeroplanes was boundless. He hoarded up information and could regurgitate it at will, apparently remembering everything she told him. He must, Jack thought, be a delight to his teachers.

One day about noon the drone of an aeroplane was heard in the distance, and Tula, summoned from his hut, dashed into the compound, shouting orders. The sentry was removed from the gate, the men with guns bundled into hiding. The captain sent someone racing towards the clearing where his men had been chopping up the trees they had felled, then took off his army cap and stood in the shadow of his hut, waiting.

He saw Jack standing outside the doorway of her hut, staring like everyone else at the distant shape against the sky, and ran across the intervening space to grab her arm and hustle her out of sight. "Please stay here," he said, his fingers biting into her arm. He peered out the still-open door as the plane drew closer. It came lower and swooped over the village with a loud roar, banked and came back again. Following his anxious eyes, Jack looked at the fence, the barbed wire and stout posts. But she realised that it had been constructed carefully to fall under the shadow of the trees at the edge of the village. An observer from the air would have to have exceedingly sharp eyes to spot it. The place must be very like hundreds of other small villages scattered throughout the island. Even the new clearing was not unusual. When the villagers ran out of space for gardens, or the soil ceased to be productive, they were in the habit of cutting a square out of the jungle for new plantings.

The plane tilted its nose and rose over the hill, and gradually the engine note died in the distance. The excited children who had run from the schoolhouse waving and shouting filed back inside, and Tula relaxed his grip on Jack's arm and said, "You will stay here, please, until I come back."

And give you permission to show yourself, was the implication, but he ignored her silent look of irony. She contemplated strolling outside anyway, and defying him to do his worst, whatever that would be. But it would serve no useful purpose, and if he thought she was biddable and obedient, she'd have a better chance of taking him by surprise if she got a real and viable chance to get out of here.

So she stayed, while he checked his men and waited a cautious half hour before returning to give her permission to carry on as usual.

She didn't thank him.

Later in the day the sentry on duty at the gate issued a sharp challenge. Watching curiously from outside Tiare's hut, where Tiare had been trying to teach her the intricacies of hand-weaving with palm leaves, Jack saw a man at the gate, his gestures as he talked earnestly to the sentry somehow conveying urgency.

Tiare's nimble fingers had stilled.

"Do you know him?" Jack asked her.

The girl shook her head. "No, he's a stranger."

The sentry called someone over, and the man was escorted to Captain Tula's hut. He had still not emerged when Jack went to bed, although a tray of food had been taken into the hut from the large outdoor kitchen that served those of Tula's men who were not members of the village community.

Sometime in the night she woke, not knowing what the sound was that had broken into her sleep. Then she heard a clinking, a rustling, a low-voiced command. Getting up, she cautiously peeped out of the window. A knot of men stood near the gate, all with rifles, some humping packs and bundles of equipment. As she watched, another command was given, and the men began filing out the gate, moving with remarkable silence and speed, and disappeared through the trees.

Uneasy, she didn't sleep for the rest of the night.

The place was strangely empty without the busy captain and his hardworking fighters. Only a few men now remained in the village, and the women's faces were shadowed with anxiety. Even the children seemed more subdued than usual, and Aroko told her, "My father has gone to fight. He's going to kill lots of bad men!" Tucking an imaginary machine gun under his elbow, he proceeded to spray the compound with bullets. "Ack-ack-ack-ack-ack."

She wondered where on earth he had gained that knowledge of guns. There was no TV in the village. But his father had probably had to learn how to use modern weapons, she supposed, he and the other villagers. Perhaps there was even a practice range somewhere nearby.

Once she thought she heard the drone of a plane far away but, scanning the sky, could see nothing. And once a distant wisp of smoke hovered in the air, so that some of the women climbed up the slope of the hill hoping to see better, shading their eyes, and a couple of children were sent scrambling up trees to report what they saw. But that was all it was, smoke, with no explanation.

Then one evening the men came back, and the women and children ran to greet husbands and brothers and fathers, some of them wearing makeshift bandages on heads and arms and legs, and one being carried by his comrades on a litter. And one woman stood and looked at the group of men and looked again and called a name on a high note of fear, and Captain Tula, with his cap missing and his shirt torn and his eyes ringed and hollow with weariness, spoke to her quietly, his head bowed as if in shame.

The woman gave one harsh shriek and then, with her hands against her heart as though cradling something there, turned from him, sobbing in great ugly gulps, and Mrs. Savusuta and two others came and put their arms about her and led her away.

For a few seconds there was a hushed stillness, and the men who had been laughing and smiling their relief at being alive, and their gladness at coming home to their loved ones, turned solemn. Then a child babbled, and a girl said something and was answered by the man at her side. Aroko's father swung his son up onto his broad shoulder, making him yelp and giggle, and the crowd of people broke up into family units as the heroes were accompanied to their homes.

About half an hour later Jack answered a tap on her door and opened it to Captain Tula.

"Yes?" she said distantly.

"Mrs. Simonson, some of my men are hurt. They need treatment."

"I'm not a doctor," she protested. "Or a nurse."

"You've been helping your husband. You must have some knowledge."

"Surely someone else must know something...."

"Mrs. Savusuta and the head teacher are with the men now, and the woman healer. I hoped that you ..."

"I would help if I could, Captain. But all I've ever done is ... is hold things for Finn and do what he tells me."

He said stiffly, "I'm sorry I disturbed you."

"If... if an extra pair of hands is any use, I'll come. But you mustn't think I have any specialised knowledge."

He gave one of his stiff military bows. "Thank you. Please come. We have taken them to Latu Savusuta's house."

There were six men there, lying or sitting on thin mattresses laid out in the large living room, and most of the wounds, she was relieved to see, were not very serious, although obviously painful. Mrs. Savusuta greeted her with quiet appreciation, nodding resignedly at her profession of ignorance. But she had, she soon realised, absorbed more than she had thought through working with Finn. She sponged and cleaned and disinfected, and picked bits of metal out of arms and legs with sterilised tweezers, and administered pain-relieving pills that she suspected came from Finn's stores. The man who had been carried in had a shattered leg, not a simple crack like the one she had helped Finn to set, but a nasty-looking mess of torn flesh and splintered bone, and she and Mrs. Savusuta looked at each other in appalled silence after they had done what they could. The man was very pale, his brown complexion turning to sickly yellow, his eyes closed as though he didn't have the strength to keep them open, and Jack whispered, "He probably needs a transfusion."

The older woman nodded. She got up and went to talk to the captain.

Tula came over to kneel by the sick man. Putting a hand on his shoulder, he said, "Your leg needs proper attention, Toma. We'll have to get some professional help for you. Okay?"

Toma opened weary eyes and said, "Okay. Thank you, Captain."

"Good man." Tula squeezed his shoulder and stood up. "I'll get on the radio right away," he promised Mrs. Savusuta.

Twenty minutes later all the patients were resting quietly, and the teacher had cleaned up the mess with Jack's help, while Mrs. Savusuta made tea and gave some to those who were awake. She bent over the man with the broken leg, and touched him, then drew back. Putting down the cup and saucer she held, she bent over him again.

When Jack walked over to her, she said almost absently, "It's too late for Toma. He's dead."

Jack stood quite still. "I'm sorry. Is he from this village?"

"No. He came from the coast. But he has a wife, and a family."

Stupid, Jack thought. *What a stupid waste!* For the first time she understood Finn's hatred of war and its consequences.

"I'll go and tell Tula," Mrs. Savusuta said, getting heavily to her feet without her usual grace.

Tula sent two men to quietly take away the body of Toma. The women took turns staying with their patients during the night, and in the morning all the others were receiving visits from their families. In the afternoon nearly everyone in the village attended a funeral service read by Latu Savusuta in a cemetery.

Afterwards there seemed to be a period of uneasy waiting. Few people went to work their gardens, and even the children were relatively subdued. Tiare came to see Jack, crying because her husband had pronounced himself fit enough to fight, now that Jack had removed the strapping from his ribs in accordance with Finn's instructions, and he had gone to tell Captain Tula so.

Jack did her best to comfort the girl, but felt there wasn't much she could say that would help. The men were determined to continue their resistance, and of course they weren't going to take any notice of the women's fears for their safety.

Mrs. Savusuta was grave as she moved among the women, who were going about their usual tasks with mechanical ferocity, and her husband was in Captain Tula's hut for a long time, coming out with a portentously solemn expression on his face. Tula himself looked harassed, Jack thought, his forehead shining with sweat as he energetically ordered his men about.

Jack returned to the makeshift hospital, relieving the schoolteacher, and found some release from the ever-growing tension in caring for the wounded men.

They were soon up and about again, showing, Jack thought, a remarkable resilience. Another messenger arrived, and this time the men left hurriedly, in broad daylight. Some hours later a plane was seen briefly in the far distance, and a drift of smoke became a rusty-coloured cloud on the horizon. It was days before the men returned, and although there were only two wounded, they were all exhausted and filthy and half starved, and several had not come back at all.

Captain Tula seemed to shake himself awake as they entered the gateway, which had been left open by the women in his absence, and started snapping orders. It seemed they were the vanguard, and the village was expected to billet more rebels who were following. Beds must be prepared, families were asked to make more room in their homes, and the gardens were to be stripped of everything that could be harvested and kept for future use. They would need a building to be prepared as a hospital.

He looked at Jack, standing alongside Tiare, and said, "Mrs. Simonson, you will know what is needed. Please consult with Mrs. Savusuta. She will instruct the women."

Jack opened her mouth and closed it again. They had been beaten back, that was obvious. He was expecting some kind of siege. He was the military commander, and this was the rebels' form of martial law. Even Latu Savusuta and his wife must bow to necessity.

She talked with the headman's wife, and Mrs. Savusuta talked to her husband, who talked to Tula.

"It will be best, we think, to use our house as a hospital," Mrs. Savusuta said at length. "We have two spare rooms, and a small storeroom that can be converted into an operating theatre."

Within the day most of the furniture had been removed from the rooms, and the storeroom cleared, scrubbed and disinfected. A narrow table was set in the centre with a clean sheet over it, and a smaller one next to it. The room was near the kitchen, with its metal stove where water could be heated quickly and easily, and which even had a hot tap at the side leading from the boiler. Tula had all the remaining medical supplies taken to the house, and Mrs. Savusuta cleared shelves and cupboards for their storage. By evening everything was neatly stowed away and Jack had made a list so that they knew exactly how much of everything there was, and where they had put it.

Outside there was a tremendous amount of activity, too. People had been stripping their gardens, carrying everything that could be harvested into the village and storing it wherever there was room. Families had crowded their beds together to make room for extras, and the smaller children, catching an air of excitement and trepidation in the air, were running wild, tearing about the compound playing "soldiers" and generally getting in everyone's way.

Tula stopped in his eagle-eyed inspection of the village as he saw Jack crossing from the headman's house to her own hut. She saw him hesitate before he came over to her. She hoped he wasn't going to expect her to share the hut. She would, she thought, draw the line at that.

Close up, he was red-eyed and his skin had a dry dullness instead of its usual brown, healthy sheen. She realised that although his men had been allowed to nap during the day, he had been fully occupied since their arrival, and was bone tired.

"Mrs. Simonson," he said, and then stood looking at her with his bloodshot eyes curiously blank, as though for a moment he had forgotten what he had been going to say. Then he went on, pulling himself together. "You will not be deprived of your husband much longer. I have given orders for him to be brought here."

Thinking she would be expected to show some appreciation, Jack nodded. "Thank you, Captain, for telling me."

He gave her one of his short, jerky bows, and seemed to hesitate. "You have been a great help," he said. "I'm sorry..." His voice trailed off, and he made a peculiarly helpless little gesture with his hand. "Sorry for everything," he said at last. "Very sorry."

Quite gently, Jack suggested, "Captain Tula, why don't you get some sleep? You'll be useless tomorrow if you don't."

He looked slightly surprised but was too tired to show much. "Thank you," he said in turn. "You're going to bed?"

"Yes. I'm tired, too."

"Sleep well," he said rather sadly.

Jack said, "You too, Captain," and went on her way.

She thought as she wearily tumbled into bed ten minutes later, *They've been beaten, and he knows they don't have a hope.*

She supposed she was in danger. That, she knew, was what Captain Tula's apology had really been about. It wasn't her fight and he had put her literally, it seemed, in the line of fire. He expected the village to be attacked. She remembered the smoke on the horizon and the plane in the distance, and the one that had come so low over the village some time ago. Wouldn't they see that there were children here? But if they did, would that stop them? Soldiers were trained to be ruthless. And if the government was as corrupt as these people seemed to think, would their commanders even think twice about killing civilians, their own people?

She didn't know. The village was remote, away from any inconvenient witness who might tell an embarrassing story to the other people of the island, and to the world.

Except me, she thought. *And I might not live to tell the tale, either.*

It wasn't exactly a comforting thought on which to fall asleep, but, strangely, she did.

* * *

The following day the first of the rear guard arrived, followed by several dozen more, not together like a disciplined troop, but in dribs and drabs of weary, often blood-streaked men, who had made their way by secret paths and quiet streams, travelling inconspicuously in small groups, easily hidden from aerial spies. They were greeted quietly and without jubilation, for it was obvious that this was a desperate remnant, rather than a fighting-fit force.

Jack was kept busy at the makeshift hospital, tending those who needed it. The work wasn't too difficult, because these were walking wounded. The casualties had been light, she assumed, without really thinking about it. And then as she was winding a bandage about a long cut on a man's thigh, she realised that of course they had left the really badly wounded behind. Their retreat had been too hurried to slow themselves down by carrying their comrades who couldn't make it on their own.

The drone of an aeroplane engine made her lift her head quickly, and she felt the man she was tending flinch.

Her heart pounding and her throat dry, she went on bandaging, finishing with steady fingers and saying briskly, "There. All done."

He limped to the window, and she knew she should tell him to lie down, but instead she followed him, and saw the aircraft bearing down on them, closer...closer. Then it veered, turning in a circle, and she slumped with relief.

"It's a spotter," the man beside her muttered.

A spotter, not a fighter plane. Not a bomber. Come to think of it, she didn't think the government had a bomber. There had been talk in Sulaka about them trying to buy a couple, but that kind of aircraft and the weapons they carried were extremely expensive, and arms dealers willing to sell them would want cash on the nail, while the governments of other countries were likely to put themselves into some hot water internationally if they supplied the means for the Tukaikian administration to blow its own people up. Bombers, Jack thought with some relief, were not so easy to come by.

The plane, still flying in lazy circles, moved away to the west. The compound, which had resembled a still from a movie for several minutes, with a few people caught in the open staring apprehensively skyward and others in the shadows of the trees and buildings stopped midway in whatever they had been doing, came alive again. Yet everyone moved with a kind of caution, and talk was hushed, as though they were afraid of attracting the attention of that ominous shape in the sky.

Captain Tula seemed to have regained all his energy after a good night's sleep, and he had some men on the hillside below the village digging what Jack assumed were foxholes. She wondered for what purpose. She didn't imagine he had gone to the trouble of surrounding the place with barbed wire so he and his men could remain outside it.

"Perhaps you should sleep for a while," Mrs. Savusuta suggested to Jack a little later. "You may be needed in the night."

Jack nodded. The man with the bandaged thigh was sitting in a chair near the window, watching the plane, which still circled in the distance, getting farther and farther from the village. The intensity of his gaze suggested that he was trying to will it to go away. "Can you get that man to lie down, do you think?" she said quietly to Mrs. Savusuta. "I'm sure he should rest his leg."

The woman nodded. "I'll try."

Walking into the sun, Jack blinked. Automatically her eyes went to the distant speck of the plane, a wink of silver now against the blue haze of the sky. It was the first time she could remember being made nervous by the sight of an aeroplane. Even after Brad had died flying his, she had not seriously thought of them as a threat.

The first time she had flown after that, she had known a moment of loss, a wrenching, angry loneliness because he wasn't there anymore. It was a long time before she had admitted to herself that the relationship had probably been doomed anyway. It had been convenient for him to have an adoring, affection-starved teenager to come home to, to make love to. He had talked vaguely of marriage some time in the future, when she was older, and would give her a tolerant, slightly amused smile when she introduced him to people as her fiancé. But he had been showing signs of restlessness, of boredom, and she had begun to feel a cold ache of anxiety even as they planned the celebration of their "anniversary."

His death had been a cruel and shocking way of ending it, and she wished, often, that Brad had been alive and able to walk away from her, as he would have done in the end. She wondered if in time she might have learned to stop loving him. As it was, he had been the only thing in her life apart from flying, and she had still been kidding herself that he would settle down if she could adjust, become the kind of woman he really wanted.

"Fool," she castigated her younger self, from a depth of acquired cynicism. What an idiot she had been, at that vulnerable age. Her mouth curved wryly. She had grown up pretty quickly then. Especially after that abortive telephone call to her parents the day after Brad's body was found, in a childish, futile reaching out for comfort, a hope that they might recognise her desolation and need, and offer her some compassion, forgiveness....

Don't think about that.

Some children scampered across the compound towards her, calling, "Hello, Jack!" They no longer giggled every time they heard her name, and she smiled at them, reciting their names, too. They grinned back at her, and Aroko asked, "Did you see the plane?"

"Yes, I did," she told him.

"It's an enemy plane," Aroko informed her with some solemnity.

"Yes," she said. "I suppose it is. But don't worry. It's not going to hurt us."

"If it tries to bomb us, my father will shoot it!" he boasted, going into his well-known imitation of a machine gunner.

Trying not to wince, Jack agreed, "I'm sure he will." No need to pour scorn on his natural if overabundant confidence in his father's ability to deal with any threat. If the battle that Tula evidently anticipated was to take place, Aroko might find out soon enough that automatic rifles and even machine guns could be matched by weapons even more deadly.

She reached her hut, and the children ran off as she went in. She had left the door and windows open because of the heat, but even so the room was very warm. She got herself a glass of water, and lay down on top of the mattress to sleep.

Some time after she had drifted off, she fell into a dream in which she and her brother Jimmy were swimming in cool water. Then a whirlpool suddenly swirled about her, and she cried out in fright. "I'm coming," Jimmy called, his fair hair, darkened by the water, lying in straight slicks across his forehead. "I'm coming, Jack!"

She struggled to keep her head above the water; he was swimming desperately, his arms going over, over, but he didn't seem to get any closer. The whirlpool was sucking her down, roaring, and her head went under and the roaring became louder.

Her eyes snapped open. She said aloud, "But that never happened!" And in the same instant she recognised the sound that still beat in her ears for what it was, the whirring, familiar droning of a helicopter.

She sat up. It could be a government one. But the shouts she could hear were not frightened, and Tula's men had not opened fire. He had said he was sending for Finn.

She scrambled up, grabbing a comb, pulling it through her tumbled hair, then smoothed the material of the pareu she wore, running her hands over her stomach and hips.

Realising what she was doing, she stopped herself, her head jerking up. *Preening for a man, for heaven's sake,* sneered an inner voice. *What's come over you?*

She made herself saunter to the doorway rather than run, as the children did, to the aircraft while the whirling blades slowed and Finn flung open the door.

He got out and stood there with the draught ruffling his hair, his eyes searching over the children's heads, and ignoring the hand that Captain Tula was holding out to him. Searching for her.

Her heart gave a thump as their eyes met across the intervening space, and she leaned on the door frame, her hands going to her arms, rubbing the inexplicable gooseflesh that shivered over her skin.

Then he looked away at Tula, who now stood stiffly at attention, and exchanged a few words with him. The pilot dropped a bag at his feet, and Finn nodded in acknowledgement, then spoke briefly again to Tula and picked up the bag and strode across to the hut.

She had never realised how vividly blue his eyes were. She had forgotten the way he moved when he wasn't limping, with an easy, confident stride, and how his hair waved on his forehead, the determined line of his jaw.

He stopped in front of the step that made her eyes level with his; then he bent briefly and slid the bag through the door onto the coconut matting. His eyes searched hers, looking for something.

"Hello!" he said, and a smile started at the corners of his eyes.

Jack looked back at him, her own eyes wide and dark, her heart pounding peculiarly. "Hi," she said, her voice very husky. She tried to smile back, but her lips felt stiff. "I'm glad you're safe."

Inane, she thought wildly. He had just been brought into the middle of a war zone.

His smile grew. "I'm glad you are, too." He stepped deliberately up beside her, so she had to move back, because there wasn't really room for two. He glanced into the compound, where not only the children but several adults and even Captain Tula were watching. "We're disappointing them," he said, and drew her into his arms.

Chapter Eleven

Finn's mouth closed on hers, and Jack unthinkingly curved her body into his embrace and opened her lips to him, her arms going up to encircle his neck. It was a long, electrifying kiss, and she totally forgot about their frankly critical audience. She didn't even hear the increased hum of the engine when the pilot took off in haste before the helicopter's presence drew unwelcome attention. There was a rushing, hectic roar in her ears that drowned all sound except her own quickened breathing, and Finn's.

His mouth still on hers, Finn swung her to one side, kicking the door shut with his foot. Jack started at the sound, and made to pull back, but his arms tightened just enough to prevent her escaping him, and his lips were coaxing and teasing hers, setting her veins on fire. He ran a hand up her back and his fingers trailed over her shoulder blades and then touched her hair. He raised his mouth to say indistinctly, "It's grown," before he claimed her lips fully again.

His fingers cradling her nape, he stroked her neck with his thumb, and his other hand caressed her back down to her thigh, taut against his. He lifted his head and bent it again to kiss her bare shoulder, her throat, her eyelids. "You seem smaller," he muttered, his hands exploring her body. "Have you been eating?"

Her eyes still closed, because she was afraid of breaking the spell, Jack said, "Like a horse. Have you?"

"When I had time." His voice was muffled, his lips tracing the line of her shoulder, savouring the taste of her smooth, tanned skin.

She leaned back a little against his hands, bringing her lower body into sweetly intimate contact with his. She opened her eyes as his head came up again, looking with a troubled gaze into his. "Was it bad?"

A shadow momentarily dimmed the brilliant sheen of desire in his eyes. "Not now," he said roughly. "Right now what I need is this!"

He brought his mouth down again in possession of hers, and she felt the thrust of his tongue and parted her lips, allowing him the freedom to do as he wanted, the texture and the taste of him exciting her almost beyond bearing.

She moaned softly, and when for a moment he broke the kiss and bent an explicit, questioning look on her, she knew the answer he saw in her eyes. He gave a satisfied little nod, and then he was drawing her down on the bed, rolling her over so that she lay beneath him, held to him, his arms underneath her solid and tight, as though he never intended to let her go.

She opened her eyes to smile at him, and a movement caught her attention, at the window that was still wide open with red curtains drawn well back.

She gasped and went stiff as a board, and pushed against him. Finn grunted, giving her a quick, surprised frown, and said, "What is it?"

Two small black heads with interested dark eyes rested on two pairs of brown arms on the sill. Jack wriggled out of

Finn's slackened hold and sat up. "Aroko!" she said, sternly. "Go away! You too, Silia!"

They giggled and departed. Finn shot her a rueful look, muttered, "Little devils!" and got up to slam both windows shut. Jack had struggled to her feet, too, her hands shakingly trying to tidy her hair.

"Now, of course," Finn said, "the place will be like an oven. But at least we'll have some privacy."

"You're kidding!" Jack said, adding, "Don't do that!" as he made to draw the curtains across the glass.

He followed her gaze to the compound. Tula had disappeared, and some of those who had gathered about the helicopter had also gone, but there were still a few groups sitting in the shade of the trees, casting covert, smiling glances at the hut and whispering behind their hands.

"They'll all know . . ." Jack said, her cheeks burning.

Finn looked at her and sighed. "I see what you mean. And it would bother you?"

"*Yes*. I couldn't . . ."

"I could." He laughed a little at her startled, warning expression, and said, "But okay. I can understand that. You wouldn't enjoy it much."

"I wouldn't enjoy it *at all*!" Jack said vehemently, appalled.

He gave her a quizzical look of exaggerated disbelief.

Silently, Jack shook her head, her mouth very firm.

Finn laughed again. He put his head on one side, regarding her. "I'm tempted to make you take that back," he drawled.

She turned her back on him, pretending she needed to find her comb. "Did Tula tell you," she said, attempting a nonchalance she didn't feel in the least, "we have some patients for you?"

"I gathered there's nothing particularly serious."

"No, they're all on the mend now. But . . . we had two deaths. I wish you'd been here."

"Odds are I wouldn't have been able to save them, you know," he said.

"But if you'd been here," she said with sudden fierceness, turning to him, "you might have done *something*!"

"I might have," he agreed, his mood altering as he searched her face. "You cared."

"I didn't even know them," she said. "It just seems a pity they couldn't have had better—more expert—attention. After all, somebody cared about them."

"I'm sorry I wasn't here," Finn said, still watching her intently.

"It wasn't your fault. I'm not blaming you."

"It wasn't your fault, either, you know," Finn told her. "Have you been blaming yourself?"

Jack shook her head. "Whatever gave you that idea? I...did try. We all did. I suppose you're...used to death."

"You have to become accustomed to it," Finn said. "You can't help the dead anymore. Only the living."

"How was it, at Kitikiti?" she asked him.

"Could have been worse," Finn said. "There were some infected injuries that shouldn't have been allowed to go untreated for so long, but I only had to do one amputation. Still, that's not much comfort for the poor guy who lost his leg. Most people had the sense to boil their water, and the danger of an epidemic of cholera or typhoid is receding, thank heaven. They had a water purifier brought in recently—the pressure from international aid agencies has paid off, and both the government and the rebel leaders have agreed to allow relief planes in, after all. The Red Cross have some people there now, who arrived about the same time I did."

"Couldn't you have got out on one of their planes?" Jack asked.

Finn said, "You mean, leave you high and dry? What do you take me for?"

"You could have!" she said. "Finn, why *didn't* you?"

"Apart from...other considerations," he said, "I'd given my word to Tula. And he was holding you against it."

"He wouldn't have hurt me."

"He's a soldier, Jacqueline. He'd do whatever he thought necessary. And sometimes that can be pretty nasty."

"You should have taken the chance," she said.

"Not without you."

She swallowed an unfair anger, knowing that in his place she would have done the same. Or not done it. "Well, now that you're here," she said reluctantly, "you'd better come and see our new hospital."

Tula's men were digging again, this time a trench right in front of the Savusutas' house, the temporary hospital. The dirt scooped out of the trench was being shovelled into bags and laid along the edge. Finn eyed these operations frowningly, and said, "I'll have a talk to our Captain Tula later."

He approved what the women had done inside, only asking for a few changes. He checked all the remaining patients, gave one man an injection, and left a few instructions for the amateur nurses, then strode off to the captain's hut, and it was some time before Jack saw him again.

She had cooked him a special meal, not so much because she had planned to, as because everyone assumed that she wanted to, and brought her the means to do it with. Tiare had killed and plucked a chicken, Kalanui's mother brought some small, sweet melons and a few tomatoes, and Mrs. Savusuta contributed a precious tin of asparagus. Other neighbours sent their children with corn and cucumbers and green bananas, and even a couple of lemons.

"They'll be hurt if we don't eat it," Jack said when Finn joined her, cocking a surprised eyebrow at the abundance of food. "And it's awfully generous of them."

"I'm aware of that," he said. "I intend to do it full justice."

When he pushed away his plate, he said, "I need a walk to shake that down. Coming?"

"If the captain will let us," Jack said, doubtfully. "He's tightened his grip, you may have noticed. Did you know he's got the people to harvest everything they could from their gardens and bring it inside the fence?"

"Well, there may come a time when it isn't safe to wander about outside, I suppose," Finn said. "I guess he's taking precautions." He pushed back his chair. "I'll wash up when we get back."

Jack said, "I'll do it. You must be tired."

He looked at her thoughtfully. "Not that tired," he said enigmatically. "Are you having second thoughts?" he added when she followed him to the doorway. His hand came up to take hers as he stepped outside ahead of her.

Automatically she took it, although she certainly needed no help to negotiate the single step. She made a tentative effort to free her fingers from his light clasp as she strolled at his side, but his grip tightened, and at her continued silence, he said, "Have you?"

She couldn't pretend not to know what he meant. She said, "Don't rush me, Finn ... please."

"I didn't think I was," he said, as they approached the sentry at the gate. "You seemed quite ... ready, this afternoon."

"I was ... pleased to see you. More so than I expected. It took me off guard, rather."

"Well," he admitted, "it kind of did me, too. I hadn't counted on such a passionate welcome. But I'm not complaining."

The guard hesitated, but let them through. Apparently there were no orders yet to keep anyone in, even the doctor and his wife. They went uphill, taking a winding route that left the village and gardens behind. As they reached a bend in the narrow path, Finn tugged her to a halt. "Maybe we're talking too much," he said. "Come here."

She didn't really try to stop him, putting up only a token resistance that he quite naturally refused to take seriously, only capturing a wayward wrist in his hand while his mouth took hers in a long, satisfying kiss. She swayed against him, and felt her mouth part and respond without any thought, and when he stopped kissing her, she rested her head lightly against his throat and licked her throbbing lips and breathed his name.

He moved, backing her into the deepening shadow of a nearby tree, so that she came up against the trunk. Then he imprisoned her there with his hands flattened on the bark and looked down at her and said softly, "Well? What now?"

Feeling almost dazed, Jack looked away. "I don't know," she said. She frowned, blinked and said almost resentfully. "I don't *want* this!"

Finn laughed. "You liar."

Jack irritably shook her head. "No, I mean . . . you know what I mean!"

He straightened abruptly, shoving his hands into his pockets. "Yes, unfortunately." He added, "I could make you forget your . . . scruples, whatever they are, couldn't I? I wish I were insensitive enough to do it."

Jack smiled rather sadly. "But you're not."

Regretfully, Finn agreed. "No, I guess not."

"Are you by any chance," Jack asked delicately, "trying a new tactic?"

He frowned, then gave a short laugh. "No, I'm not. What a nasty, suspicious mind you have, Grandma!"

"I don't," Jack informed him, "see you as Red Riding Hood."

"Well, I'm not the big bad wolf, either," he said. "Believe me."

Their eyes met with a flare of understanding, of sudden, amused tenderness. *Danger,* flashed the automatic warning signal in Jack's brain.

"I've had enough walking," she said. "I'm going back."

If he noticed her use of the singular, he didn't heed it. They walked back side by side, without talking, and when in the quickly growing darkness Jack turned her foot on a stone and stumbled, he shot out a hand to steady her but removed it as soon as she assured him she was all right.

"You're not limping anymore," she commented, as the village came into view down the slope.

"Good as new," Finn said. "The scar on your arm hardly shows, either. I must have done a better job on that than I thought."

"I don't scar easily," she said.

"No?" he said after a short silence. "I'd have said you probably do. But then, some wounds go deep."

They had reached the gate, and Jack said hurriedly, "I'll wash up, if you want to go and check on things at the hospital."

He hesitated, then said casually, "Okay, I'll do that." And sauntered away, not looking back. Jack conquered a brief, fierce regret and went to do the dishes.

When he came back she was already in bed. He had been quite a long time, perhaps giving her the chance to pretend sleep on his return. Instead, she rolled over onto her back and said in a deliberately impersonal tone, "Everything all right?"

"Yes. You women didn't really need me."

"We're glad you're here, though. And Captain Tula is expecting more wounded, obviously."

"The situation looks bad for the rebels."

"Did you hear things in Kitikiti?"

"Rumour, gossip. Tula's lot are losing badly, being pushed back all the time. They got overconfident, I think, having harried the government into going on the defensive with their guerilla tactics, and began to get too close to the capital. Instead of their usual sniping and melting away, they stood and fought the army. That frightened the administration, and they hit back with more force. They've been investing heavily in the war effort in the last six months."

"I think Tula is going to try and hold the line here. There have been other guerilla units coming in."

"Yes, I know. He hasn't got a hope." Finn moved restlessly.

"They don't have bombers, do they?" Jack asked. "Fighter planes?"

"I've heard rumours. Tula must have, too. They do have highly trained army units with very sophisticated weapons. Long-range artillery, for instance, with a pretty accurate range. And some helicopters. I think the one the rebels use is a 'liberated' army machine delivered to them by a pilot who changed sides."

Jack said, "I just hope they realise that there are civilians here. Children."

Finn said, "I just hope they respect that."

The next morning he was up early, and when Jack went over to the hospital, she saw him standing on the ground, apparently directing a couple of men on the corrugated iron roof doing something with string and chalk. At the foot of a ladder they had used stood a tin of paint.

"What are they doing?" she asked curiously.

"Painting us a red cross on the roof," Finn answered.

"Good idea. Did Captain Tula agree?"

"Absolutely."

She saw that the bags that yesterday had been piled by the newly dug trench were now arrayed along the walls of the building. "And that?"

He took his attention from the roof to grin down at her. "He also agreed that his sandbags are more use there, protecting the patients from stray bullets."

"You must have done some fast talking," Jack commented.

Finn said, "It was straight," and then lifted his head, gesturing as he called something to the men above them.

That day, Jack thought afterwards, was a kind of hiatus. The helicopter returned twice, bringing more men, fresh and fit and not war weary. Most of them were also very young.

"Soldiers generally are," Finn told her, when she made a comment on the fact. "That's one of the most tragic aspects of any war."

The village was bursting at the seams, but the people found room and welcomed the newcomers in the tradition of the island, even putting on a special feast in the evening, with roasted whole pigs and flower leis, and girls in palm leaf skirts and floral headdresses performing the local version of the hula.

Jack sat with Finn at a long board loaded with food and decorated with flowers, flanked by Tukaikians who smiled and laughed and sang as though they hadn't a care in the world, and passed little coconut shell bowls of the traditional *kawa* made of fermented gingerroot.

Jack drank sparingly, knowing from experience it was wise to leave the *kawa* until after the food, but even so she found her mouth going numb, and experimentally ran her tongue over her lips.

Finn smiled down at her. "Okay?" He raised his brows, and took a cautious sip from the bowl she had handed on to him.

"Can't feel a thing!" she assured him gaily, and he laughed.

"It does have that effect." He handed the cup to his neighbour.

"I suppose," she said, "it's all thoroughly unhygienic. Doesn't it horrify your medical mind?"

He said, "I imagine that stuff would kill any bugs in short order."

"Well, at least it won't give us a hangover."

But it did make one sleepy, and after a while the crowd of chattering, laughing and singing people began to blur before Jack's eyes. She shook her head and opened her eyes wide, seeing Captain Tula, with a wreath of waxy white blossoms rakishly awry on his head, sit down with a beaming smile to accept a dish of fresh roasted peanuts, throwing them expertly into his mouth. He was attending the party, but every fifteen minutes or so he disappeared. Checking, Jack figured. Making sure that no one was creeping up on them in the darkness, under cover of all this happy noise.

She shivered, and Finn put a casual arm about her shoulders and said, "Cold?"

"No. Why do you suppose Captain Tula's allowing this?"

"Morale," Finn suggested, following the direction of her eyes. "It could be a long time before these people can party again."

"It could draw attention, though."

"Maybe. But the government troops probably know there's a village here, anyway."

"Yes, they do. There was a plane one day... reconnaissance."

"And villages do have celebrations. Maybe that's the idea. Tula's lot have been beaten, they've lost men. They don't have anything to celebrate, do they? Perhaps he hopes to put the army off the scent. Make them think this is a perfectly innocent community going about its perfectly innocent daily life."

"Do you think they're that close? The army?"

"I don't know. Tula's playing his cards close to his chest. But if his scouts thought the enemy was within attacking range, he certainly wouldn't be letting half his men get legless."

Jack giggled. It was a good description. Her own legs, when she experimentally shifted them, felt rubbery. "I doubt," she confided, "if I could walk to our hut just now. And I haven't really had much, you know."

"I know," Finn said, his eyes glinting with humour. "You do seem more mellow than usual, though."

"How do I usually seem, then?"

"Guarded," he answered. "Like someone who's retreated into the castle and pulled up the portcullis."

"Down," Jack said.

"What?"

"Down. You let *down* a portcullis. It's a grating, that slides down to close the entrance to the castle."

"Oh, yes. You're right ... I think."

"Of course I'm right. You meant the drawbridge."

"Ah, yes. Pulled up the drawbridge, then."

"My tongue's gone to sleep," Jack informed him thoughtfully.

"I'd never have guessed. Although the rest of you looks as though it wants to follow suit."

"May I borrow your shoulder for a minute?" she asked very politely, thinking that it was comfortably broad.

"Feel free." He pulled her closer to it, and settled her head against him. "That okay?"

"Great," Jack said, and fell asleep.

Five minutes later she opened her eyes. Only it might have been more than five minutes, because the noise had died down, and a number of people seemed to have left, although there were still children picking at leftovers and women quietly gathering up dishes while the after-party lingerers chatted to one another. Captain Tula had gone again, and the headman and his wife, who had been sitting at the centre of the table, had disappeared as well.

"Where's everyone?" Jack enquired.

"Party's over. You should be in bed," Finn told her.

"If I try to walk," she said doubtfully, "I think I'll disgrace myself by falling all over the table."

"Very likely."

"You're no help."

"What can I do? Carry you?"

"I don't think so." She removed herself slowly from his encircling arm and cautiously stood up.

Finn stood up, too, and caught her as she staggered. "I think I'm going to have to," he said, laughter in his voice.

Crossly, Jack said, "You were drinking the stuff, too. And I didn't have much! It's not as though it's the first time."

"I ate more than you. It dilutes the effect."

"I suppose," she said. She licked her lips. "Someone's taken my legs away and replaced them with wet clay."

Finn chuckled, and hoisted her up in his arms. "This is the only way, I'm afraid. It'll give our hosts a thrill, anyway. Look at them."

She looked and shut her eyes. Talk about elbows digging into ribs! Although to give them their due, the islanders' interest was not in the least sly, but openly approving. She buried her suddenly hot face against Finn's shoulder. "You know what they all think . . ." she choked.

She felt him shake with silent laughter. "They think it's incredibly romantic. If you weren't drunk and incapable, I might think so, too."

She lifted her head indignantly. *"I am not!"*

"You are so," he argued. "Can't even walk straight. Can't walk at all."

"Oh, yes I can," she said. "Try me!"

"Right," he said promptly, and put her down. Her feet found the ground, and she wobbled dangerously.

"No!" she said sharply as he made to put out his hand. "Don't you touch me, Finn Simonson!"

He retreated exactly two paces, watching her critically, and she drew a deep breath and fixed her gaze on the door of the hut about twenty yards off. She took a step. Okay. Another. Her legs didn't belong to her, but never mind. They were working, she'd make them. Another big breath. Keep the eyes straight ahead. Don't look down, don't look to the side. And especially don't look at Finn, keeping pace an arm's length from her side and grinning like the Cheshire Cat every inch of the way.

She got to the step, and carefully lifted one foot over it, then the other, and stood for a moment triumphant as Finn applauded softly behind her. Very cautiously she turned in the doorway and with a hand surreptitiously clinging to the jamb, made him a formal, not very deep bow. "That," she said, with great dignity, "is stone-cold sobriety."

Then, as he shouted with laughter, she spun on her heel, almost ruining the whole effect as the room in turn spun around her, found the edge of the mattress more by good luck than good management, and thankfully allowed herself to fall facedown on its welcome softness.

Finn followed her in, and stood looking down at her for a full minute.

"Jacqueline?" he said, his hands on his hips. "Jack?"

She moaned and turned over, staring up at him with her brown eyes made luminous by moonlight.

"Jack," he said, and dropped to his knees on the mattress beside her, looming over her with his hands on either side of her shoulders. "That," he told her, with laughter still colouring his voice, "was sheer willpower."

He bent and dropped the lightest of kisses on her lips, and was drawing away when she hooked a hand softly about his neck, and murmured, "Mmm."

He kissed her again, warmly, lingeringly. Then he reached up and unhooked her detaining hand from his neck, and sat back.

"So," he said rather unsteadily, "was that."

Jack sighed disappointedly, and her eyelids fluttered down. He sat watching the gentle rise and fall of her breasts, confined by the pareu.

"Jacqueline," he said. "Oh, Jacqueline. Stone-cold sober you are not."

He lay back beside her with his hands behind his head, and admired the copper-edged moon hanging at the corner of the window until it inched out of sight. Then he sighed, touched the black smudge of Jack's hair on the pillow, and closed his eyes, deliberately blotting out the tantalising sight of her.

Chapter Twelve

Jack woke clearheaded and clear-eyed.

"There's no justice," Finn complained as he came back from the bathroom to find her slicing fruit for breakfast. "By rights you should have a thick head."

"Not with *kawa*," she replied. "Anyway, if there was any justice, you'd have a hangover, not me."

He grinned. "You may be slightly dehydrated. Make sure you drink plenty of water."

"Yes, Doctor."

"You can't fool me with that meek tone," he told her, helping himself to a slice of orange.

"Coming to the hospital later?" he enquired as they finished eating.

"Yes. Right away, if you like."

"You said once," he reminded her, as they crossed the compound, "that you were destined for one of the professions. Did you ever think of becoming a doctor?"

Jack laughed. "Hardly. Although I suppose that's one thing that . . ."

"That...?" Finn queried as they walked over a plank bridge spanning the trench in front of the building.

"...that my parents would have approved of," she said lightly, pushing open the door before he could get to it.

"They didn't approve of you taking up flying?" he asked.

"Oh, no! That was one reason I liked it so much."

"Teenage rebellion?"

"I was a trial to my parents," she said drily. "A horrible brat, really."

"Mmm," he said. "I can imagine."

"I'll bet." She smiled and moved away from him as Mrs. Savusuta greeted him and stood ready to bring him up to date on the patients.

There was more smoke that day, distant but not so distant as before, and again a plane came swooping low over the village.

"I hope they've hidden that gun well," Jack muttered to Finn as they watched the aircraft head for the far horizon.

"I'm sure they have. One thing I'll say for Tula, I think he knows his stuff," he replied.

The place still looked, Jack hoped, like an ordinary village, except for the larger population, though half of them had been indoors, and the armed guards had hurried into the trees at the first sound of the plane. Parents had called children to their sides, and stood watching apprehensively, but after one pass the plane didn't come back.

Otherwise the day progressed without incident, except that the helicopter returned near dusk, and settled not in the compound but at the new helicopter pad, disappearing among the trees, and Tula sent some men to hide and guard it.

The red cross on the hospital roof had been covered over with palm leaves as soon as it dried. "No need to advertise that we're expecting casualties," Finn had agreed when Tula suggested it. "But they come off as soon as an attack seems imminent."

Jack found it hard to sleep. An oppressive sense of impending disaster seemed to hang over the village. Finn had stayed late at the hospital, coming in well after midnight. She heard him as he shed his shirt and slipped onto the mattress beside her, but she lay still and quiet. Presently she knew by his breathing that he was asleep.

Towards dawn she dozed, only to be woken by the harsh challenge of the sentry, and a murmured answer. She heard the faint creak of the gate even as Finn sat up beside her, alert and listening.

There were more voices, and Finn went to the window.

"Reinforcements?" Jack guessed, joining him. There were shadowy figures filing through the gate, some with bundles on their backs.

"Refugees, more like," Finn said grimly, and turned, reaching for his shirt. There were small children among them, she saw now, trudging wearily as though they had walked a long way. "I hope Tula's prepared for this!"

If he wasn't, he soon remedied the omission. Tula, Jack decided, was in his element when he had a huge job of organisation on his hands. He shifted most of his fighting men, including a number of recruits from among the newcomers, to the huge copra-drying shed, and the families who flowed in through the gate until dusk were accommodated within the village.

"The soldiers burnt their homes," Jack told Finn after talking to some of the women. She had been helping to distribute food to hungry children and their mothers. "They drove the people out and set fire to the entire village. Their gardens, too."

Finn nodded. "Back in Sulaka, remember, you said that starvation would do the government's dirty work."

"Yes. But this is worse than just doing nothing to prevent it after the cyclone. This is actively, deliberately destroying people's food."

"I know," Finn said. "It's worse, but the results are the same, in the end. That's what we have to deal with."

"I wonder how long our food supplies will last," Jack mused. "They used an awful lot at that feast the other night. You don't think they'll turn on another one for these people, do you?"

"I doubt if Tula would allow it. The army is definitely closing in."

"So it won't be long now," Jack guessed.

"Of course, if they have heavy equipment it could slow them down."

"But they're on their way, aren't they?"

Finn nodded. "I'm afraid there's not much doubt about it. They can't afford not to press their advantage. It would be bad strategy to allow the rebels time to recover and regroup properly."

"I almost feel relieved," Jack said slowly. "We've been waiting for it for so long . . . preparing."

When a plane appeared again, heading straight for the village, and making several passes this time, some of the refugee children screamed and ran to cling to their mothers. Everyone else stayed quiet and still, as though they could make themselves invisible. Even the local children refrained from their usual shrill excitement, understanding now that the sight of a plane made the adults inexplicably nervous.

Tula, to Finn's great relief and approval, had moved all his men outside the village. They were deployed down the hillside, ready to repulse an attack well away from any danger to the noncombatants.

The first shots came at midday, a rattle of gunfire that echoed up the hillside and brought all movement within the village to an immediate, petrified standstill.

Finn, dealing with an infected foot on one of the refugees, glanced up at Jack, who was holding a bottle of disinfectant for him. She had jerked her head up at the sound, spilling a little of the stuff over her hand.

"Careful with that," he said. "We can't afford to waste it." Then he returned to his swabbing.

"Sorry," she said automatically. Their patient had gone briefly white-eyed, and she smiled at the young woman in what she hoped was a suitably reassuring way.

After a while she got used to the gunfire, and a deeper, explosive sound that Finn said was grenades, adding, "We might get some nasty wounds."

The red cross on the roof had been cleared of its covering. It might stop the hospital becoming a direct target.

And then another plane came, faster and much more deadly than the spotter, swooping low over the green hillside where Tula's men were concealed, and spraying the trees with bullets spitting from its wings. When the casualties began to arrive, Mrs. Savusuta recruited extra nurses from among the village women. Finn had been right, Jack thought, deliberately shutting off all feelings of horror and gritting her teeth against a desperate need to be sick. "Nasty" was hardly the word for the things they were dealing with now.

She worked on by Finn's side. She seemed to have developed a sixth sense that allowed her to provide what he needed almost before he had finished asking for it. There was some satisfaction in knowing she was performing well, and Finn was, too—they were a team.

Even the fact that they were in the middle of a war didn't lessen the feeling of elation that buoyed her through hours of backbreaking and unpleasant work. When Finn said, "Want a rest?" she shook her head and kept on going. Sometime during the evening she gulped down coffee and a bowl of chicken and rice while standing up in the kitchen, and went back to the ward.

But when at last there was a lull, and he said, "Come on, you and I have earned a break," she followed him back through the darkness to the hut and fell on the bed and slept.

All through the next day the fighting continued, and now a new note intruded. The warplane came back, and as it banked away up the hillside, the antiaircraft gun that had been so carefully hidden spat streams of bright flame, and the plane veered, lurched and then lifted over the top of the hill and disappeared.

"They missed," Jack said. She was standing at the doorway of the hospital with Finn at her side, taking a breath of fresh air.

"Yes," Finn answered. "And they might not get another chance."

Next time the plane made a pass, spitting flame, the bomb doors opened as the gun on the ground returned the fire with equal ferocity, and there was a loud explosion followed by a dull *crump*.

Finn was staring uphill at a thick cloud of smoke rising from the trees. "I think they knocked out the gun emplacement."

The plane was roaring upwards, skimming the surface of the hill, but it dipped to the right as they watched, and ploughed into the side just short of the summit, erupting immediately in a bright banner of flame.

"Oh, God!" Jack said. "No one will have got out of that!"

"No," Finn said unemotionally, looking at her white face. "I don't suppose they will. Come on, let's go back to work."

He held her arm firmly until they were inside.

"It's coming closer, isn't it?" she said in the afternoon.

"It has been for some time," Finn told her. "Tula's in retreat."

Mrs. Savusuta passed by them, carrying a bowl with a white cloth over it. Her usually serene face was puckered with anxiety.

"Hold this for me," Finn said, and Jack wrenched her attention back to what she was doing.

Late in the afternoon the firing seemed to lessen, becoming a desultory sniping. No new casualties had appeared for some time, and Jack and Finn had a cold meal provided in the Savusutas' kitchen and returned to their hut, hoping to snatch some sleep.

But sleep eluded Jack. She tossed and wriggled, feeling hot and prickly and uncomfortable in spite of the shower she had taken. After a while Finn touched her arm and said, "Try to relax."

"I am trying!" she snapped, annoyed at such trite advice. Then, shamefaced, "Sorry, did I wake you?"

"Doesn't matter." He pushed a pillow up behind him and leaned on it. "Want to talk?"

"What about?"

"Anything. It might help you unwind."

"I don't want to talk about the hospital—or the war."

"Your childhood?"

"No!"

"Okay," he said easily. "Tell me where you met your friend Abe."

"Abe?" It seemed a long time since she had seen him. Another world. "I met him five years ago, in Sulaka. I'd arrived crewing on a yacht, but the skipper figured one of his perks was the right to sleep with his female crew. We didn't see eye to eye, and I was sick of fighting him off."

"So you bought a plane instead?"

"Not exactly, no. I didn't have enough money for that. I won it. Or at least, half of it. I bought out the other half later."

"*Won* it?"

"I was always a natural at cards. I used to beat my brother all the time, and he was three years older and a lot smarter than me. And Brad... Brad taught me a lot about poker. He was good. I didn't beat him nearly so often. We played regularly with his friends. I picked up a bit from them, too."

"Who did you win it from?"

"From Abe. That's how I met him."

"He didn't know how good you were?"

She grinned in the darkness. "He had no idea." She sat up, too, hugging her knees. "It was *beautiful*!"

"You took him."

"I bet my entire wages, which I'd just collected, against a half share in his plane. He thought I was a sucker, and he fell for it." She chuckled. "He said afterwards he wouldn't have taken my money—not all of it. He figured he was going to teach me a lesson. You know, don't play with the big boys."

"Poor Abe."

"Yeah. Still, he was a sport about it. And it taught *him* not to take anything for granted."

"You must have been a pretty bright kid."

"Not bright enough."

"Why do you say that?"

"I never . . . came up to expectations."

"You mean your parents' expectations?"

Jack shrugged. "Who else?"

"What about your brother who died? Older and smarter, you said."

"Older, brighter, better-looking, better-tempered. My parents adored him. So did I."

"Were you jealous?" Finn asked softly.

"No! I just told you, I adored him!"

"One needn't necessarily preclude the other," Finn told her. "And it's nothing to feel guilty about, either."

"I don't feel guilty, and I don't want to be psycho-analysed," Jack said tightly.

"Sorry, I didn't mean to probe. Want to change the subject?"

"Yes. What about *your* childhood hang-ups? Or were you too well-adjusted to have any?"

"Well—I was never much good at baseball. That's a big thing where I come from. It led to some . . . grief, when I was small."

"Were your parents disappointed?"

"Probably not. But I always imagined that my dad must be. He was quite a player himself when he was in school. One day he sat me down and told me he thought I should stop trying to make the team and do something I could be good at. By that time we'd gotten into a kind of vicious circle. He coached me and helped me because I was so determined I was going to master the blasted game. And because he spent so much time and effort on it, I figured he was going to be really disappointed if I never did get the hang of it. He was appalled that I thought I was letting him down in some way. Said he was proud of me just for trying so damned hard, but the only approval I had to look for was my own. He figured it was time I found some activity I could enjoy and get a sense of achievement from. Because it was pretty obvious that I didn't really like baseball.''

''It's hard to like something if you're never good enough,'' Jack commented. Nothing had ever been good enough for her parents. Not after Jimmy died and they had turned all their attention on their remaining child. They had tried to bring her up to his standard, to make her take his place. Their plans for him had all been transferred to her, and she had been coaxed and coached and encouraged and exhorted to do better, better, better.

The eternal refrain of her childhood. *You can do better.* No matter how well she had done, and her marks were always in the top third, the pleased smiles and congratulations would be followed, sometimes immediately, by, *But you can do better, I'm sure....*

Until she had rebelled one day, shouting at them both, *No, I can't do better! I don't want to do better! I'm sick to death of mathematics and French and physics, and exams, exams, exams! I want a life of my own—I'm leaving school!*

Predictablly, her father had replied, *You're doing no such thing!* And that had been only the start of it. After a series of rows, each noisier and more recriminatory than the last, with her father's cold logic and implacable authority backed up by her mother's shrill reproaches, after Jack had fled in the middle of the night and been returned to her home by the police, the final straw had been when finally they brought into the open the thing that had lain under all their ambitions for her, all her fruitless striving to please them.

You're all we have left now. Jimmy would never have done this to us.

And behind that, still unspoken, she read as clear as a banner headline what she had known all along, ever since the black days after Jimmy's death, when her father had carried on as though nothing had happened, and her mother had looked at her with absentminded detachment as though she wasn't there. Until one day when, bewildered and frightened and distressed by the stark announcement of her brother's death and the total silence on the subject after the funeral, during which she had been left in the care of an aunt, she had indulged in a bit of silly nine-year-old naughtiness. And her mother had turned on her with hatred in her eyes and snarled, *Why couldn't it have been you!*

Perhaps her mother, too, had later been appalled at that. She had tried to retract it almost immediately. *Mummy didn't really mean it. Mummy's upset. We all are. I know you didn't mean to be naughty, either, did you? You see, we all do things we shouldn't.*

But the explanations and excuses were much less convincing than that moment of naked venom, and of course the child knew that she *had* meant to be naughty as the only, desperate means of regaining her mother's attention. Which she had, with such devastating results.

So when on her sixteenth birthday she had declared her intention of leaving school and her mother had flung at her bitterly, *Jimmy wouldn't have done this to us!* she had retaliated with a teenager's ruthlessness and intention to wound.

Jimmy would never have had the guts! He was always a boring little prig, anyway, and I hate him!

That had been very satisfying, and after it there was, of course, nothing to do but leave home.

Her father had brought her back that time, convincing her that by law she couldn't leave unless he approved of her living conditions, which of course he hadn't. Sponging on a friend with a flat wasn't her idea of living, either, and jobs weren't as easy to find for sixteen-year-olds without qualifications as she had hoped. So she had returned home reluctantly, and punished her parents by being a surly, trying teenager, abusive and disobedient, acquiring a boyfriend among a rowdy bunch of young tearaways who drank too much and smoked pot occasionally, and frequently taking illicit days off school. A teacher called her parents and suggested counselling. They were glad to agree, and she had attended the first session with a sulky air of coercion hiding the fact that she was utterly miserable with herself and harboured a secret hope that the counsellor might be able to help her. After that she attended regularly with only a minor show of reluctance, because contrary to all expectation the counsellor was a youngish, good-looking man with fair hair and a thin, sensitive face, who treated her like an adult and encouraged her to think like one. He made the rowdy boyfriend seem callow and uncouth, and Jack developed a secret, full-blown crush on him.

When he left the school for a better job six weeks into her sessions, she felt betrayed and angry. She sat through sessions with his replacement, an experienced middle-aged woman, refusing to cooperate, sneering at the woman's patient questions, and putting up a total blank wall between them until she missed one appointment, then another, and finally stopped going altogether.

The fact that she passed her exams at the end of the year quite comfortably didn't do much to mollify her parents. It was to their credit, she supposed, that they had not changed their minds about their desire to have her stay with them. She wouldn't have blamed them for throwing her out.

She stayed home for another year, in an atmosphere of daily recriminations, often unspoken but loud for all that. She went out every Friday and Saturday night and occasionally didn't come home until morning. When her father tried to impose a curfew she laughed in his face and dared him to make her keep it. She knew that they'd put up with a lot if she just got through the year at school. They said it was for her sake, that she would be grateful to them for forcing her to gain some qualifications, that when she had recovered from her present admittedly unpleasant phase she would realise that she was destined for a career in one of the professions—law perhaps, or even science. When she mentioned engineering, they gulped and demurred, but agreed unconvincingly that maybe that was an option, too. Perhaps architecture, her mother suggested daringly. Now, that was something different for a girl.

She had never believed they were doing any of it for her. They were doing it all because death had cheated them of their son, and if a daughter was second best, she could still be moulded into a convenient if not quite perfect substitute. But she played along for a while because her brief foray into the world outside of books and exams had taught her that in one thing they were right. She would have a better chance at freedom and independence if she could prove that she had at least a basic education. She cruised through her classes, did the minimum of work she felt was necessary, and completed further exams with flying colours, and her parents breathed a sigh of relief and suggested university.

You've got to be kidding! Jack said, and got herself a job and a place in a flat and moved out.

"Did you ever go back?" Finn's soft voice came.

She wasn't even aware of when she had started to put her memories into words; she had scarcely known that she was talking. The question jolted her into a realisation of what she had said, and she thought, *I've never told anyone all that. Never.*

"Once," she said. But she wouldn't tell him any more. Her head was swimming with fatigue. That was why she had talked so much, she supposed. "You must be bored rigid," she said, trying to sound a light note.

"Far from it," Finn answered. "Think you can sleep now?"

"Yes." It had been a catharsis of sorts, she supposed. Damn the man, he had got her to open up something she had kept locked away for years. Memories that could still make her shudder and shrink if she ever allowed them to surface, as they did sometimes in that twilight zone between sleeping and waking.

She had gone back once, taking Brad with her. She had told him she wanted to introduce him to her parents. "Don't worry," she had said, laughing at him in the early, confident days of their relationship. "I want to show off my fiancé. I want them to know that I'm happy. I wasn't very nice to them, you know. I'd like to tell them I'm sorry."

Perhaps she had also wanted his moral support for this first meeting with her parents since she had left home.

Her father had stood in the door and regarded them both coldly, and refused to let them in. It had been one of the most humiliating experiences of her life. But she had held her head high and turned away, and put her arm through Brad's on the walk back to his car. *I guess I deserved it,* she had told him, shrugging it off. *I can't really blame them.*

And Brad had said, *Middle-class creep!* Which made her laugh more than was necessary. And then he had taken her flying.

A sudden light spilling into the room through the windows brought her into startled wakefulness. It was white and then purple, filling the corners and making her blink, and Finn beside her had flung an arm over his eyes.

"Flares," he said. "I wonder what they hope to see?"

"It's been quiet for a long time."

"It's still quiet. Either they didn't find anything or they're just doing it to keep the guerillas awake and make them nervous."

Four of the flares went off, spraying the sky with coloured stars and throwing everything into stark light. Jack lay awake until dawn, when the gunfire started again, closer, she thought, than ever. She got up and showered and then stood at the doorway of the hut, watching the sky grow pink, and listening to the sinister sounds of battle.

It was no surprise, really, when some of Tula's men came running up the hill towards the village and burst through the gate, flinging themselves into the trench behind the fence. Others were still firing from outside the gates when Tula himself appeared with another bunch of men.

By this time Finn was standing behind her. "This is it," he said. "I guess they've got Tula and his men where they want them, now. Right on our doorstep."

Some of the men needed urgent medical treatment and were carried straight into the hospital. A pile of automatic rifles was soon stacked at the corner of the house, because Finn wouldn't allow them inside. He kept Jack too busy to see what was going on outside, but every so often there was a burst of gunfire, then silence, and the occasional ominous thump of a grenade.

"I don't hear any heavy artillery," he said once, lifting his head during a lull.

"That's good news, I suppose," Jack said, with dry doubt in her voice.

Tula himself appeared in the doorway, filthy and haggard, and Finn crossed the room to speak to him.

"Are you hurt, Captain? What can I do for you?"

There were streaks of blood on Tula's face and clothes, and he had a handkerchief tied roughly around one wrist, but he said, "No, Doctor. I tried to keep the fighting outside the boundaries, but we have been driven to our last defences. I came to tell you that I'm instructing all the women and children to come here. It's the safest place for them. The army may respect the red cross."

If he had expected an argument, Finn didn't give him one. He only said, "You realise that the space will be very limited."

"I know. But Latu Savusuta has agreed."

"I'd appreciate it if you'd ask them to keep away from the room we're using for surgery. It should remain sterile, and we need it. And I need one other room for my seriously ill patients."

Tula nodded. "I understand. I'm grateful for your cooperation." He bowed and went away.

"As if I had a choice," Finn murmured as he returned to his work.

By the time whole families had crowded into the house, filling every available space, and even the broad verandah along the front, the noise of crying children and anxious mothers almost drowned out the renewed shooting around the fence.

"Why don't they surrender?" Finn muttered as another soldier was brought in, supported by two of his comrades. "Put him down here," he said, pointing to one of the few mattresses left on the floor. "I'll get to him as soon as I can. And get his gun out of here," he added as he glimpsed the rifle swinging from the man's shoulder.

He assessed the man's wound, and told Jack what to do while he went to inspect someone else. She gave the man an injection for the pain, reflecting that only days ago she had not known how to do that, and dressed the wound. The man slipped into sleep, and Finn came back and touched her arm and said, "Take a break with me. We seem to have hit a quiet patch, but it can't last."

They stood on the verandah steps side by side. Day was fading, and she hoped that with the night there would come a cessation in the fighting. Some children were playing about the so far unused trench in front of the house, scrambling up the sides and jumping down again, sometimes running along its length. Even now, Jack thought with detachment, the children were irrepressible. Too young, she supposed, to understand the gravity of the situation.

She saw her young friend Aroko run along the trench and waved to him before turning to peer across the compound to the trees outside the fence. A single shot showed as a rapid flash of red, and someone from inside the compound fired back, a quick tattoo.

She hadn't seen Aroko climb out of the trench near the corner where they had stacked firearms taken from the wounded, nor seen him snatch at one of them before he dived back into the trench, staggering under its weight. And by the time he scrambled out of the other side, with the weapon now balanced and held at the ready in imitation of his father and other men, it was too late.

She heard Finn say, *"That kid's got a—"* even as she shouted, *"Aroko—no!"*

But he was immersed in his favourite game, perhaps thinking that this time he was a real fighter like his father, helping to save his people. He ran across the bare ground shouting at the top of his childish voice, *"Ack-ack-ack-ack-ack!"*

Jack was down the steps and running before the answering, much more deadly and horribly real, gunfire came spilling out of the trees in a lethal horizontal arc, and she didn't even notice the spurt of dirt kicked up almost beneath her feet, or hear Finn shout her name as Aroko seemed to jump into the air, legs lifting in a quick kick behind as though he were swinging on a liana as she had often seen him do. Then he fell backwards and sprawled on the ground.

She noticed that there was a lot of blood, even before she reached his side and fell to her knees, with Finn behind her saying, *"Down, for God's sake!"*

Tula's men were keeping up a rapid fire now, and Jack said, "Tell me how to move him. We've got to get him to the hospital, Finn!"

Even as Finn leaned over the boy his body curved protectively about hers, shielding her. He touched the child briefly, then gripped her shoulders and said, "It's no use. He's dead."

Chapter Thirteen

Seconds, she thought. *Seconds!* That was all it had been.

"He can't be. He *can't* be!"

"Come," Finn said. "It's not safe here, Jacqueline. There's nothing we can do for him."

"But—"

"Come *on*."

She looked down and saw that Aroko wasn't Aroko anymore. But she couldn't just leave him there. "I'm taking him," she said, and picked up the body, heedless of the blood, of a renewed burst of fire from the outside that raised a line of dust spurts across the compound, and walked steadily, with Finn at her back all the way, to the hospital.

Aroko's mother had appeared from inside the building, where she had been putting her smaller children to bed, and her friends were holding her, making her turn her face away. Finn snatched up a blanket and wrapped the child in it and took him from Jack before gently laying him down in a corner. He spoke to the mother, and to her friends, and looked around for Jack.

"Are you all right?" he asked.

"Yes," she said, her voice perfectly steady. She turned away from him, going back down the steps and along the front of the verandah, on the narrow path between it and the trench.

"Where are you going?" Finn asked sharply.

And she said calmly, "I'm going to get a gun."

By the time he had followed her, she had picked one up, along with a clip of ammunition.

"Jacqueline!" he said.

"You see, I know how to use it," she explained. "I don't think it's just a toy, like Aroko. He didn't even know how to fire it."

"And who," he asked, "are you planning to use it on?"

"Those bastards out there, of course!"

"Have you ever killed anyone?"

"Not yet. But I'm going to now."

Finn said quietly, "No."

She turned on him with a bleak flame in her eyes. "Don't try and stop me, Finn!"

She realised that he was in her way, and made to leap across the trench. He hauled her back, upsetting her balance, and she found herself against the railing of the verandah. The gun, held tightly in her hands, the barrel pointed upwards, was between them, and he had her fast by the upper arms. "Are you prepared to shoot me first?" he asked her.

Her unnatural calm was shaken by a sudden, all-consuming anger. "Let me *go*, Finn!"

"Give me the gun, then."

"The *hell* I will!" She brought it across her body, holding it like a bar to push at him. "I'm not a spineless fence sitter like you!" she panted. Finn sidestepped, and grabbed at the gun, too, and as he twisted it so the barrel pointed earthwards, she felt her hands lose their grip. Finn tossed the gun into the trench, and Jack hit out at him with a fist.

"Calm down," he said, deflecting it with his arm. He snatched at her wrist, and then the other one, wrestling them down, shoving her back again.

"*You* be calm if you like!" she blazed. "You're inhuman! How can you be *neutral* when you've seen a child gunned down before your eyes!"

"What should I do?" he demanded furiously, giving her a hard shake. "Go out and kill more people, maim more people? That's what you want to do, isn't it? Why? It isn't going to do a damn thing for Aroko. Only for you. It'll make *you* feel better, temporarily. Because you'd rather get out there and kill someone than cope with a normal, healthy emotion like grief. Because while you've got a damned gun in your hand, you don't have to think, or feel, just be a finger on a trigger! Because you're an emotional coward, lady, and that's your whole trouble!"

"What the *hell* are you talking about?" Jack demanded, her voice rising.

"You!" Finn shouted at her, his rage easily matching hers. "You and your damned death wish! You're so sorry for yourself because your parents didn't love you the way you wanted them to, that you can't think of anything better to do than dice with adolescent fantasies of danger and hope that when you're dead everyone will be sorry! Well, go ahead, get yourself killed! I've got patients waiting for me, and I personally think that making sure *they* don't die is a hell of a lot more useful than shooting the guys who did it to them."

He abruptly let her go and stalked off inside, and Jack slumped against the rail, feeling as though she had just been hit by something large and lethal. She shivered, and gulped in some air, and braced her shoulders. Damn him, she thought, a deep rage building inside her. How dare he call her a coward, the self-righteous bastard? She should never have told him all that stuff about herself. If she hadn't been so tired she wouldn't have. And now he had turned it against her with a cruelty that took her breath away, used her confidences as a weapon.

Oblivious of the stares of the children and the few parents who had witnessed the row, she straightened her shoulders and stiffened her spine, and thought, *I'll show him. Nobody calls me a coward. Nobody!*

Two people were lurching across the compound, one supporting the other. She walked towards them, put her arm about the injured man, and helped to guide him inside. In the ward, she looked about until she found Finn's bent head where he was talking to one of the patients. "Doctor?" she said.

His eyes briefly met hers before they slid to the man at her side.

"Over here," he said. "There's a spare mattress in the corner."

He helped them lower the man, and dismissed his comrade with a nod.

"Scissors, water, disinfectant, bandage?" Jack queried crisply.

Finn looked up and this time his eyes held hers a fraction longer. She fancied there was a certain warmth in them, but her face stayed remote and cold, shut away.

"Yes," he said. "Thank you."

The helicopter had been captured by an advance party of the government forces, the pilot killed as he tried to take off. Jack heard Captain Tula giving Latu Savusuta the news.

Finn sought out the captain and urged surrender. "You're just going to lose more men and make the army more determined to take a harsh line when they finally overrun the village. You know it's only a matter of time. If they make an all-out assault on the village the women and children will be in real danger. One child is dead already. Let Latu Savusuta negotiate with them."

"They'll shoot him on sight," Captain Tula said.

Finn paused. "Do you really believe that?"

Tula was silent for a long time. At last he said, "I am really afraid of that."

"All right, then—I'll do it."

"You, Doctor?"

"I'll try to negotiate with them. Surrender on condition that they spare the village. Would you agree to that?"

"I would," Tula said heavily. "But they may shoot you, too."

"I'm willing to risk that. I just hope they hold their fire long enough to listen."

Finn wore a white coat, stained and rumpled, and hung a stethoscope about his neck. "Credentials," he explained, as Jack, tight-lipped and pale, lifted her brows.

They found a white cloth and tied it to a broomstick, and as soon as it was light, Finn picked it up and marched out of the hospital and down the steps, and steadily crossed the compound.

Captain Tula himself opened the gate, and saluted as Finn passed him, to stand outside, holding his flag of truce and waiting.

It was a few minutes before anything happened. Then a voice from the trees called, "Who are you, and what do you want?"

From the verandah, where she waited with a crowd of women, all of them seemingly holding their breath, Jack heard the answer clearly on the still morning air. "Finn Simonson. I'm a doctor and a United States citizen, working for the International Volunteers for Emergency Relief. I have a message."

Another short silence. Then, "Come forward."

Jack swallowed, suppressing a quick desire to shout, "Be careful!" A murmur of apprehension ran through the assembled women as he walked down the slope and into the trees. She waited, dreading the sound of a shot, a bullet that could snuff out Finn's life as quickly and horrifyingly as Aroko's.

Instead, the white flag reappeared, and Finn came back, flanked by two men in grubby uniforms, looking as exhausted and battle-worn as Tula's tattered troops.

They marched through the gate and stood in the centre of the compound, and Finn said to Tula and Latu Savusuta who stood facing them, "They've agreed. No burning of the village. No reprisals. But . . . the surrender of all weapons, and you two are to be taken back to Sulaka for trial on charges of treason, sedition, and armed rebellion against the people's government." He added, "I'm sorry."

Savusuta nodded sadly, and Tula stood stiff as a ramrod and said, "That was to be expected."

The officer on Finn's right said harshly, "Do you accept the terms?"

Without looking at Tula, Savusuta said, "We accept . . . if my people are spared any further hardship. They have suffered enough."

"I have given my word to the doctor."

Tula handed over his pistol, leaving the holster empty.

Savusuta said, "Last night a child was shot. That was not an action worthy of a soldier."

A woman sobbed, and Jack saw that it was Aroko's mother. Another woman put an arm about her heaving shoulders.

"I regret that," the officer was saying with apparent sincerity. "The light was bad, and one of my men acted perhaps too hastily. But the boy had a gun."

"That is true," the headman admitted. "But he was only ten years old. He was not firing the gun. He was too young to know how to do that."

The officer said, "The man will be disciplined. We don't make war on children."

Savusuta nodded. He was playing the only card he had, Jack realised. And he'd play it for all he was worth. The Tukaikian army and government didn't want to get a reputation for shooting children. That would help the rebel cause, both at home and abroad.

The officer looked up, and started when he saw her standing there. *Another witness, mate,* she told him silently. *Another foreigner, who might have friends in high places, here or at home. And you daren't shoot us out of*

hand and dispose of witnesses and evidence. Finn isn't stu-
pid. He's told you that several people with influence back in
Sulaka know where we are and will create a fuss if we don't
reappear there soon.

Finn was looking at her, too, fixedly, as though trying to
beam a message from his brain to hers, but she wouldn't
respond, wouldn't receive it. She wasn't going to let him into
her mind ever again, she had decided. Not ever.

But there was one moment when he nearly got through.
The rebels were disarmed and government troops brought
several of their wounded soldiers to the hospital.

Finn examined them and looked up at Jack standing rig-
idly by and said, "Bandages, please."

Her face frozen, she stayed where she was.

Finn said, "*Bandages,* Jacqueline . . . *Jack!*"

She shook her head, and his eyes narrowed and he got up
from beside the stretchers and came over to take her arm in
an iron grip. "Come here." He pulled her unwillingly towards them. "Look at them," he said. "*Look at them!*"
His fingers hurt her arm, and reluctantly she looked, her lips
set in an unforgiving line.

"All right," Finn was saying quietly in her ear. "Maybe
one of them saw someone with a gun running towards him
in the dusk, and fired before he realised it was only a kid.
Because he was frightened. They're hardly older than
Aroko!"

He was right. She saw the tears on the unlined, dirt-
streaked face of the nearest one, the frightened appeal in his
pain-filled eyes. Her shoulders slumped. "Yes," she said
tiredly. "Bandages."

Everything happened rather fast after that. The officer
proposed to transport Finn and Jack back to Sulaka in the
captured helicopter, with a refuelling stop on the way at an
army depot.

Finn said no thanks, not until he was sure all his patients
were being properly cared for.

"He'll take you," he told Jack, finding her on the verandah. "I've told him you're a hostage, that you weren't ever here by choice, and that I faked the story of our marriage, and why. You might still be in some hot water about our original flight being unauthorised, I suppose, but they've got bigger fish to fry. I'll give you a cheque for the money my organisation owes you. You can cash it in Sulaka."

"I don't want a cheque."

"I didn't bring that much in cash—"

She looked at him then, and he almost flinched at the expression in her eyes. "You hired me to fly you to Kitikiti," she said.

"You did your best, you're entitled—"

"No! I don't need your money, and I won't take it."

He seemed to hesitate, but she refused to meet his eyes again.

"If you take my advice," he said, "you'll get out of Sulaka and out of Tukaiki as soon as you can. There's nothing to hold you, now that you've lost your plane, is there?"

"No," Jack agreed coldly, "I don't suppose there is."

"Do you know where you'll go?"

"I've no idea."

He looked at her in a rather nonplussed way, then reverted to a crisp, impersonal manner. "Would you deliver a message for me? Telephone our headquarters in New York and let them know that I'm safe? Reverse the charges and use my name. After all," he added, with an experimental smile, "you've been using it for a while now."

"I'll do that," Jack answered, obligingly but with no particular inflection.

"You can get in touch with me through them, any time," he said, and scribbled on a bit of paper. "That's the phone number."

"When do you think you'll be getting out of here?" Jack asked him, folding the paper.

"I have no idea. It depends if the army people will arrange proper medical treatment for some of the serious cases. Even if they want to, I don't really have much hope of that."

"Well," she said, "if there's nothing else . . ."

They were standing in full view of half the village, but he said, "Yes, there is. There's this."

And he took her into his arms and kissed her rather hard and quite thoroughly.

It hadn't taken long. But when he drew away and his hands slipped over her shoulders and down her arms, and he picked up her hands and for a moment gripped hard before he released them, she felt as though he had tried to tell her something important, only she couldn't absorb it just then. In the last few days she had taken an emotional battering such as she had not experienced for years. She had the strangest conviction that if she allowed anything to penetrate the wall she had deliberately erected around her heart something would give way, and a structure that had taken her years to build up piece by piece would shatter forever. Somewhere inside her there was a mortal fear of what that would do to her.

She was touched when Mrs. Savusuta presented her with a beautiful woven basket as she left. Tiare, too, pressed on her the gift of a special pareu, surveying with veiled disapproval the shorts and threadbare shirt that Jack had donned for the journey, and Aroko's mother begged her to take a piece of carefully folded tapa cloth, "Because he loved you, and you were so kind to him."

That threatened to crack her composure, but she boarded the helicopter dry-eyed, along with a gaunt Captain Tula and dignified Latu Savusuta and their guards.

It was not a comfortable journey, and when they got to Panaki airport at Sulaka, there were officials waiting, and more army people, and although Jack tried to insist on knowing where the two men were being taken, and when they would be allowed visitors, she was whisked off to be questioned in a small, stuffy room by a large, sweating and unfriendly officer.

Yes, she said, she had been in the rebel stronghold, but not by choice.

Yes, her name was Jacqueline Victoria Renton, Australian by nationality, resident of Tukaiki, and yes, she had a passport and other documents to prove it, but they were in her house in Sulaka. For which the rent, she remembered, had not been paid since she left. So they might not still be there. The landlord might well have removed her things and relet the place.

No, she had not been aware that her passenger had no permission for his cargo and himself to leave Sulaka when she had flown out. He had passed through the checkpoint at the gate, after all, with a truck. It was hardly something you could sneak through unnoticed. She'd seen some sort of document herself, with a seal—very impressive, very official. No, she had not been aware of any effort to stop her takeoff. She had got clearance from the tower, but then there had been some static, she remembered. What army truck? She had been concentrating on the runway and her plane, as a good pilot must. Distractions caused accidents.

No, the accident to her plane had not been caused by any distraction. She thought it must have been due to contaminated fuel.... No, she wasn't accusing anyone of deliberately tampering with anything, only there had been the cyclone, and groundwater might have seeped into the fuel tanks.

Finn would be proud of her, she thought. She had been patient and polite, and given her answers with the utmost respect. Not raised her voice once.

Yes, she said, her plane was insured. Thank you for your concern. (Was that a little too ironic? Watch your mouth, Jack—it's got you in trouble before.) And yes, it was a total wreck. (Did they think she was going to sneak back into the interior and resurrect it, perhaps?)

Yes, she realised that she had been flying over rebel territory, but her passenger hadn't planned to land there; they had been downed by accident, so they had no choice in the matter. The plan had been for her to fly into Kitikiti, off-load her passenger and cargo, and fly out again. She had already told him that....

At last she was allowed to go, and she found some coins at the bottom of her knapsack and tried to phone her landlady.

There was no reply, and she humped up her knapsack and hailed one of the island's battered and much-travelled taxis to take her into town. By that time it was getting dark.

She had given the driver the address of her house, but as they hit the main street of Sulaka she changed her mind and said, "Take me to Rosie's Bar instead." She didn't feel like a possible confrontation with new tenants, and the hassle of finding out where her stuff was stored, or if it had been sold. Not that she had much, but there were some rather nice shells, and some carvings she wouldn't willingly have parted with, and there were papers that were important. Her passport, and the plane's ownership and insurance papers, for a start.

The streets were crowded and very noisy. More so than she remembered. But it was at least a less frightful noise than the near sound of gunfire.

The cab left the main street and travelled down a familiar side street, and stopped in front of the garish neon sign. Rosie's was a cheap, badly furnished and not terribly well-run place, but at least it didn't attract tourists and the prices were therefore not artificially inflated. And, as Abe had taught her when he had first taken her into a reluctant partnership and realised she was serious about eventually running her own one-woman airline, it was a good place to pick up business.

She stepped out of the cab, gave the driver some money and stopped, hit by a feeling almost of affection for the place.

She had forgotten about the dim lights, a feature that Rosie, who was not female, fair and flouncy as the name suggested, but male, paunchy and Polynesian, seemed to think denoted class, citing various superior establishments that he claimed to have visited in the major cities of the world; or perhaps that was just an excuse, and the real reason was an attempt to hide the general shabbiness of the place.

The awful shell lampshades revolved slowly in the wafting tobacco smoke, and she grinned up at them with new appreciation, and fought her way through to the bar and threw some money on the stained counter. "Get me a beer, Rosie," she yelled to the man standing behind it. "And a packet of cigarettes."

"Jack?" Rosie almost dropped the bottle he held in one huge hand, and a couple of the bar's regular drinkers nearby gawped at her with equal disbelief. "Jack Renton! Where did you spring from, eh? You sure you're not *atua*?"

"No ghost, Rosie. It's me. Beer?" she reminded him gently.

Rosie smiled then, a very wide, very white grin of joy. "Beer. It's you, all right, Jack. Well, I tell you what—this one's on the house. The cigarettes, too."

"Thanks," she said. "My poker partners in yet?"

"I think so," Rosie said. "Yeah, I remember seeing Abe, anyway, at the corner table. And I think I saw a redhead going by. They're sure gonna be surprised to see you. They been saying nice things about you for weeks now."

Jack laughed. "I'm not dead yet. Takes more than a little ole plane crash to put me six feet under, you bet!"

She took a sip of the beer, followed by a good swallow, and closed her eyes as though savouring the nectar of the gods.

"Good?" Rosie asked unnecessarily.

"You have no idea, Rosie, how good it is." She hoisted her bag up on the counter. "Do me a favour and take care of this for a while, will you?"

"Sure, Jack. Glad to."

She winked at him. "Thanks. I'll just go and say hello to Big Abe and Red."

Rosie shook his head, the wide grin still fixed on his face, and turned to serve another customer who was showing signs of impatience.

She didn't hurry, holding her beer with care as she nego-
tiated a forest of oblivious backs, and living the moment in
anticipation. Fat Little Louey wasn't here yet, but there was
Abe, scowling as he expertly shuffled a deck, a cigar between his teeth, and Red with his shoulders hunched inside
a plaid shirt that badly needed ironing. Not that she should
talk, Jack reminded herself, remembering her own much-
abused clothes. She stopped to tear off the cellophane
around the cigarettes and shake one out, one-handed,
shoving the rest into her pocket. Abe was absorbed in the
cards, straightening the pack, shifting the cigar from one
side of his mouth to the other before he began dealing.

Jack sauntered over to the table, plonked down her beer
as she took the cigarette from her lips, and pulled out a
chair; and as two heads lifted, with every sign of displeasure at the intrusion, she drawled, "I hope one of you guys
has a match. I forgot to buy some. Deal me in, will you,
Abe?"

The effect was everything she could have hoped for.
Probably for the first time in his life, Abe dropped a deck
in the middle of dealing, as well as his cigar, which rolled off
the edge of the table and disappeared soundlessly and irre-
trievably onto the floor. Jack regarded the performance with
well-hidden delight and turned her attention to Red, who
blenched. She had never actually seen anyone do that before, but she was sure that was what it was. He paled, and
jumped, and closed his eyes, and opened them again as if to
assure himself that she was still there.

She studied them coolly, leaning back in her chair, and
trying to appear mildly surprised at their reactions.

Then Abe growled from somewhere deep in his throat,
"Holy bleedin' hell, Jack! Where in tarnation have you
been?" And without waiting for an answer he jumped up
from his chair, never mind that it tumbled behind him, and
hauled her up to wrap his great arms about her in a bear hug
that threatened to crack all her ribs.

Red got up, too, and was thumping her back, the grin on
his mouth practically hanging itself from his ears, and when

Abe finally decided not to crush her quite to death, she had to hug Red, as well.

"You're supposed to be dead. We were sure you were dead!" Red babbled when they were all sitting down and relatively calm again.

"Yeah, so I gather," Jack said, leaning over to the match he held for her. She took a puff and was surprised to find her cigarette tasted horrible. Grimacing, she removed it from her mouth and looked at it sternly. "Damn."

"Thought the rebels'd got you," Abe rumbled, the scowl settling back on his face. "What'd you give us a fright like that for?" he asked reproachfully.

"Well, they did get me—us," Jack told them. "Or you could say they rescued us. It depends on which way you want to look at it, I guess."

She gave them an edited version of events, very laid back, very casual, and laced with much humour that had them roaring with laughter.

"I saw you get waylaid as we left," she told Red. "Did they hassle you much?"

"Nah," he said. "No sweat. Told them I was only asked to deliver the stuff, the other bloke handed me a bit of paper, and the guard seemed to think it was all right, so what were they getting heavy with me for? I'm just the dumb delivery boy, right?"

She heard the remembered note of aggrieved and slightly dim-witted innocence in his voice, and smiled. Maybe Red should have made a career on the stage or in films. It was what she had told Finn, that Red could talk his way out of any tight corner, but at the back of her mind there had always been a slight, niggling doubt. She was relieved to have it finally put to rest.

"I haven't been back to my place," she said. "Do you know if it's still got my stuff in it?"

They both looked down at the table. "Well...no," Abe said at last. "We kept an eye on it, saw the landlady about the rent, paid it for a while, but...well, there didn't seem much point, in the end. So we took it away, your stuff. It's all at my place. Didden know what to do with it. Didden seem right to sell it.''

"Thanks, Abe." Jack gave his arm a squeeze. "You're a real friend."

"Well, I did think your folks might like it, but . . ."

Jack cast him a quick look. "What folks? I told you, I don't have any family."

"Yeah, I know but..." Abe shot a glance at Red, and said hastily, "Well, I don't have to worry about it now, 'cause you're back, large as life and twice as—" He stopped and looked at her and blinked, as if seeing something he had never seen before. Perhaps something in her eyes gave him pause, and he finished, rather feebly, "Cheeky. You've grown your hair!" he added, rather as though he was making a statement against his better judgement but was quite unable to stop it coming out.

Jack shrugged, embarrassed. "Just never got round to cutting it," she said. "I'll do it tomorrow."

Red said unexpectedly, "Don't do that. I like it."

Jack scowled at him. "Tomorrow," she said firmly, "it comes off."

"You're a stubborn cow, Jack," Abe told her comfortably.

"I know. Where's Louey?"

"Louey got married," Red told her mournfully. "Met this real nice rich American lady, and he just up an' married her. They had a bang-up wedding, too. Living in Hawaii."

"Married?" Jack wondered what other world-shaking events might have happened in her absence. "Hawaii?"

Abe nodded. "You know Louey. An eye to the main chance. He ain't no oil painting, I'll grant you," he added judicially, "but still, neither is his bride. It sure was a good do, that reception," he added wistfully.

Jack blinked. At a guess the wine, and possibly other beverages, had flowed freely, to create this apparent sensation of awe in her companions. She said, "I take it you were both invited?"

"You betcha!" they chorused.

"Pity you weren't there," Abe told her sorrowfully. "Darn shame. We said so at the time. Thought ole Louey might have had a two-minute silence or something," he added with vague disapproval.

Jack choked on her beer and put it down on the table with a thud. "At a *wedding*?"

"Well," Red explained, "friends, and all that. Show a bit of respect."

Jack grinned. "Since when did you guys show any respect for me?"

Doggedly, Red said, "I do respect you, Jack, as a friend and as a woman. But especially," he added firmly, "as a friend. I said so when you were...away. Didn't I, Abe?" He appealed to the big man for confirmation.

"He certainly did," Abe said. "And we toasted you. We toasted you royally! Rosie even gave us a discount on the beer."

She looked from one to the other of them, and decided they weren't pulling her leg. A gleeful smile curving her mouth, she said, "You had a *wake* for me, didn't you?"

Abe gazed about him, as though for inspiration, and Red almost buried his nose in his beer, mumbling something totally indistinguishable.

Jack began to laugh. "You did!" she said. "Oh, I bet it was a great night. I wish I'd been there!"

"If you'd been there, we wouldn't have had it, you silly cow!" Abe grumbled, and she shrieked, helpless with laughter. After a minute or so Abe started to grin, and a rumble that started somewhere in his ample stomach turned into a chuckle, and then a roar, and Red was whinnying and choking and thumping the table, while all about them people turned and smiled in sympathy, and for a little while Jack thought that maybe everything would be all right, after all.

Chapter Fourteen

After Rosie's closed, Jack spent the remainder of the night on a sofa in Abe's cluttered and untidy sitting room, which doubled as his office. She slept late, and woke to find Abe blundering about the room on tiptoe, breathing heavily and swearing under his breath as he lifted piles of books and riffled through stacks of papers, and opened a filing cabinet drawer that gave a long, subdued squeak.

Abe winced, glancing at Jack's still form.

"What on earth are you doing, Abe?" she demanded sleepily.

"Sorry, Jack, didden wanta wake you," he apologised. "Got a job to do at eleven, and I can't find the damn form I filled in for the airport wallahs."

"What form?"

"Aw, they got this new system," he said disgustedly. "More red tape. Every time you go up, you have to produce this authorisation form before they even let you in the airport gate. Martial law, and all that. First you go to the government office in town, then you fill in the form, they send it upstairs for approval and some jumped-up civil servant signs it, then when you go out to the airport you hand it over at the gate and it gets stamped and handed back, and when you're ready for takeoff someone else comes and takes it from you and stamps it again, and when you come back they drag it out and log the time and stamp it *again*. Then I s'pose they file it. Anyway, I can't find the damn thing.''

Jack wriggled upright, absently smoothed her hair, and swung her legs off the sofa. "What's it look like?"

"It's just a white bit of paper," Abe said despairingly. There were white bits of paper everywhere, it seemed. "Headed, you know—whaddya call it?"

"Letterhead paper?"

"Yeah. Y'know—Republic of Tukaiki, Aviation Department."

"Okay." Jack joined in the search, lifting cushions, sifting along shelves, moving a small heap of yellowing newspapers. "What on earth do you keep these for, Abe? Hey, is this it?"

"How on earth did it get there?" Recovering from his amazement, he seized on the printed sheet she had found under the newspapers, and planted a kiss on her cheek. "Thanks, Jack. You're a true friend! Sometimes I wish we'd stayed partners."

She laughed at him. "We're both too independent. You need a secretary."

"I know. How about applying for the job?"

She made a face. "Oh, sure! Can you see me?"

"No." He grinned happily.

"I'll tidy this lot for you, though," she offered. "In return for the bed, etcetera." She picked up the newspapers again. "Starting with these—you want them for some reason?"

A strange expression flitted across his face. "I guess—no, not really," he muttered. "Here, I'll get rid of them."

"No, it's okay, I will. But are you sure ... ?"

Because of his hesitation, she glanced down at the top one, and saw a heading halfway down, just above where it folded. *Doctor and Pilot Presumed Dead.*

"Oh," she said. "I see. Well, I'm not dead."

"Yeah," he said. "I was gonna cut them out. But no point, now, is there? We'll just chuck 'em, eh?" He put out a hand as if to take them.

"No!" Jack said. "Is there more?" She lifted the top paper so that she could see the others. Some of them were Sydney papers. The Tukaikian papers printed almost exclusively local news, heavily biased in the government's favour, and Australian papers—often a week old—were sold freely in the capital. One had her photo on the front. "I might like to put them in a scrapbook," she said, grinning at him.

"Aw, you don't wanna read that stuff, Jack! It's—whatchacall—morbid!"

"Where did they get the photo?" she wondered, peering at it. "Hey, it's from that one of you and me together, isn't it? They've cut you out of it, Abe!"

"Yeah, well, it wasn't me they were interested in." He shrugged.

"You gave it to them?"

"Not them!" he protested. "Only there was this reporter, and...well, I figured there was no harm...." He frowned as though trying to remember what had prompted his capitulation to the reporter's persuasion.

"Did the reporter interview you?" she asked interestedly.

"Yeah, but...I didden say much," he assured her. "Dunno much, do I? Sorry, Jack, if I shoulden have, maybe. Only we all thought..."

"I know, Abe. It's okay. You'll be late," she added, looking at the clock sharing a shelf with a pile of old letters, a sprawl of ballpoint pens and for some strange reason a much-dented saucepan.

"Sure you'll be all right?"

"Abe, I've been downed in the jungle, and captured by rebels, and caught in the middle of a civil war. I think I can manage to survive being left alone in your apartment, even if it does bear a distinct resemblance to a bomb site. Go on!" She raised one hand and gave him a push.

Not that it had any real effect, of course; it was like pushing a bulldozer. But he gave her a doubtful smile, stuffed the government form into his breast pocket, and said amiably, "Okay, okay. I'm off."

When he had gone, Jack threw the papers on the sofa and set about making herself a cup of coffee. She would forgo a cigarette, she had decided. Last night's had made her feel queasy, and she seemed to have lost the urge to smoke. Finn would approve, of course. . . .

Finn. The name rang in her head with an echo that set her whole body tingling. She wouldn't think about Finn. Maybe she wouldn't even read those papers. She'd throw them out, as Abe suggested.

But curiosity was too strong. She sat on the sofa with the coffee and picked up the papers, choosing first the one with the earliest date. *Plane Goes Missing,* said the headline.

Fifteen minutes later she had finished the coffee, and the papers lay discarded on the floor. "That'll teach you," she muttered to herself, and reached for her bag, rummaging for the pack of cigarettes she had bought the night before. Then she had to search the place for matches, which she finally found in a drawer of the poky kitchen, along with scissors and a ball of string, some loose stamps and a variety of screws, nails, clamps and unidentifiable small metal objects.

She lit the cigarette and dropped the matches back in the drawer. She hesitated as she made to close it, then took out the scissors and pushed the drawer firmly shut.

Marching back to the sofa, she picked up the newspapers again. The cigarette tasted foul, but she persevered with it as the scissors flashed through paper, cutting around columns and borders.

By the time the cigarette was half-smoked, she felt sick. The cuttings lay on the sofa, and she gathered them up decisively and folded them together, stowing them flat at the bottom of her knapsack. She stubbed out the remains of the cigarette among others in an ashtray on Abe's desk, and looked about. She emptied the ashtray into a bin, which was already almost overflowing, under the desk. She found a paper garbage sack in the kitchen, and upended the contents of the bin into it, then returned to the other room and began a rapid tidying and cleaning operation. Gradually her stomach settled down.

When Abe returned some hours later, he surveyed the regimented rows of books and papers on his shelves, the desk with its clean ashtray set on a surface clear except for two stacks of forms and letters with edges all aligned, the battered chair set dead square behind the desk. The floor was clean, and uncluttered except for the stack of cartons holding Jack's belongings from her house. The shabby sofa pillows had been plumped, and Jack had stowed her bag behind the sofa out of sight.

"That you, Abe?" she called from the kitchen.

"Better be," he answered, going to loll in the doorway. Jack had tied her hair back with a piece of string, and was on her knees before a cupboard. Here, too, a transformation had taken place. He looked about him and whistled. "Sure you don't want a job?"

"Uh-uh! I haven't touched your bedroom," she said. "You can do that yourself, you slob!" She stowed a last pot in the cupboard, and said, "I've sprayed this. You have cockroaches."

He grinned. "Everybody in Sulaka has cockroaches, Jack! You know that."

"Not like you do." She pushed back a strand of hair that had fallen over her face, and put a hand to her back.

"You okay, Jack?" he asked, searching her face.

"I'm fine," she answered cheerfully, "except for a crick in my back."

"What'd you do with those newspapers?"

"Threw them out."

Relief flickered in his eyes. "You read them first?" he asked.

"Some. Bit of a laugh, weren't they?"

Giving her a feeble grin, he said, "Yeah. I guess. Had any lunch?"

"I opened a tin of bacon and beans."

"Good. That's all right, then. Tell you what, we'll go and have dinner at one of them fancy tourist places tonight. How about it?"

"Thanks, Abe. Sounds great. But I'll have to go out for a while soon. I need to fix up about the insurance on my plane, and find somewhere to live."

"You can stay here, long as you like," Abe offered.

"I know." She gave him an affectionate pat in passing. "Thanks, but I need my own place."

"Sure." Abe understood that. He was a loner himself.

The insurance people were inclined to make difficulties, but in the end conceded reluctantly that it "appeared" there had been an accident and that "if" the plane was actually a total and irrecoverable wreck, she was entitled to full compensation.

"What do you mean, 'if'?" Jack snapped. "You can send your assessor in there to inspect it, if you like. I expect I can give him reasonably precise directions!"

"That is the usual procedure," the clerk said austerely, and in the end reluctantly gave her a form to fill in, which had so many questions on it that it took her the best part of an hour to complete it.

Then she went to the army headquarters building in the main street and tried to find out what had happened to Latu Savusuta and Captain Tula.

Here she was regarded with even more suspicion, and after undergoing what she could only regard as an interrogation, was told that they were being held in an army detention centre outside the town.

"May I visit them there?" she asked.

"Why would you want to visit your former captors?" the uniformed man behind the desk asked suspiciously.

Jack swiftly considered her answer. *None of your business!* would hardly suffice.

"We were not badly treated," she said. "And Latu Savusuta and his wife were kind to us. I'm concerned for his welfare. He's not a young man."

"I see. And what is your concern for this rebel, the man Tula?"

"He . . . well, after all, it was Captain—I mean, Mr. Tula who . . . who rescued my passenger and myself after my plane was wrecked. We might have died out there, of . . . starvation or exposure, if we hadn't been found by *someone*. My passenger was injured, you know, and I was ill after eating poison fish. And my friends were prevented from searching by the application of martial law." They had tried, Abe said, but the new regulations had hampered their efforts, and although the government, prodded by Finn's relief organisation, said they had mounted a search, obviously it had not been a very thorough one. "I owe Captain Tula my life," she said, exaggerating. "So even if he is a rebel, I don't feel I can turn my back on him."

"What are your feelings about the uprising against our democratic free republic, Miss Renton?"

Republic maybe, she thought. Lately it's been getting progressively less democratic, and certainly less free. She said, "I'm a commercial pilot, Major—" she glanced at the nameplate on his desk "—Limisi. I'm not interested in politics. All I do is fly my plane."

"You have no rebel sympathies?"

"I'm an Australian, not a Tukaikian. I told you, politics don't interest me."

He flipped open a folder on his desk, and read out a date.

"Last year," she said. "Yes?"

"You flew a cargo to Kitikiti for a man named Kano."

Jack thought back. "Probably. The name sounds vaguely familiar."

"A cargo of arms, destined for the rebels."

Jack said, "I'm not a gunrunner."

"By your own admission, you are a mercenary. A pilot for hire to anyone who will pay you—including gunrunners. Our information is reliable."

"Tractor parts," Jack said slowly. "I remember. The crates were exceptionally heavy. He said they were tractor parts." And it was in the very early stages of the war, when she wouldn't have thought of questioning that.

The major gave a small, disbelieving smile. "You didn't check?"

"Of course not! I'm not in the habit of opening my clients' cargo."

"Perhaps you should," the man said. "This file was closed, because at the time the information came to hand you were missing, presumed dead, Miss Renton. Now, of course, there is the possibility that it could be reopened."

He looked at her penetratingly, and she said, "In other words, watch my step."

"That would be wise."

"Thank you for the warning," she said, although she suspected it was more of a threat. *Keep your nose clean, or else....* "And I would still like to see Latu Savusuta and . . . Tula."

He shrugged as though, having done all he could to save her from herself, he washed his hands of her. "Ask at the detention centre," he advised her. "The officer in charge may give you permission."

She wondered, but thanked him politely and left. By that time it was too late to do anything more that day, and she went back to Abe's apartment.

Next day she borrowed Abe's ancient motorcar, a rattling box on wheels that had been modified so much to his idiosyncratic needs that it was no longer of any recognisable make.

The commandant of the detention centre was equally as suspicious as his colleague, at first refusing even to see her.

She used Major Limisi's name as a lever, and was eventually ushered into the commandant's office.

After going over the same ground once more, she was told that the prisoners were not allowed any visitors.

"Not even family?" she asked, although she didn't know if either man had any family in Sulaka. "What about lawyers?" she persisted. "They're entitled to have their legal representatives visit them." She was sure of that, having read it somewhere. One of those useless bits of information that stick in one's mind.

The man's eyes flickered, and she blessed the authority with which she had trotted out her bit of recondite knowledge.

"The country is now under martial law," he said evasively.

Not allowing a tremor of doubt to enter her voice, she said, "Martial law doesn't alter basic human rights." She remembered now; she had read an article in the local paper about how the Tukaikian government had only recently ratified the United Nations Declaration on Human Rights, adopting it into the constitution. Less than a couple of years ago. They had been very proud of that, she recalled, and it was there that she had seen the provision about legal representation mentioned.

"The Tukaikian constitution," she said confidently, "specifically protects a prisoner's right to legal advisers of his own choice. Have Latu Savusuta and Cap—and Tula been given that opportunity?"

In the end she was allowed five minutes with each of them. Latu Savusuta looked tall and dignified and a shade thinner, but said he had no complaints about his treatment. She thought that the humiliation of imprisonment itself, and the toll that last battle had taken on his people, were probably responsible for the shadows haunting his eyes. He was most anxious to let his wife know he was well, and Jack promised to do her best to get a message through somehow.

Tula looked fit, although he had a bruise on his cheek that he shrugged off when she enquired about it.

"Sometimes the guards are a little rough," he said, "but there is no organised brutality." He thanked her formally for her concern, but had no messages.

"I'm trying to persuade them to let you see a lawyer," she said. "Do you know anyone?"

Latu Savusuta didn't, but Tula named one instantly, and she nodded and said, "I'll contact him."

"Her," he said, and gave her the address. "Thank you, Mrs. Simonson."

There was a guard standing in the corner of the room, less than six feet away. She thought that Tula probably knew how to get a message to the village, but she couldn't ask. She took her leave without touching him, as she had been instructed.

The lawyer was a tall, stately young woman who listened gravely and said, "Thank you for contacting me, Miss Renton. I will go and see these men."

"You may have trouble," Jack warned. "The commandant is a bit obstructive."

The woman smiled serenely. "I'm used to that, Miss Renton. I'll see them."

She would, too, Jack thought. This was not a lady to mess with. She said, "I would like to get a message to Latu Savusuta's wife."

Perhaps she imagined the slight hesitation before the lawyer said regretfully, "I'm afraid I cannot help you there. But the other matter you may leave in my hands."

The army was still fighting rebel units in the area south of Kitikiti. According to the papers the government was on top of the situation, and all that remained was a mopping-up operation. But Jack regarded the reports with some scepticism. It seemed to her that the rebels were part of a popular movement. There was no recognized leader, and no central command, which might lead to disorganisation, but which also made it difficult for the government to win decisively. As soon as one area, like Latu Savusuta's, was subdued, another erupted to take its place.

One night in Rosie's Bar as she turned from the counter with a glass of beer, someone jogged her elbow, and the stuff splashed down her arm and onto her khaki shirt. The man said, "Sorry!" and grabbed a paper napkin from the bar and wiped her arm, muttering apologetically all the while. He discarded the sodden paper in an ashtray on the bar and took another, pressing it into her hand with more apologies.

She looked into his earnest dark eyes and said, "It's okay. Don't worry about it, it'll wash."

She fought her way to the ladies' room and locked herself into a cubicle. The note, folded small and hard-cornered, was concealed in the crushed napkin.

A name and address, that was all. The man who spilled her drink had muttered between his embarrassed apologies only, "Hold this carefully, don't lose it." His eyes had said the rest. The lady lawyer was cautious, Jack thought. Well, no doubt she needed to be.

Jack dabbed some water on the wet stain on her shirt, and went back to the table. "Whose deal?" she asked Red and Abe. It was hers, so she took the deck from their new fourth, a journalist who had been sent by one of the Australian papers to cover the war. He had wanted to interview her about what he called her "return from the dead," and about life in a rebel village, but Jack had refused. "There's already been an article on that, anyway," she said, citing the woman journalist who had written up her own experience of being kidnapped by the rebels. In the end he gave up trying to persuade her to change her mind, but stayed to play poker. The subject of the interview was closed, and he had accepted that.

That night Jack left the bar earlier than usual, saying, "I like to smell beer in my glass, not on my shirt. I need a bath."

Chapter Fifteen

It was two months before Finn arrived back in Sulaka. He had held out as long as he could against army pressure to remove himself from the war zone, but his credentials, as they well knew, were impeccable, and his organisation had influential contacts. As for his safety, which they cited as a reason for their anxiety for him to return to Sulaka, he had told them, "I'm willing to sign all the waivers you like absolving the army and the Tukaikian government from any responsibility for my actions."

At last it was possible to hold out no longer. His patients were going on as well as he could hope for, and there was nothing more he could do on his own. He asked to be taken to Kitikiti, his original destination, but was told that international aid and the government's own efforts had relieved the situation there. He was glad to hear from his own people, when he contacted them after the army had returned him to Sulaka, that this was substantially true. The government had not acted quickly, but with some pressure from both inside and outside Tukaiki, the wheels of officialdom had at last turned.

He took a room in the same hotel as before, and phoned New York.

"Yeah, the Tukaikian government informed us you'd been found," he was told. "Are you coming home?"

"A couple of things I'd like to clear up here, first," he said. "I may take some time off."

"Sure. Things are fairly quiet just now. Got an address where we can contact you?"

He gave it, and asked them to pass on a couple of messages, and said, "You haven't heard from the pilot of my plane, have you?"

"There was something, but I didn't take the call. Just a message on my pad. A guy called Jack?"

"Yes," Finn said drily. "That's the one."

"Well, as I said, it was just a message to say you were okay. Came just after the official call. It was nice to have it confirmed."

"Any address?" Finn asked. "Or telephone number? Where was the call placed from?"

"No, no, and no idea," his colleague replied unhelpfully. "Is it important?"

"No," Finn said shortly. "It's okay."

With some trouble he found the house where Jack had taken him that first night. It was occupied by an elderly couple who didn't have any idea where she had gone, but gave him the landlady's number. She was no help, either. He didn't have the name of the bar where he had met her, he realised. His memory wouldn't dredge it up for him. Nor the name of the street. Still, he knew the general direction, and Sulaka wasn't that big a place.

By the time he registered that there was something familiar about the flashing neon rose outside a building that bore a close resemblance to a couple of others he had already entered with a disappointing shock of nonrecognition, he was becoming not so much despondent as frustrated. The shell lampshades had a definitely familiar impact, quite apart from the natural impact of their sheer awfulness. His spirits lifting, he skirted the bar and sought out the table that he gathered had been her usual one.

He saw the big man, Abe, and the redheaded one whom he knew, and his eyes quickly leaped to the chair opposite Abe. A dark head, but it fooled him only for a moment. The fourth man at the table was a stranger, too, not the rotund individual who had called Jack a "loony bitch" with laconic tolerance.

Abe placed his cards on the table with a satisfied air. A heap of money changed hands, and the big man removed his cigar from his mouth, picked up his glass and pushed his chair back, meeting Finn's eyes as he rose.

A frown of puzzled recognition creased his brow, and Finn offered his hand and said, "I'm Finn Simonson. We've met before."

"Right!" the man said, the frown clearing as he wrung the proffered hand. "Jack's passenger!"

"I thought you might know," Finn said, "where she is. Did she leave the island?"

"No, mate. At least, only long enough to get herself a new plane."

"She's got a new plane?"

"A little beaut. Almost enough to make me go back to flying a fixed-wing crate myself."

"Well, good," said Finn, not sure if it was. And the dark-haired man at the table, who had been regarding them both with interest, suddenly stood up and said, "Dr. Simonson, my name's Dave Clayton. I'd really like to talk to you."

"What about?"

"You and Jack. The crash, the rebel village, the clash with government forces."

"You know Jack?"

"I play poker with her." The man smiled. "She's quite a girl."

"Woman," Finn said. "She doesn't like being called a girl."

"Woman," Dave Clayton amended agreeably. "Can I buy you a drink? Here, take my chair. I'll grab another one."

Finn let him. Abe had gone off to get his glass refilled, and Red regarded Finn with shrewd eyes and said, "Jack didn't want to talk to him. Not for the papers."

"Clayton? He's a reporter, is he?"

Red nodded. "He's an okay poker player, though," he conceded. "Jack said, long as he didn't try and print anything about her, he could play."

Finn nodded. "I won't talk to him about her."

Red relaxed. "She said you're an okay guy," he confided.

Ridiculously pleased, Finn said, "Thanks. Do you know where I can contact her?"

"Give you her new address if you like. Want to write it down? 'Course, she's not there now. Got a job on with her new plane. Up-country somewhere, I reckon."

"In the war zone?" Finn asked, his skin going cold.

"Didn't say. Plays her cards close these days, Jack does. Some things it's better not to talk about, you know."

"What things?" Finn asked, but the other two men came back and Dave Clayton began to ply Finn with questions.

He answered some, parried others and bluntly refused to talk about Jack except in general terms as "the pilot." When he made to leave, saying, "I interrupted your game," even Clayton didn't try to detain him. IVER wouldn't mind the publicity, sometimes the right kind was useful, but he hadn't given Clayton much, and the reporter must have decided that there was no more to be wrung from him tonight.

But, kicking his heels in an outer office while he waited for an audience with a government official the following day, Finn saw Dave Clayton again. The newspaperman passed the door, did a double take and came over to him. "Hi," he said. "What brings you here?"

"What about you?" Finn asked, without answering. "Sniffing out a story?"

Dave laughed. "Not really. Just prowling on the off chance. Not much happening these days, unless our friend Jack . . ." His voice trailed off as though he were nervous of being overheard.

"What?" Finn asked sharply.

Dave glanced about him, then dropped down on the leather-covered bench beside Finn. Very quietly, he said, "She's not too popular around this place, I can tell you. She's strongly suspected of consorting with the rebels, I gather. Not to mention gunrunning."

The ugly word leapt in Finn's brain. "She wouldn't . . ." he said involuntarily.

"Why not?" Dave asked. "You know Jack. I heard that before I ever met her. You're a friend of hers, aren't you? So I can tell you, I happen to know it's true."

"How?" Finn asked coldly.

"I can't divulge my sources, but believe me, they're impeccable. I was going to do a story on her, you know. My paper isn't one of your sensationalist rags that'll accept any dirt their people dig up. I have to produce hard evidence. And it's there, solid as a rock."

"You're not going to do the story now?"

"Wouldn't be the same without some cooperation from her," Dave said regretfully. "And besides . . . she's still here on the spot, and I don't want to make things sticky for her, not if it could mean jail . . . or worse. My paper isn't that sort, either. Stodgy, some people call us. She'd make a great story, though. Even before I met her, I thought so. They told me, 'Mad Jack would fly anything anywhere.'"

"That's what they told me," Finn said, remembering.

A door opened, and a young woman in a dark skirt and white blouse, with a hibiscus nestled unexpectedly in her glossy hair, said, "Dr. Simonson? You may come in now."

He took a taxi and went to the address that Red had given him. He found a white stucco house, Spanish-style, near the beach, not particularly large, but with a new, low-slung sports car parked in a carport with an arched doorway, and a glimpse of a swimming pool visible through a black-grilled gate. He remembered the shabby little house she had taken him to the night they met, and felt sick.

The driver turned and said, "This it?"

"Yes," Finn said, with a hollow feeling in the pit of his stomach. "Take me back to town."

Jack had heard that Finn was in town. After she returned from her latest job, and turned up at Rosie's, Red confessed to giving him her address, having had anxious second thoughts in case for some reason she objected.

"It's okay," she said carelessly. "I don't mind." And put down the wrong card, so that Red crowed and Abe looked at her with heavy suspicion.

She expected to hear from him, daily rehearsing what she would say, how to say it.

When the days passed and he didn't contact her, she began to get a curiously blank feeling of surprise. He must know she was in town. Word got around, and the last few days all she had done was a couple of short hops, a few hours' flying.

She phoned the hotel where he had stayed before. Yes, Dr. Simonson was still registered.

"Tell him . . ." she said, and paused to frame a suitable, noncommittal message, "Jack Renton phoned. I heard he was trying to contact me." She recited her phone number and rang off.

She waited for the phone to ring all that evening, but it was totally silent. After a few days she had to acknowledge to herself that Finn didn't want to have any more to do with her.

Dave mentioned him one night. "Seen your doctor friend lately?"

Jack shook her head, keeping her eyes on the cards in her hand. She slid one out and replaced it with another. "Not since he got back."

Red looked up. "I thought he wanted to get hold of you."

"Apparently not. I left a message at his hotel. He never got back to me."

"Funny," Red mused.

"Maybe he just needed a pilot, and found someone else. I wasn't available when he was asking," she reminded him.

"Still, after what you two went through . . ."

"He's probably left town. Are you playing, Red?"

"He's in town," Dave said, frowning at his cards. "Saw him yesterday. He was at the government offices, meeting the Minister of the Interior."

Jack looked up in astonishment. "Whatever for?"

Dave said, "Well, it's no secret. He's trying to help negotiate a peace deal with the rebels."

"*Finn* is?"

"The whisper is, he's just about got them to agree to meet with representatives of the rebel groups, under the auspices of the UN."

"He said his organisation is nonpolitical!"

"Well, I guess he's messing with politics, all right, but I didn't hear that IVER had anything to do with it. Not officially. I think this is his own personal peace initiative. Be interesting to see if it works."

She had agreed to take a journalist on a flight along the coast, with a small, illegal detour inland. He was working with a world-renowned journal of political and social comment, and was one symptom of the growing interest the rest of the world was showing in Tukaiki. She enjoyed flying him, finding his astute comments on the situation added to her own understanding, and when he asked if she would mind if he printed some of her remarks, especially insights gained during her captivity, she agreed on condition that he didn't use her name.

"No problem," he answered promptly. And when they arrived back at the airfield and she had taxied the plane to a halt, said, "How about you have dinner with me this evening, and we continue to talk? The Sulaka Sunshine Inn has a great restaurant."

"I'm told it's very good," she said. "But if I'm going to eat there, I'll have to dash out and buy something suitable."

He raised his brows. "It's not that high-class."

"No," Jack laughed. "Only they won't allow trousers. And pareus are the only other thing I have."

"Wouldn't you like an excuse to buy a new dress?"

Jack shrugged. It was years since she had bought a dress.

The one she found was a perfectly straight tube hung on very narrow straps, that she bought because it was cool and comfortable, not noticing how it skimmed her figure while subtly defining it. It was white silk with a brown batik pattern like fine cobwebs and flowers, and she realised that she would have to buy shoes to go with it. She settled for a pair of white sandals, although the heels were higher than she would have liked and she'd have to walk slowly for fear of tripping, but time was short and she still had to get home and showered and changed. Passing a makeup counter with mirrored pillars on her way out of the department store where she had bought the shoes, she noticed a grease mark on her cheek, and paused to wipe it off with her fingers.

"Try this," said a smiling salesgirl, dabbing a bit of lotion on a tissue and handing it to her. "You won't get rid of grease like that."

She had made a dirty smudge instead of a black streak, it was true, so she accepted the tissue, and when she handed it back, the girl said, "Were you wanting makeup?"

"No," Jack said. Then, "Well, perhaps a lipstick."

It was buying a dress that had done it, she decided afterwards. It had gone to her head or something. Resurrected a lot of buried female conditioning. Still, when she had applied the scarcely visible lipstick and the cloud-soft eye shadow and the mascara that mysteriously lengthened her already dark lashes, she recognised that there was a perceptible difference in her. And that she didn't dislike it.

Neither did her escort. He greeted her with quiet appreciation, and when they were seated at their table he said with only the faintest hint of surprise, "You look lovely."

It would be boorish to reject that. She said, "Thank you," and opened the menu the waiter handed to her.

They were eating early, because he planned to relax in the lounge afterwards and talk over coffee, he said. When they had finished the meal he held her elbow lightly as they left the restaurant and crossed the tiled foyer, passing a huge bowl of tropical flowers that occupied a plinth in the centre.

He said, "Just a minute," and his hold momentarily tightened. He quickly plucked one perfect white bloom from a stem of fragrant frangipani, and tucked it behind her ear so that the waxy petals kissed her cheek. "Finishing touch," he said, smiling down at her. "You don't mind, do you?"

She scarcely heard, because she was staring past his shoulder at the two people who had just come in the wide glass doors. Captain Tula's lawyer, regal in a garment resembling a very upmarket, ankle-length pareu falling in shimmering folds of finely beaded black satin to her black high-heeled sandals. And Finn.

Finn, returning Jack's sudden stare with a cold, oddly furious stare of his own.

He turned away, looking towards the door of the restaurant, and she knew with a shock that he would have cut her dead if his companion had not recognised her and, smiling, tucked a hand in his arm and brought him over.

"Miss Renton!" A slim hand, scarlet-tipped, was held out to her. "How nice to see you. You know Finn, of course."

Jack cast Finn a glance that she knew was full of astonished questioning, but he nodded briefly, his eyes looking at something over her head, and turned to the man at her side, so that she had to introduce them.

"Are you dining here, too?" Finn's companion asked.

"We have," Jack said briefly, hoping that would end it, but her escort broke in with an invitation for the other couple to join him and Jack later. "We'll be there for couple of hours at least, I hope," he said, smiling down at Jack.

She smiled back and nodded, trying to seem enthusiastic, and then they were walking across the foyer again, to a welcome cup of coffee.

Bewildered, she tried to put the incident out of her mind and concentrate on the discussion with her companion. In the end, she said she was more tired than she had realised, with a headache coming on, and would he please make her excuses to the doctor and his friend, but she would like to get a taxi and go home.

She didn't think she could stand sitting across from Finn and making small talk, while he sat beside the regal, exquisitely gowned lawyer, who was by any standards a fine figure of a woman, and looked at Jack with that inexplicable, cold, angry stare.

She sat rigid in the taxi all the way home and when she got to the house she turned her ankle on the step, and found her hands were shaking so much she could hardly get the key into the lock.

"Pull yourself together, you fool," she muttered fiercely to herself, and went into the bedroom to haul off the silk dress and hurl it into a corner of the room, kicking the shoes after it. She grabbed a bathing wrap and a towel and went out to the kidney-shaped pool, muttered, "More ornament than use," and changed her mind, returning to the bedroom for a long shirt, which she pulled on in place of the wrap, then flung the towel over her shoulder and started for the beach.

It was a short walk, and when she got there no one was about. The islanders, in spite of their frankness about sex, were modest and didn't care for the more crass tourists' exposure of the human body, so she checked carefully before discarding the shirt near the water's edge and running into the surf.

She swam strongly and fast for quite a long way, and then back to the shore, panting as she picked up the shirt and dropped it over her wet body before rubbing the towel over her head, face and legs. She felt better, more like herself. Damn Finn Simonson. Damn all men. With the possible exception of Big Abe. And maybe Red. She didn't need Finn, she didn't need anybody. Whatever was bugging him, let him sort it out. He wasn't her problem.

On that thought, and ignoring the leaden, lost feeling that centred somewhere about her midriff, she walked briskly home, rinsed her sandy feet under the shower, removed the damp shirt and fell into bed.

And dreamed of her mother, saying, *Why couldn't it have been you?* with hatred in her eyes. When she woke the pillow under her cheek was damp.

The next day, as she did once a week, she went to the detention centre outside of town. The officers and guards knew her now, and she was surprised and angry to be told she would be unable to see the prisoners.

"What's happened?" she asked. "Why can't they have visitors?"

"I didn't say they can't have visitors," the officer on the desk replied. "They have had a visitor already. Only one visit per day."

"Both of them?" she asked. As far as she knew, the only other visitor who came, except for one of Latu Savusuta's cousins on Sundays, was the lawyer.

"A meeting with their legal representative doesn't count as a visit," she said firmly, having no idea what the United Nations or the Tukaikian constitution had to say about it.

The man shook his head. "They have had a visitor. In fact, he is still with the prisoner Tula."

"He?" Jack repeated blankly.

Then the inner door swung wide open and the man stood up. "Have you finished, Dr. Simonson? This way." He motioned Jack out, too, and she found herself standing outside the firmly closed door with Finn.

"What are you doing here?" she asked.

"Visiting Tula and Latu Savusuta."

"Well, I wish I'd known. I've just made the trip for nothing."

"What do you mean for nothing?"

She repeated the officer's words. "Only one visit per day. That's the rule."

"I'm sorry," he said. "I didn't expect you to be here, either."

"I come every week."

"Really?"

"They know that," she said crossly. "They might have stretched a point. Anyway, why are you so surprised?"

They were walking down the path when he said, "Because it doesn't seem to fit. Or do you have an ulterior motive? Arrangements to make, perhaps?"

She detected a sneer in his tone, and pushing aside a stab of hurt, said, "What are you talking about?" They were standing by her car, and she fumbled for the key in her pocket.

"I know one shouldn't mention it out loud, especially around here, I suppose," he said, "but it seems to be common knowledge what you're up to these days. I'd be careful if I were you."

"What *are* you talking about?" she asked again, totally at sea.

"Whatever else, you were never stupid," he said contemptuously. "Your escort the other night might have swallowed the wide-eyed feminine innocent manner, but it won't wash with me. I know you better—Jack!"

"You stayed in the interior too long," she decided. "It's affected your mind."

"Something did," Finn said with unwonted cynicism.

"I wish you'd tell me what the hell you're on about," she said sharply. "I've better things to do than stand here listening to you blethering."

"I'll bet you do," he said, and looked up suddenly and swore as a bus roared by, brown faces peering from the windows, and a cloud of sandy dust settling in its wake. "That's my bus!" he said. "It's early!"

Island buses were not noted for keeping strictly to time. Often they were late, but occasionally, just to keep the commuters on their toes, one took off minutes before schedule, apparently on the theory that to make it to the depot according to the advertised timetable was a praiseworthy deviation from normal practice.

"I'll give you a lift," Jack offered. "If you'll just refrain from making snide comments until we get there."

"No," he said, as though the idea of sharing a car with her was repugnant. "No, thanks."

"Suit yourself." She shrugged and opened the driver's door. "You'll have to wait an hour for the next one, though."

He checked his watch, and as she put the key in the ignition, bent and said, "I'd like to take advantage of that offer, after all. I've got an appointment in half an hour. Do you mind?"

"Get in."

She waited for him, then turned the key and said mockingly, "Say thank you nicely to the lady, then."

"Thank you." His voice sounded stiff, but he added, as if making a conscious effort to modify it, "And I do mean that. It's an important meeting."

"With your minister?"

"My minister?" He cast her an unreadable look.

"Of the Interior, isn't it? I believe you've been talking to him about a truce with the rebels."

"Who told you that?"

"Is it supposed to be a secret?" she asked. "You should know by now, there are no secrets in Sulaka."

"Maybe that's something *you'd* be wise to remember," Finn said.

"What do you . . . ?" She glanced at him frowningly.

"Watch out!"

But she had already seen the child, shooting out of a gateway on a bicycle, and swerved violently, narrowly missing a couple of chickens scratching at the side of the road.

When she had straightened the wheel, and quickly checked on the child, serenely cycling in the opposite direction as though nothing had happened, he said, "Maybe you'd better concentrate on your driving. Road skills here are nonexistent."

She laughed, and he glanced at her with irritation. The near-accident had put a flush on her cheeks and a sparkle in her eyes. She was, he thought, actually *pleased* with herself.

He shut his lips tightly on a stupid urge to shout at her. It wouldn't do any good, and it certainly wouldn't help her driving. Not that there was anything wrong with it, he conceded; she had averted a nasty incident very cleverly. She had excellent reflexes. But driving on Tukaiki was always hair-raising. No one seemed to have any idea of rules of the road, and tourists, often slightly wild-eyed, were apt to return their scratched and dented rental cars asking plaintively, "Didn't you tell us that you people drive on the *left*?"

Jack said, "I tried to get messages through to the village, to let Mrs. Savusuta know how her husband was. Do you know if they reached her?"

"Yes, I know she received them. She was grateful. Did you . . . send any others?"

To him, for instance. "No," she said. She had thought of it, once, but there wasn't anything she could say to him that could be transmitted through a third person.

"I see," he said quietly, and they lapsed into uneasy silence again.

"Government Building?" Jack asked as they entered the outskirts of town.

"If you're going that way," Finn answered formally.

"No problem," she assured him with equal courtesy.

When she drew up outside the building, leaving the engine running, he seemed to be hesitating, and she said, "Good luck with your talks."

"Thank you," he said. And then added bitterly, "But gunrunners don't help. Supplying more weapons only prolongs the agony for people like Latu Savusuta and his wife, and Tiare and her husband."

"I guess you're right."

"Because it's obvious now they're not going to win. We can only try to get them some concessions, a chance for a peaceful policy in the future."

"I remember you saying you were not political."

"I'm taking no sides. My stance is strictly neutral. I just want to stop the killing and bring them together to talk."

"Still doing good?" she mocked gently.

"I try. What about you?" he said. "You said you were apolitical, too. Are you doing what you do for some noble motive?"

Jack laughed. "Not me. Do you know a Major Limisi?"

"I've met him."

"He called me a mercenary, for hire to anyone for anything. He was right."

"I see." Finn paled, his lips very straight. He got out of the car and said, "Thanks again for the lift," and slammed the door very hard.

"You're welcome, I'm sure!" Jack said, astonished, to his retreating back. The strain must be telling on him, she thought. Maybe she should make allowances and be charitable. But dammit, he didn't seem ready to make any for her. So he condemned her for not having a high-minded and self-sacrificing job like his. Too bad. She'd never been attracted to holier-than-thou types, anyway.

So why was she quietly, secretly, achingly, breaking her heart over Finn?

Chapter Sixteen

Jack attended the trial of Latu Savusuta and Captain Tula. By that time the papers had printed the news that a cease-fire had been declared, and all the rebel groups appeared to be observing it. Representatives from the UN had arrived in Sulaka, and preparations were under way for the peace talks.

Tula was convicted of taking up arms against the government and returned to the detention centre to await sentencing, but Latu Savusuta, to Jack's surprise, was discharged without conviction on the lesser charge of aiding and inciting rebellion.

She went up to him afterwards and shook his hand, congratulating the lawyer. "I must admit I didn't think you would get an acquittal for either of them," she said.

The woman said, "I can't really take the credit. It was . . . arranged."

"Arranged?"

"The insurgents are insisting that Latu Savusuta be one of their representatives at the peace talks. The government won't sit at the table with a convicted man. So a compromise was reached. It took a lot of talking. Your friend Finn Simonson has been busy."

"What about Tula?"

"He'll be sentenced to several years in prison. But he won't have to serve the complete term. Latu Savusuta wouldn't have agreed to the deal if he hadn't been assured of that. If the talks succeed, the rebels will be given suspended sentences, as part of the agreement, on condition they never take up arms against the government again. And if the government's policies change to give the people what is needed for their prosperity, then they needn't fear another uprising."

"As simple as that?" Jack commented drily.

"No, of course not. It isn't simple at all, and it may take months and years of negotiation, but that's better than months and years of fighting."

Finn was in court, too, but he had not approached Jack, and when she gave him a tight little nod, it seemed to be all he could do to give her one in return.

That night in Rosie's Bar she played cards with Abe and Red and Dave Clayton, her eyes sparkling in a way that made Abe study her covertly over his cards, and exchange a meaningful glance or two with Red. Dave bought the regular drinks that Jack demanded, and eyed her with bemused fascination.

When she left the table to visit the ladies' room, Dave said, "What's up with Jack tonight? She celebrating something?"

"Something's upset her," Red told him shortly.

"She doesn't seem upset, exactly," Dave objected, taken aback.

"And you can take that look off your face," Abe growled. "It isn't what you think. If you make that pass you've been planning for the last half hour, you're likely to get a glass of beer over your head. Or a fist in your nose."

"I wasn't . . ." Dave protested, flushing.

Abe looked at him ironically. "Just warning you," he grunted.

"Anyway, what gives *you* the right to punch me in the nose?"

Red gave a snort of laughter. "Not him," he said. "Jack."

Later Abe took Jack home to his place, telling her bluntly that she had no right to be driving a car.

"I'm not drunk, Abe," she said clearly, walking a perfectly straight path to the door without his help.

"I know," Abe replied. But she had drunk more than her usual quota. "I just want your company."

She looked at him, prepared to be indignant, and found him staring back at her stolidly with no particular expression on his face. "All right." She sighed, knowing who it was that he thought needed company. Abe knew her too well. "You're a fussy old dope, Abe." Which was the nearest she would come to thanking him.

He settled her on his sofa, and pulled a blanket over her shoulder and gave it a pat. "You know," he said, "if there's anything I can do..."

"Thanks, Abe. I'm okay." She closed her eyes, and he stood there for a while, and sighed heavily.

Making his way to his room, he rumbled quietly, "You're not okay. You haven't been okay since you came back." He glanced at her as he reached the bedroom, but she hadn't stirred. He sighed again, and went into the room and shut the door.

She had a flight the next morning at eight o'clock, and she picked up her car before seven and drove home, showered and changed hurriedly, and then drove to the airport. The job was to take a party of tourists to one of the outlying islands where there was an exclusive holiday resort, and no sign of war. She was back for lunch, and was making herself a salad when there was an imperative ring at the door.

Finn stood there, with a strange expression on his face. "May I come in?"

"Sure." She stood back. "I'm in the kitchen, making lunch. Want some?"

"I...no, I don't think so. Don't let me stop you, though."

She led him into the kitchen and went on tearing up lettuce and slicing tomatoes at the counter under the window, because it gave her something to do and that way she had her back to him. He didn't sit down, although she indicated a chair drawn up to the table in the middle of the room.

He said, "Where were you last night?"

"At Rosie's." She was too startled by the question to ask him what it had to do with him.

"Not all night," he said tightly.

"No," she said, putting down the knife, an ominous sparkle in her eyes as she turned to face him. "Not all night. I spent the night with a friend."

"Male?" he shot at her.

"I don't have female friends," she told him mockingly. "You know that."

His mouth took on an ugly twist. "No, that's right. How could I have forgotten? I guess you don't have much to talk about. Most women wouldn't understand your...line of work." He looked about the kitchen, at the wall oven and the gleaming stainless steel and laminated plastic, the swimming pool visible through the window. "But it pays well, doesn't it? Nice place, this. Pity your trade is about to dry up."

"Dry up? Actually, business is getting better. As a matter of fact—" About to tell him that now the war was over she had cargo flights booked to take seed and farm implements into the war-torn area, and bring back copra and coffee that would help rebuild the economy of the inland communities, but not that she was quietly doing some of those flights for aid groups at the cost of her fuel alone, she was stunned by the white fury in his face.

He strode over to her and took her shoulders in a bruising grip. "What the hell do you mean by that? They're using the truce to build up an arms supply, is that it?"

She gazed at him blankly, remembered conversations racing through her brain, falling chillingly into place. She realised, blindingly, the reason for his hostility, his puzzling contempt since his return. He had heard some rumour...and believed it. "Who told you," she asked him, with sudden comprehension in her eyes, "that I was gunrunning?"

He released her as though she were contaminated. "Does it matter?" he asked.

"No, I suppose not." What mattered was that he had believed it. Believed it and condemned her, without even asking her for the truth. He really thought that after all they had been through together, after that strange intimacy they had shared at the crash site and later at the village, she had flown arms in to the rebels, knowing that it could only prolong the agony for people who had suffered enough.

The hell with him! she thought angrily. Did he really know her so little? She lifted her head. "Well," she said, her eyes glittering, "I warned you that you were bound to be disappointed."

"Yes," he said. "So you did. Does it ever occur to you that you'd make a more honourable living on the streets in Sulaka?"

The silence stretched. She said, "That's hard work. And it doesn't pay so well, especially since the downturn in the tourist trade...."

"Shut up!" A muscle twitched in his cheek as he bit off the words.

"You started it," Jack said, her voice very husky. "Why did you come here, anyway? Just to call me a whore?"

His already pale face went paler. "I've been asked to find a plane for some IVER work. Everyone says your new machine is ideal for the job. But on second thought, I don't think I can stomach putting more money in your pocket, even for a good cause."

He turned on his heel and went out, and Jack stood listening for the snap of the front door, the sound of an en-

gine starting up outside. Did he have a taxi waiting, or had
he rented a car? Irrelevant, of course. What did it matter?

Think about something else. Anything. Anything at all to
stave off the pain. But it came anyway, in waves, and she sat
down on the chair that Finn had scorned, and crossed her
arms over her midriff, as though that was where the pain
was, although she knew it wasn't really. And rocked back
and forth, gasping with the force of it.

The next time she saw him was in Rosie's. She heard his
voice before she realised he was standing behind her chair,
and she went rigid, not even hearing what he said.

But he was apparently talking to Abe across the table, ignoring her completely. "I believe you have a helicopter," he
was saying in clipped tones. "Is there somewhere we can
talk?"

Abe glanced curiously at Jack, who was staring at her
cards as though if she took her eyes off them they might
disappear. Abe raised his eyes again to Finn. "I'm busy
right now," he said. "Can it wait?"

"This is the only place I could find you. I could meet you
tomorrow morning."

Abe nodded. "My place. Got a pen?"

He scribbled the address, and handed it to Finn.

"Thanks." Finn pushed the paper into his pocket and
walked away.

Dave was looking curiously at Jack. "I thought you two
were friends?"

"Did you?" she said shortly. "Just because we got caught
together in a situation that was unavoidable, that doesn't
make us friends."

Abe was scowling at her across the table.

"Still, he didn't even say hello!" Dave said.

"The good doctor has a one-track mind," Jack told him
lightly. "He probably didn't even notice I was here."

Abe grunted and said, "Are you two playing or what?"

"Yes," Jack said, and carefully laid two cards on the
table.

* * *

The game broke up early, and Abe followed Jack out to her car.

"Can I drop you off?" she asked him.

She had offered before, but he had usually declared a preference for walking, to clear his head. Tonight, however, he said, "Yeah, thanks."

"You okay?" he asked as she started the engine.

"Of course." She checked behind the car and swung out of the parking space.

"I don't have to take his job," Abe said gruffly.

"Not if you don't want to," she agreed. "But you don't even know what it is yet."

Abe grunted. "What I mean is, if you'd rather I didden deal with the feller..."

Jack gave a peal of laughter. "Why on earth should I care? It's no skin off my nose. He said he wants a helicopter. Well, *I* don't have one!"

She was willfully misunderstanding him, he knew. He should shut up, if he knew when he was well-off. But his concern for her, which he dared not show too openly, made him go on, doggedly, "What'd he do to you, Jack?"

She drew in a sharp breath, her hands tightening on the steering wheel as she guided the car round a corner. "Nothing," she said coolly.

Abe gave a short, disbelieving growl.

"He called me a few names," Jack admitted carelessly. "We had a bit of a row. Nothing earth-shattering."

"Uh-huh." Jack wouldn't take that lying down, he thought. She had probably flung a few choice names at Dr. Simonson, too. "You liked him, didden you?" he said. "What was he calling you names for?"

"He thinks I've sold my soul to the devil." Jack laughed, drawing up outside Abe's apartment. "Here you are. I'll see you at Rosie's."

In other words, no private conferences, no pouring out her troubles to a helpful friend. Abe sighed heavily, and opened the door. "Get yourself a decent-sized car," he advised grumpily, negotiating his way out of the bucket seat.

Jack gave him a friendly shove. "Ungrateful sod!" she said, and laughed again as he closed the door.

When Finn arrived Abe was halfheartedly tidying his office. He shouted, "Come in!" and turned off the transistor radio on one corner of the desk, fixing his visitor with a belligerent stare as Finn closed the door behind him.

"Yeah?" Abe said, shoving a cigar between his teeth and lighting a match rather ferociously, waving to a chair as he did so.

Finn sat down. "I want to fly some food and seed and other supplies to a place inland, where there's space for a helicopter but no place a fixed-wing aircraft can land. The army's agreed we can use one of their depots for refuelling."

"The place where you were with Jack?"

Finn hesitated. "As a matter of fact, yes. Now, there'll probably be three or four flights, and you'll be paid at the rate of—"

"What'd you call her names for?" Abe demanded.

"What?" Finn flushed, startled.

"What'd you—"

"Yes, I heard. That's between Jacqueline and me."

"Jacqueline." Abe stared at him fixedly. "Nobody calls her that."

Tempted to say, *I* do! Finn instead said, "A slip of the tongue. Look, this has nothing to do with—"

"You want my helicopter," Abe said, his eyes narrowing behind a cloud of cigar smoke, "you answer my questions."

Finn moved as though about to stand up. But privately owned aircraft of any sort were not so easy to come by on Tukaiki. The war and the drop in tourist trade had put paid to several operations. He sat still and stubbornly silent.

Abe drew a deep puff of his cigar. "So," he said, "what's been going on between you two?"

"Nothing," Finn said coldly. "Do you mind explaining just what your interest is? I'll bet *Jack* didn't put you up to this."

He'd be right there, Abe thought dispassionately. She'd skin him alive if she knew. "I'm fond of Jack," he said simply. "I don't like to see her hurting."

"Hurting?" Finn said. "Jack?" He gave a short, harsh laugh.

"Yeah," Abe said, clamping the cigar between his teeth. "That's right. Jack. She was living with me..." He stopped abruptly for a second, taken aback by the instant leap of angry pain in Finn's eyes. "...for a few days," he went on. "When she came back." Giving himself time to think, and Finn time to recover, he said, "Her house was relet, you know, while she was away. She had nowhere to go."

Finn had recovered all right. "She soon found something, didn't she?" he said bitterly. "Quite gone up in the world, I'd say."

Feeling his way, Abe said, "You've seen her new place?"

"I've seen it. And the new car. And the new...style. I wonder how long she'll slum it at Rosie's with you and your friends, now that she's made it in the big time."

Abe snatched the cigar from his lips and got to his feet, roaring, "Now you listen here, mate!"

Finn leaned back in his chair, folded his arms and, with his blue eyes cold and watchful, said, "Yes?"

Abe leaned across the desk, big and dangerous. "You might be a doctor and a big shot with the UN and the government and all that, but none of it'll stop me giving you a thick ear if you talk about Jack like that in front of me! Or anywhere else, for that matter. 'Cause I'll get to hear about it, and I'll come after you!"

Finn said calmly, "I'd just as soon not talk about her at all. It was your idea." And he pointedly closed his mouth.

Abe sat down and replaced the cigar, chewing on it viciously while he scowled across the desk. "Just tell me," he said heavily, "without calling her names or anything," he warned, "what you've got against her."

"All right," Finn said. "I don't like gunrunners."

The bobbing cigar came to a stop. Abe's brows drew even closer together. "Gunrunners?" he repeated. "You think *Jack* was freighting *guns*?"

"She admitted it."

"She *did*?"

"Ask her yourself," Finn said shortly. "Now, can we get on with the business I came for?"

The subject of Jack was not mentioned between them again until after the job was finished, and Finn asked Abe to come to his hotel room and collect a cheque for his work.

"Would you like a drink?" he asked, as the big man stowed the cheque away in his pocket.

"No, thanks."

Finn smiled. Since that first day Abe had been formally polite all through their dealings with each other. "Won't sup with the enemy?" he asked. And then, unable to quell his curiosity, "Did you ask her?"

"Yeah." Abe looked at him penetratingly. "She said no."

"And you believe her."

"That's right." Abe's jaw thrust forward. "I believe her. Jack wouldn't lie to a friend."

"It's not what she told me," Finn said. "Did you tell her where you got the information?"

Shaking his head, Abe said, "No. Told her I'd heard it at Rosie's. She said there was one time . . ."

"*One* time?" Finn repeated jeeringly.

"Listen, will ya? There was this one time last year, the guy told her it was tractor parts. She didden have no reason to think any different. But the army, they reckon it was guns."

Finn made a small sound of disbelief. "It's a nice story," he said sarcastically. Then, "Hasn't it occurred to you to wonder why she's got so much money all of a sudden—how she could afford a house, a car, new clothes, as well as a new plane?"

"Insurance!" Abe said, surprised that Finn hadn't thought of that.

"That might have bought the plane," Finn said impatiently. "But all the other stuff?"

"She'd been saving for another plane," Abe explained. "She had quite a bit stashed away for a deposit on it. But she'd insured the old one for its replacement value, and when she'd bought the new one with the insurance money, she still had most of her savings. She told us at Rosie's one night, after coming so close to dying she figured, what's the use of saving more money, why not enjoy it? She's got her plane, she doesn't want to employ another pilot, like she'd have to if she bought a second one. So—a nice house near the beach, a good car. It's all she wants. And she's damned well earned it," Abe finished. "Without any help from anybody." He added, "You're sure she said right out she was gunrunning?"

Finn opened his mouth and closed it again, thinking. *Who told you I was gunrunning?* he heard her saying. And then he had practically called her a whore, and seconds later walked out. He closed his eyes and sank down in the nearest chair. "Oh, God!" he said.

"She didn't," Abe said flatly, knowing. "So why'd you jump to conclusions?"

Finn said, "It sounded as though... I thought she was admitting it."

"She said you called her names. Musta bothered her, and it's not like Jack to be bothered. Heck, I call her names, and she just comes right back with something worse."

"That's different," Finn said. "I was... brutal."

Abe grunted. "And she didn't hit you?"

"No. Maybe she should have."

"Maybe," Abe agreed. "I don't know what's going on between you two, but it's tearing her apart. When you came in that night, and looked right through her... I saw her face."

"I didn't look at her at all," Finn said. "I didn't dare, in case I... well, never mind."

"I've never seen Jack look like that. Not ever before. I've been wondering what's buggin' her, lately, thought maybe it was losing her plane, getting caught in the war and all that. But that night, I thought, nah. It's something else. Something to do with you.''

Finn swallowed, his face drawn and tight.

Abe looked at him piercingly. "You love her?" he asked bluntly. "Real stuff, like till death do us part, all that?''

Finn smiled faintly. "For all the good it may do me," he said. "Yes. All that.''

"Jack's always been running scared," Abe said bluntly. "I never knew what from. And she's taken a beating lately, what with the crash, and ... whatever else happened out there. She's been walking on hot wire ever since she came back. Something happened then that ... well, I reckon it must have been worse than losing her plane. And I know how she'd feel about that, even if it was an old crate that should've been retired to the scrapyard years ago if we hadn't both nursed it along. She loved that old heap like it was her very own baby.''

"What happened?" Finn asked him. "What do you mean, it was worse than losing her plane?''

"Well, when it looked like Jack was dead in that crash, Dave—you know Dave, he's a reporter—well, he was trying to find out about her. He traced her parents.''

"They're alive?" Finn asked, unsurprised.

"Yeah. He told the police first, so they could go and break the news, y'know. So it wasn't much of a shock when he phoned them. He wanted to talk to them about Jack, 'cause he was doing this backgrounder, I think he called it. Y'know, something about where she came from, her childhood, and that.''

"And?" Finn prompted as Abe paused unhappily.

"They said ... her father said, they didn't have a daughter. And when Dave pressed it, he told him they weren't interested. She was never any good, he reckoned, she was always totally selfish and useless, ever since she was a kid she'd been getting into trouble. He knew she'd get herself killed sooner or later, the kind of life she'd been leading, and far as they were concerned, she'd been dead for years anyway, so it made no difference. Said she'd finally got what she deserved, and she'd asked for it. The way I read it in the papers, and from what Dave said after he'd talked to the man, he was glad she was dead. Seemed to think it served her right. Dave asked if her mother felt the same way, and he put her on. She said yes she did, their daughter had never brought them anything but trouble and heartbreak, and she never wanted to hear Jack's name again.''

Finn's face was pale, his eyes appalled. "Dave didn't tell her any of this, did he?"

"It was in the papers," Abe muttered. "Well, everyone thought she was dead, see?"

Finn frowned; then his face cleared. "But that would be while we were in the interior. She can't have seen them."

"Yeah, she did," Abe confessed, his face lined with guilt. "I kept them, and she found them in my flat. She told me she'd thrown them away, but I found them in the rubbish later, and she'd cut out the bits about her."

Finn passed a hand over his eyes. "Oh, God!" he said. "Did you talk to her afterwards?"

Abe shook his head. "Tried to. You've got to be careful with Jack. Push it, and she shuts up like an oyster."

"Yes," Finn said. "I know."

"Never said a thing about it. Not a word. A loner, Jack, always was. Took her out for a meal, and pretended everything was sweet. We were telling jokes all night. Broke my heart, though, every time she laughed. You know, I think Jack decided a long time ago not to get close to anyone...not let anyone get close to her. Maybe she's been hurt too much by people she loved. Reckons it's not safe, loving someone, thinks she's better off without."

"You know her better than anyone, don't you?"

Abe thought about that, and nodded. "Guess so."

"Do you think she's better off without . . . love?"

Abe said, looking straight at him, "Maybe she'd be better off without someone who doubts her word."

"I don't doubt her word. If she'd given it, I'd have believed her instantly, no matter what evidence there was. She didn't deny it, Abe! I should have asked her when I first heard it. It was Dave who told me, and I was impressed with his certainty. I know he believed it, he had what he called rock-solid evidence. And when I confronted Jack with it I thought she was telling me it was true!''

Abe chuckled. "Yeah," he said. "That'd be right. She'd be so mad you believed it without asking, she'd just let you go on thinking it. Cut off her nose to spite her face. That's Jack."

Finn gave a faint smile. "Yes," he said grimly. "You're right. But at the least I owe her an apology. Do you know where she is right now?"

"Out on a job, I think. Flying someone back to Sydney. Won't be back until late. She said she'd see us at Rosie's to-night."

"She'll see me, too, then," Finn promised.

Finn was there before her, sitting at the table with the other three when she walked in. She was practically there before she realised her chair was taken, and as Abe looked up with a slightly apprehensive smile, she stopped short. Finn turned his head and got up, and she said, "I see you've got a fourth," and turned her back on them and walked away.

Finn dropped the cards in his hand and went after her. Because she was smaller, she was able to wiggle out through the crowd faster than he, but he caught up to her on the pavement outside.

"Jacqueline!" he said. "Jack! I want to talk to you."

"Sorry," she said. "It's not mutual."

She kept walking, not looking at him, and he grabbed at her arm. "Please," he said. "I want to apologise. I was wrong."

"About what?"

"Just about everything, it seems," he said ruefully. "We can't talk here. My hotel isn't far—will you come back there with me? Please!" he said again.

She looked up at him then, and said sarcastically, "In spite of the falloff in the arms trade, I'm not yet reduced to earning my living that way, thanks."

"I didn't mean that!" he said, holding her by both arms, a treacherous rage threatening. "You *know* I didn't mean that!"

"If you want to apologise, you can do it here," she said coldly.

"All right. I apologise for thinking you were running guns. I apologise for not asking you if it was true. I should have given you the chance to set me straight. I don't know why I didn't, except that...the information seemed conclusive, and when we met, I thought you were tacitly admitting it. And I apologise for as good as calling you a whore. Is that comprehensive enough?"

"I guess so," she said, still in that cold, brittle voice. "If that's all, I accept. Will you let me go now, please?"

He dropped his hands. "It's not all," he said. "There's a whole lot more."

Someone coming out of the bar jostled his back, and he looked about and said, "Can't we go *somewhere*? We can sit in the lounge at the hotel, if you like. It's only a short walk. Where's your car?"

"Over there. I'll give you five minutes," she said reluctantly. "We can sit in the car."

He got in beside her and shut the door. The hood was up, and he wound down the window because it was warm.

She sat stiffly upright, with her profile turned to him, remotely. She wished now that she hadn't suggested the car. She had forgotten how big Finn was. He seemed very close, and she could feel the tension inside her rising to meet his.

"I love you," Finn said, and her heart seemed to leap straight from her chest and into her throat, beating like a mad thing, almost choking her.

"Jacqueline! Did you hear what I said?"

"Yes," she said. Her voice sounded quite calm, but she wasn't sure where it had come from, perhaps a great distance.

His hand came up, fingers lightly gripping her chin, and she slapped him away, unthinkingly, snarling, "Don't touch me!"

But she was facing him now, her eyes gleaming, her back against the door.

"I wasn't going to attack you." He sounded annoyed, trying to hide it. "What are you frightened of?"

"It isn't fright," she said in an accent of loathing. "I just don't want you near me!"

"I wouldn't blame you if you hated me," he said, "but I don't think that's it." He might have doubted, but for Abe's conviction. Abe was no fool, and he knew Jack, knew her very well. He said, "I want to marry you. I want us to be together all our lives."

"No-o!" she cried, and a car passing by threw a wash of light across her face, showing him a mask of what could only be anguish. She gritted her teeth against it and said harshly, *"Not if you were the last man on earth!"*

The words seemed to echo in the darkness left behind by the flash of light. *Cut off her nose to spite her face, that's Jack,* Abe had said. How very true, Finn thought. She would never *allow* herself to be happy, like other people. Because her parents in the throes of their grief had wished her dead instead of her brother, and because she had spent years unsuccessfully trying to win their love and approval, she wouldn't accept it from anyone else. If she didn't succeed in killing herself by constantly courting death, she would turn her back on life in another way, by refusing to accept Finn's love, and denying him hers. And make herself miserable for the remainder of her almost certainly short life.

Shaken by a wave of anger at her headlong, stubborn urge to self-destruct one way or another, he reached for her and pulled her towards him, because he knew now that talking was going to do no good. There was only one way to get to her, and if she hated him for it, he had to take the risk.

She fought, silently and with determination, and she knew some tricks, but Finn knew them, too, and how to combat them, and he was strong and, for once, utterly ruthless. In a minute he had her hands locked securely in his grasp, her head thrown defiantly back against the curve of his arm against the seat, his body crowding her against it.

"I'll bite!" she warned him, as he lowered his head.

"You would, too." His lips went to her throat, and his own teeth grazed her skin. He felt the swift intake of her breath, the shudder that passed through her, and he laughed softly, and nuzzled her throat with his lips, sliding them up towards her ear, nipping the lobe briefly before turning his attention to her cheek.

She tried to turn her head away, but he kissed the skin near her eye, and pressed his lips to the beating pulse in her temple, and she said hoarsely, "Don't!"

He raised his head, waiting. Confused by his silence and stillness, she turned to him, her mouth parted on an indrawn breath, and he captured it under his, very briefly. She drew back, and he let go of her hands, but immediately they were trapped against his chest as he leaned over her, his breath light on her cheek. "I want your mouth, Jacqueline," he murmured. "Stop fighting me, darling."

"Never!" she said between her teeth. "I won't give in to you, Finn! Why are you *doing* this?"

"I love you."

"That doesn't give you the right . . . !"

"No," he agreed. "But this does. . . . *You* love *me*!"

She gave a shaky laugh. "You've got a nerve! What the *hell* makes you imagine that I—"

"Jacqueline!" he said. "Shut your beautiful mouth or I'll do it for you."

She gasped. "Don't you threaten me, you arrogant *bastard*!"

His mouth swooped down on hers, hard and insistent and angry, and she opened her teeth to bite him, and then a great flood of heat swept over her, and she found herself kissing him fiercely back instead, her hands fighting from their imprisonment to go around him, her body straining every nerve to get closer to his.

When they parted at last she was shaking, unable to speak at all. She made to pull away, but he held her, and his lips traced the line of her throat, while one hand found the wild beating of her heart, and then settled warmly on her breast. She sighed, and her head moved back, her eyes closing.

"You love me," Finn breathed against her cheek. "Say it, Jacqueline. I want to hear you say it."

Her head moved aside, her teeth sinking into her lower lip.

Quite gently, Finn laid his hand along her cheek, his thumb lifting her chin. "Say it," he insisted. "Be brave. You'll take a chance on anything but love, won't you? For years you've been playing games with death, gambling with your life. But you're afraid of loving, in case you get hurt. I can't promise never to hurt you, but I can swear that I'll always, always love you. I know it scares you, I know that love for you has meant impossible demands, and pain, but don't turn your back on it out of fear, because I know you've got more guts than that."

She moistened her lips, staring at him, and nodded slowly, and he said almost sternly, because he wanted no last-minute retreats and evasions, "I want to hear the words."

And they came at last, in a rush, a sigh of sweet capitulation. "I love you, Finn."

He let out a tensely held breath and kissed her again, his mouth moving over hers. "And you'll marry me," he said, momentarily lifting his head.

She hesitated, and Finn brought his mouth down to hers, punishingly. She shuddered, and closed a fist and tried to hit him, but he caught her wrist again and went on kissing her. "Come on, love," he said, when at last he relinquished her mouth. "The whole way. Say you'll marry me."

"If you think you can bully me into..."

"Yes, I do," he said coolly. "Now stop stalling and say yes."

Jack wriggled, and looked away. "Yes," she muttered.

"What? I can't hear."

She glared at him, full in the eyes, her mouth sulky. *"Yes!"* Her eyes shot angry sparks. "I'll marry you! Although I can't think why! It's completely crazy. Everyone will think Mad Jack has finally flipped her lid."

Finn sat back and let out a long sigh. "Perhaps you have," he said. "But it feels good, doesn't it?"

"Yes," she said. "No. I think so—I don't know! You've got me all mixed up."

"With respect," he said drily, "it wasn't me that did that. You've been mixed up all your life, not surprisingly."

"I know. So why on earth do you want to marry me?"

He took her hands in his. "Because you're brave, and intelligent, and forthright, and beautiful..."

Jack made a scornful little sound, which he ignored.

"...and because in spite of being a little mixed up, you're strong, too. And I admire your courage, your determination, your humour.... Shall I continue?"

"Please!"

He laughed. "That's enough to go on with. Can I take you back to the hotel now? We have plans to make. Wedding plans."

"I hope you don't want me in white satin and a veil," Jack said edgily, not sure how he had gained her consent to something that filled her with a sort of delighted dismay.

Finn laughed. "I can't imagine it. I don't care what you wear, but I'd like the wedding to be very soon."

"Before I have time to change my mind?"

"Something like that. You're still unsure, aren't you?" he added wryly as she opened the door. "Where are you going?"

"Let's walk," she said. "It clears the head."

"Okay. We'll walk to the hotel."

Locking up, she said, "Are *you* sure? It seems so—unsuitable for someone like you."

Finn shouted with laughter. "What, marriage?" he asked.

"To me," she replied soberly, not even smiling.

He came round to her and surveyed the doubt in her eyes and gathered her into his arms for a long kiss. "I've never been surer of anything."

He looked up as Abe and Red emerged from the doorway under the flashing neon rose.

"Hey!" Red called. "That you, Jack?"

She gave Finn a look of resignation as the two men approached. He still had an arm about her, and after an embarrassed, reflexive effort to free herself, she stayed within its warm, protective circle.

Red peered at them in the darkness. "You all right, Jack? What's going on?"

Abe said witheringly, "Don't be an idiot, Red. You can see what's going on. Everything all right, then?" he asked Finn hopefully.

Finn shook with silent laughter. "Yes," he said with satisfaction. "It's okay, Red, my intentions are strictly honourable. Jacqueline has just agreed to marry me."

Red gaped, and Abe grinned broadly, kissed Jack soundly on the cheek and wrung Finn's free hand. "Great!" he said. "That's great!"

"Yeah," said Red belatedly. "Great. Congratulations! Never thought Jack was the marrying sort."

"Neither did she," Finn told him. "But she was wrong."

"When's the wedding?" Red asked.

"Soon," Finn answered promptly. "We thought of a quiet ceremony, and a few drinks afterward."

"Uh-uh!" Abe said decisively.

"Whaddya mean, quiet?" Red demanded with suspicion. "A few drinks? For *Jack*? Listen, Doc! If you think we're letting Jack tie the knot without a decent hooley to celebrate it, you've got another think coming! She missed her wake, and that's a shame, 'cause it was a good do, but we can at least give her a proper send-off for her wedding! When Louey got married—"

Finn gave in quietly. "I'm sorry," he said meekly. "I didn't think. We were just going to walk back to my hotel to plan the ... the do. Why don't you come along and give us the benefit of your advice?"

"Sure thing!" Red and Abe fell into step beside them. "Now, as to the service," Red was saying kindly, "that's up to you an' Jack, but when it comes to the party afterwards, you leave that to us. Now I know Rosie'll give us a good deal on the grog.''

"Wine," Abe said. "A wedding ought to have wine. D'you s'pose Rosie can lay his hands on some cheap champagne?''

Finn felt Jack's shoulders quivering under his arm, and paused to grin down at her, letting the other two walk ahead, oblivious.

"You'll have to stop them," she said.

"Why? Don't you want a send-off from Rosie's?''

"Wouldn't you hate it?''

"I think it sounds fun. But if you want something more...traditional?''

Jack shook her head. "Not for me.''

"My mother will love you," Finn said suddenly.

Jack stood quite still. "Will she?" Her voice held a tremor of uncertainty. "How do you know that?''

"I know," he said confidently. "She will. She'll know instantly that you're exactly what I've been waiting for. She's been trying to marry me off for years." He kissed her, lingering when her lips answered his, clinging, almost pleading for reassurance. Compassion softened the desire in his kiss. She was so unsure of herself; it was going to take a lot of convincing to make her believe that she was loved, desperately and forever, and that she fully deserved it. He was anticipating that gentle persuasion with a great deal of pleasure.

Red turned around and said plaintively, "Aw, come on, you two! Plenty of time for that after the wedding.''

"All the time in the world," Finn agreed, as he lifted his head, smiling down at the woman in his arms. "All the time in the world.''

* * * * *

Available now from

TAGGED #534
by Lass Small

Fredricka Lambert had always believed in true love, but she couldn't figure out whom to love . . . until lifelong friend Colin Kilgallon pointed her in the right direction—toward himself.

Fredricka is one of five fascinating Lambert sisters. She is as enticing as each one of her four sisters, whose stories you have already enjoyed.

- Hillary in GOLDILOCKS AND THE BEHR (Desire #437)
- Tate in HIDE AND SEEK (Desire #453)
- Georgina in RED ROVER (Desire #491)
- Roberta in ODD MAN OUT (Desire #505)

Don't miss the last book of this enticing miniseries, only from Silhouette Desire.

Wonderful, luxurious gifts can be yours with proofs-of-purchase from any specially marked "Indulge A Little" Harlequin or Silhouette book with the Offer Certificate properly completed, plus a check or money order (do not send cash) to cover postage and handling payable to Harlequin/Silhouette "Indulge A Little, Give A Lot" Offer. We will send you the specified gift.

Mail-in-Offer

Item:	A. Collector's Doll	B. Soaps in a Basket	C. Potpourri Sachet	D Scented Hangers
OFFER CERTIFICATE				
# of Proofs-of-Purchase	18	12	6	4
Postage & Handling	$3.25	$2.75	$2.25	$2.00
Check One				

Name _____

Address _____ Apt. # _____

City _____ State _____ Zip _____

ONE PROOF OF PURCHASE

To collect your free gift by mail you must include the necessary number of proofs-of-purchase plus postage and handling with offer certificate.

SSE-2

Harlequin®/Silhouette®

Mail this certificate, designated number of proofs-of-purchase and check or money order for postage and handling to:

INDULGE A LITTLE
P.O. Box 9055
Buffalo, N.Y. 14269-9055